Christian Doellner

FRANK BILL

BACK TO THE DIRT

Frank Bill is the *New York Times* bestselling author of *The Ravaged*, with Norman Reedus; the novels *The Savage* and *Donnybrook*, the latter of which was turned into a film in 2018; and the story collection *Crimes in Southern Indiana*, one of *GQ*'s favorite books of 2011 and a *Daily Beast* best debut of 2011. He lives and writes in southern Indiana.

BACK TO THE DIRT

BACK TO THE DIRT

FRANK BILL

FSG ORIGINALS

FARRAR, STRAUS AND GIROUX   NEW YORK

FSG Originals
Farrar, Straus and Giroux
120 Broadway, New York 10271

Hand-lettering by Matt Buck.

Library of Congress Cataloging-in-Publication Data
Names: Bill, Frank, 1974– author.
Title: Back to the dirt / Frank Bill.
Description: First edition. | New York : FSG Originals / Farrar,
    Straus and Giroux, 2023. |
Identifiers: LCCN 2022055242 | ISBN 9780374534431 (paperback)
Classification: LCC PS3602.I436 B33 2023 | DDC 813/.6—dc23
LC record available at https://lccn.loc.gov/2022055242

Designed by Abby Kagan

Our books may be purchased in bulk for promotional, educational, or
business use. Please contact your local bookseller or the Macmillan Corporate
and Premium Sales Department at 1-800-221-7945, extension 5442, or by
email at MacmillanSpecialMarkets@macmillan.com.

www.fsgoriginals.com • www.fsgbooks.com
Follow us on Twitter, Facebook, and Instagram at @fsgoriginals

1 3 5 7 9 10 8 6 4 2

For my father, Frank Merritt Bill Sr.,
First Engineers, C Company, Third Platoon
(Thunderin' Third Herd), US Marine Corps,
who served in Da Nang from December
of 1967 to January of 1969

We didn't expect to live. Nobody out there with any brains expected to live . . . The way to live is to kill because you don't have to worry about anybody who's dead.

—WILLIAM DOYLE

PART ONE

SEEDS

BEFORE

THE

TEMPEST

IN MILES'S WORLD there was no God. That belief had been destroyed by the vigilance of the NVA, the North Vietnamese Army. Sometimes it was the gunfire traveling football fields of distance across rice paddy crops or exploding from the jungle brush that lined the rutted roads of Da Nang. Gunfire that ripped a grunt's brain from his skull as he swept the roads for land mines leading in and out of Hill 37 or Hill 65. A five-mile trek where explosive devices were constructed of scrap wood or bamboo, tied together with rope or vine. Buried beneath the earth with an oxidized nail touching a blasting cap that, when weighted down by the pressing of a marine's boot, the trespass of a vehicle, or a tank's heft, metal and human would become one and the same, an explosion that dispersed body parts into unrecognizable shapes.

But then, there was that other enemy. A host of rogue soldiers that had once trespassed the same territories as Miles. Breathed the same air. Enjoyed the same freedoms. They were the one memory he tried to keep buried, some days with booze, other days with iron. On days away from the 6:00 p.m. to 6:00 a.m. shift, he cruised the county back roads when his irritation level redlined, when it inflamed the memories of a war that to this day still offered more questions than answers.

Lance Corporal Miles Knox had been a combat engineer in the US Marine Corps. Schooled in demolition. Taught how to use TNT and C-4, he blew up bridges traveled by the NVA, destroyed their ammo caches and food supplies, and torched the villages where they were stored and hid.

Using C-4 he'd mold the gray puttylike explosive, set a blasting cap, pack the plastic explosive on the nose of an unexploded ordnance, cut a length of detonating cord based on how far he could run, and yell, "Fire in the hole." And then hope to hell he didn't get disintegrated into human dust before he got away.

Miles left for Vietnam on December 18, 1967. His tour of duty was twenty-four months. Three Christmases and three New Years in Da Nang. His time ended on January 3, 1970, but the images and the voices of war still haunted Miles's waking and sleeping hours thirty-four years later, leaving no good for this man who still conversed with the dead.

That was what Miles was doing as the voice of Childers questioned him with, "Gonna make him pay up, Turtle?"

Miles felt the shadow of Childers grace him as he grumbled, "With interest."

Standing outside of the sheet-metal walls of the dirt

plant—a night-shift factory job he'd worked since the early eighties, landed after the tobacco plant down the street where he'd worked for ten years folded—he watched strangers appear from the shadows on Thirteenth Street like cockroaches. Staggering and stumbling over the pavement at 2:00 a.m., tilting a paper sack with lights honing their paths, the soles of their shoes dragging and scraping the pavement. Others pushed corroded shopping carts loaded with dented plastic bottles, their hole-worn boots, and ragged blankets they used to live off the streets. They appeared like nocturnal animals, only to disappear back into the stagnation of night.

The smell of sewage swelled up from the steam of manhole covers. Reminded Miles of how the dead smelled in the Da Nang heat. The rot and spoilage from decomposition. Their lost eyes sunken into yellow skin. Flies zeroing in on a decomposed landing strip to dump their spores. Porous clothing split by the bark of an M16, mortar round, or grenade. Some men took souvenirs: ears, fingers, or scalps. Others posed with the dead. Lined them up like cutout paper dolls, saying "Cheese" or singing "M-I-C-K-E-Y M-O-U-S-E" and snapping pictures. Not Miles. He dealt with the war day by day. Word by word. Cracking movie lines from his favorite up-and-coming actor at the time, Clint Eastwood. When in a firefight, Miles always quoted, *You shoot to kill, you better hit the heart.*

But Miles knew that for those soldiers who severed ears, digits, and scalps, who snapped pictures—that was how some men dealt with the repercussions of war. They found taking from the decomposed or posing with the breathless to be, in some form, humorous. Not Miles. Other than taking gear, he felt the dead's body parts should be left intact; why stoop to the level of the inhumane, the cannibalistic, let the dead be dead. At peace.

Truck lights bounced down the city street next to the factory. A barnacled Ford Ranger with a goose-sounding suspension turned into the blacktopped area before Miles. The engine killed. A hulking shape weighted down the driver's side, tilted his head back. Looked to be sucking down a bottle of water. Through the rolled-down window Miles heard the mash of plastic. Thump to the floorboard. The door opened. It was who Miles'd been waiting on. His coworker Kimball. He owed Miles six hundred dollars' worth of steroids. He was nearing his next ten-week cycle. Needed his juice. His roids. Kimball had faltered on repaying Miles with the vials of Deca and testosterone. Kept telling Miles over and over, "Don't got it tonight, get you tomorrow, bro."

Tomorrow had turned into two weeks, and two weeks was becoming a blur. And he wasn't nobody's *bro*.

Miles was fifty-seven, fighting age. Needed his stack. Trying to keep his frame as strong and muscular as possible.

Each man worked the same job, renting their wares for coin every week. Miles wondered why one working man would fuck over another. Knowing the rigors that each encompassed night after night. Sacrificing sleep, time, and health inside the tin prison that was the factory. He estimated it was part of their generation gap. Older man coming from an era of earning and offering respect. Knowing he was owed nothing, that he had to earn and work his way through life. There was no self-entitlement. The younger generation ignored respect, believed that respect was no longer earned, but given regardless of stature and sacrifice. It was some disillusioned entitlement, wanting to pick and choose what they would or would not do, regardless of a job's responsibilities.

Miles had quit school at seventeen. He wasn't drafted, as some had been, he enlisted in the US Marines. Having a chip on his shoulder, something to prove, wanting to be a tough guy, he wanted to be a rookie cop in New York but couldn't, as he'd dropped out of school and there was a height stipulation. He was five-eight and needed to be five-ten, so he took the next option. Remembered the words a friend spoke when the heifer wagon wheeled into the barracks of Parris Island, South Carolina, after that long-haul overnight. Eugene Clemmons sat next to him nervous as a whore in church when the drill instructor stepped onto the bus, a chiseled but crazed, pale-faced, box-topped hard-ass. He read them the riot act with a bullhorn voice: "No more sucking your mother's tit and filling your socks with cock jam, you fuckin' parasites, move your pathetic asses now!" Seats of young men yawned and knuckled crust from their sockets. Hesitant and slow, Clemmons whispered to Miles, "Think we fucked the pooch, buddy." Bodies were herded from the bus to the burn of barrack lights and a yellow-footed path to a building where cots were lined up, no sheets. They were ushered into another room full of tables. The DI barked, "Remove every goddamned thing from your pathetic bodies except your fuckin' ID. No carrot-cracking pics of Tootsie-tits playing with her honey hole. No shaving kits. No money. Leave it! You're now property of the United States Marine Corps, maggots!"

With that memory seared in his mind, Miles knew Kimball and he were divided by the duration of time. By age. Kimball was twenty-eight. His father, Dannie, worked the day shift at their factory. Got his son this job by blood affiliation and good attendance. The other side of showing up to work on time was, Dannie'd been busted for suspicion of child molestation, sleeping with a girl under the age of eighteen. Was somehow holding on to his job until his next court date. Then there was his spawn, Kimball, who'd had a child from his first marriage that didn't pan out because of the unplanned second child he planted in the babysitter one night while his wife was out with her hens at a Tupperware party. He'd come home early from the gym. His libido bouncing, he offered the eighteen-year-old the fuck-me eyes. She accepted, he gave her the dog and pony show before the wife came back.

The apple didn't fall far from the family tree.

Six weeks later, the sitter gave him the EPT test and his wife filed for divorce. Now he had a girlfriend who watched his two kids while he worked, weight trained, and saturated his body with illegal hormones. Whored around on her during his late-night lunches working the night shift, in between snacking on Rally's burgers and chicken sandwiches for his five-thousand-calorie-a-day dirty bulking diet.

Probably hit the drive-thru couple blocks over, Miles thought, for a sack of plain burgers, down past Cousins Liquor store on Thirteenth and Hill, where men hid their booze in a paper sack. Picked up young whores for a five-dollar hand job or a ten-dollar suck-and-fuck. Money earned initially to care for their children; instead, they slung dope or fought turf wars to defend their affiliations, men without fathers, raised without the guidance of two parents, young men raised in an underprivileged environment where only the strong survived and the weak perished and the city ignored them both.

Miles believed Kimball needed his temperament recalibrated. To be reminded that Miles was overdue on what he'd paid for. Roid rage amped through his hands. Fingers tensed as he raised his cigarette to his lips, pulling a final draw of nicotine from his cancer stick. He knew if he got caught handing Kimball his ass he could lose his job. But by now he was beyond consequence and knew a way around the guidelines. Union or no union.

The company may own the building and property in which he worked, but they didn't own the street.

With the steel entrance door to the plant behind him, Miles knew Kimball would have to navigate through him or past him, or he could run to Miles's right, where two metal silos stood housing the amine that was pumped into the building, next to the railcars full of clay that traveled from the Dakotas. The clay was vacuumed into the plant through a three-inch line where impurities were washed from it. Mixed with amine, dried, bagged, and sold as a paint additive that made paint adhere to a surface. Didn't matter. However this was going to go down, Miles was no longer asking.

Miles heard Childers ask, "You gonna tug on that cancer stick all damn night or you gonna light his ass up?"

"I'm gonna ignite his ass like napalm, motherfucker. Just sit tight and watch," Miles said as he glanced to the charcoaled silhouette of Childers, then coiled his left hand. Homed in on Kimball. Flipped the smoke into Kimball's chest with his right. Got his attention as ashes Tic-Tacked orange.

The two men made eye contact. "The fuck's your damage, Knox?"

Miles divided Kimball's frame from head to toe. Made an imaginary line just as his trainer had taught him in Puerto Rico, circa 1970. Halve the opposition's torso, create your opening.

"Been two weeks too many. Need my fucking juice."

Kimball chuckled. Held a double hamburger in his one hand, which swelled with veins, muscle, and a bit of water retention, a paper sack with several more burgers in his other hand. Miles could smell the whore-stank and cheap CVS perfume smoldering from his T-shirt. He told Miles,

"Crazy ole bastard. Out here carrying on a conversation with yourself. No idea what a girl like Shelby sees in you but look—"

Shoving the remaining burger into his mouth, cheeks chipmunked-out as he chewed, he buried his hand into his one sweatpants pocket, then the other, reaching across his pumped chest, forearms bulged as he pulled the pockets out. Pulled the white lining from the cotton inside the pants like two ears dangling above his groin.

Bread and beef particles fell from his mouth as he said, "—I's broke as a whore in a recession. Why don't you get on your bum knees, old man, kiss the fucking bunny between his ears."

The knob of a blowtorch turned in Miles's mind, created a canvas of red-butchered outlines barking, *KILL! KILL! KILL!* That was all Miles could hear, all he could see, taste, and smell. He came with two open hands, clenched them into Kimball's chest, twisted a grip into his shirt, planted his foot, pivoted, and swung him out into the middle of the street and off company property. Kimball found his balance, stood crooked. Miles was loaded up and combusted into Kimball's face with his left. Immediately felt the ache of old age shoot through his knuckles to his sculped forearm and into his rounded shoulder of stitched fiber. Watched Kimball drop the sack of burgers and spit a regurgitated wad of bun-meat as he staggered backward.

Shaking the spin of having his clock cleaned, eyeing Miles, blinking and salting up in his eyes, he raised a forearm to his nose and mouth. Trembling, he wiped the warmth that showed under the vapor lights homing from above the street. "Think you're gonna beat my ass, ole man?" he shouted.

Smirking, Miles told him, "Know I'm gonna use your ass to wipe the grime and grit from your truck's hood when I'm finished using you as a rag to clean my knuckles."

"Well bring it, you ole motherfu—"

Miles cut Kimball short. Came forward, faking a right. Flushed his hearing with a left hook to his right ear. Dug his hips in. Twisted a right cross into his chest that sounded like a ten-gauge shotgun holing out a rotted stump with buckshot.

"Nice one," Childers said to Miles.

The guy was spewed from a generation of backward-backwoods racists. Some would say inbred. Just because you were white, poor, and scraping to get by didn't mean you were inbred, Miles knew. But Kimball's people were a lineage of men who'd developed a history of thieving, beating, and molesting those they felt were weaker and who held something they wanted. Meaning whatever they gave or dished out they believed was deserved in order to take what they wanted. And if you were kin to their bloodline, they felt they owned you.

Miles agreed with zero of that semblance.

Kimball groped his ear with his right. Came back with a wild left that bit Miles's chin. Miles spit and returned fire with a straight right of his own. Kimball caved in and shelled from the cross. Glared between his forearms. Tasted pain and hurt, met the afflicted eyes of Miles, who'd beads raining down his graying complexion of gritted teeth and heaving lungs wheezing from the pack of Marlboro reds he inhaled every day.

Miles saw it in Kimball's eyes. Fear. And Childers told him, "Got his soft ass now."

Kimball lowered his arms, shouted, "Crazy gook-killin' fuck." And swung a whooping right.

Miles coughed a nicotine glob, spit a chunk of tapioca yellow, and stepped back. Watched the haymaker miss by two rungs of a heifer's backside. Calculated his distance. Placed his left hand in front of Kimball's view, blocked his sight of the right hook he speared into the bulky tissue below Kimball's armpit, his lung point. Then fired a stiff left jab into his esophagus.

Kimball gagged for air, dropped down to one knee, as a Ford F-150 came barreling by and honked the horn, brake lights beating red and slowing as it turned right just before the railroad tracks.

Winded, Miles paused. Yelled, "Take a picture, mother-fucker, it'd last longer."

Kimball sucked up the hurt. His back butterflied wide. He came with rage from his knees. "Ahhh!" Speared his bowling-ball shoulder into Miles's abdomen. Pushed him backward.

"You gonna take this weak-ass football charge?" Childers questioned Miles.

Miles spat air. Gritted his teeth. "Shut the fuck up. Got him right where I want him."

His lower back and knees jarred and popped with ache. He gained his footing, brought his thick elbows down into Kimball's spine like two ball-peen hammers. Took whatever glow the man had left, listened to the undigested grease and meat patties splash and pile from Kimball's mouth to the pavement.

"You got this motherfucker now," Childers told Miles.

Miles's lungs flared like an enflamed throat being doused with rubbing alcohol. He reached into Kimball's wad of sandy locks. Feeling his shoulders and back knot and cramp, Miles lifted the man's complexion to viewing, watched the crimson pulp from Kimball's nostrils and lips. Spun him around to face the parked Ford and dragged him from the street's center to where Kimball's own vehicle was parked.

Miles didn't trust the pilferer, he'd learned his lesson with the VA pretending to be farmers in Da Nang. Give the fuckers an inch, they'd take a mile. Shoot you in the back.

Kimball slurped and whined, "Crazy old man, told you I'd get it to you next—"

Miles huffed and chuckled. "—You'd be correct, you bent-lip bastard, you gonna get it and it won't be next week. We're going for a ride, *bro*."

Opening Kimball's passenger door, Miles glanced to

the other truck, which sat idling down across the tracks, a shadow watching.

Shadrack palmed the busted screen door, causing it to slap the side of the house. Leaped out into the void that was night. His ears purged with explosions. Screams rang in his ears as he took to the hillside barefoot. He retreated into the dankness and spoils of timber, wondering if any of this was real or if it was a madcap juvenile dreamscape, a make-believe cartoon.

His heartbeat contorted in his temples like when he ran in PE class, catching and dodging the red rubber balls, never catching his breath, only fueled by adrenaline.

He thought back to what he saw. The frail shape of a man had come in with the bill of a ball cap poking out from beneath a hooded sweatshirt. Hiding features and smelling like soil, mildewed vinyl, and a hint of something saccharine, like rotted perfume.

Shad's father, Bedford Timberlake, had called the man *a regular*. Someone who tended to come by the house early in the day. Now he'd shown up late, unexpected, sometime between when David Letterman started but before he signed off for the night. The man jerked and turned to his right, then his left. Kept pacing in place, saying he was sold a bad batch of pills and demanding more of what Shad's father told him he did not have. The cotton. White pills in caramel-colored bottles with ivory lids that Bedford and his partner got from one of several pharmacies in Kentucky, Ohio, Indiana, Tennessee, and West Virginia.

The shape balled his slender fist into Bedford's Ozzy Osbourne T-shirt and squealed with a Bob Dylan–esque voice, "Done told you that batch was bad. You promised me a hundred pills, ain't near fifty in here, you Gumby-mouthed motherfucker!"

Shadrack's father had worked for Keller Manufacturing until he'd hurt his back nearly five years ago. Gotten hooked on painkillers. Found disability. His wife waited tables at the local Waffle House. What she earned in addition to Bedford's disability checks wasn't enough to get by on, let alone support their son nor their pain pill habit; they chewed on the cotton as though it were bubble gum or a tough cut of steak. That was where Bedford's partner came in, Carney Dillman, a friend since birth, someone his baby brother, Nathaniel, never liked him running around with. That was why Bedford kept their dealings to himself. Carney explained that he had connections, could help line up the doctors who were easy, not thorough when it came to giving prescriptions throughout the different states; he knew which doctors held little concern to whom they wrote prescriptions for. Bedford was disabled, so all he needed to do was show up, show his disability paper, get the prescription, and move on to the next one. Doctor shopping. They never researched a person's disability or pain. Around coal country this practice had become more and more popular. And, Carney told Bedford at the start, he had a line of customers ready to buy plenty of cotton.

Along with the government checks, that was how Bedford earned a living, peddling eighty-milligram tablets of Oxy for forty to eighty bucks a pop, unless he landed a higher dosage, then it was eighty to a hundred bucks.

"Keep it down, don't do deals in front of my boy," Bedford had said to the regular. "Nothing wrong with what I sold you, and I didn't promise you shit, I don't got a hundred pills I can part with. You want more, gonna take a few days to round all that—"

"—You lyin' fuck!" Coyote barked.

Shadrack's mother, Judy, sat nervously sucking on her Camel Wide and sipping her peach schnapps from a mug that stated I'M NO CACTUS EXPERT BUT I KNOW A PRICK WHEN I SEE ONE. Shadrack lay on the mangy carpet beside his father's feet, reading a Batman comic book.

"Coyote, calm down, come back Monday, we'll have more cotton, straighten this out, everything else I got is spoken for, you're sounding a bit hoarse, not like you gonna eat all this up in one night." Wrinkling his left cheek up into his eye, he said, "And you could use a good washing, you smell like a soured horse's ass."

Bedford chuckled.

Coyote fingered his forehead, hidden by the dim light of the trailer, and said, "Ain't gonna be no more Mondays for you, you pilfering son of a bitch. Selling me bad shit, not making them others wait, I'm here now, and you're gonna make things right."

Everything happened quick as an unexpected thunderstorm, when heated pressure meets cooling pressure. Conditions were perfect and Mother Nature exploded.

The earthy shape pulled a revolving piece of steel from his lower back.

Shocked, Bedford raised his hands up and spit, "Now hold on a damn minute—"

Shadrack looked up as the air exploded within the home and became a ricochet of combusted energy. The side of his father's face scattered red with wormy chunks. Bedford's DNA warmed Shad's arm and cheek. Judy screamed. The voice told Judy, "Bitch, be quiet!" Gave her the same scattered silence as Bedford.

Shadrack bucked with fear. Fought the stiffness that contorted his hands and knees as he got on all fours. Knew only the words his father had warned into his boyhood retention: *If your mama and me ever get in a pinch, you run to the timber, boy. Don't glance back till you reach Devil's Elbow, till you're knocking on your uncle Nathaniel's door.*

And that was what he did. Crawled down the hallway, hands, elbows, and knees grinding into the carpet, one following the next like an athlete doing bear crawls in spring training. Worked upward to standing and bolted out the back door. Shadrack couldn't feel his feet but knew he needed distance. Knew he couldn't stop. Once in the woods,

he overwhelmed himself with worry, worry that every snap
of a tree limb, every rustle of a bush, wisp of wind, was the
outline of Coyote hunting him down.

With charcoal-colored hair, complexion smooth as a freshly
waxed vehicle, and the music of the band Prodigy pulsing
from the walls, floors, and tables, the young man was well
groomed and held a wad of cash. He'd been buying table
dances from Shelby McCutchen all night until the bouncer,
Mel, a meaty bruiser with Schwarzenegger arms and a
beer belly, manhandled the young man after he grabbed
Shelby's arm, telling her, "Come with me, you don't have to
work here. I'll buy you a townhouse, pay for your car, your
food, clothing. All of it. You're too beautiful to work here."
Shelby jerked from his grip. Only to have the man reach for
her again. By then Mel was on him like fumes to fuel,
dragged him to the EXIT door. Tossed him out onto the
pavement, scratching and scraping up his palms and knees.
Shelby and Monica, a bleach-bottle blonde with shoulder-
length hair, fake-and-bake tan, toned and shapely, laughed.
"The hell, girl? That was insane."

"It was." Shelby yelled over the music, "Guy comes in
here to blow off steam. Blow some money, don't mean they
own us."

"No shit. It's all fantasy. We're not looking for Mr.
Right in this place, only here to get paid."

"For real, who wants to date a customer?"

Monica chuckled from her hot-pink lips as Shelby suddenly checked out, stared off for a moment; everything went dark in her head and Monica said, "Hey? Shelby? Girl, you hear me?"

Shelby didn't answer, just stared off into nothing while the music vibrated her body and around her other bodies danced, money was transferred into hands or fingered into G-strings from the surrounding tables, and Monica snapped her manicured fingers in front of Shelby's face.

Shelby came to behind Bedford's home, sitting in a '68 Camaro, her mind flickering between her memories at work, where she'd been zoning out, losing track of time, going incoherent, and the memories of the bluing flesh, the cellophane lips, and the twist of curdled milk that had haunted Shelby's mind all week. She remembered an empty rig hanging from the bend of a tapped-out vein. A turned-over bottle with crushed pills chalky and smeared over a reflection . . . Her head was reeling and ringing from the tunes she pole danced to at Déjà Vu, a topless dive off Taylor Boulevard in Louisville, Kentucky. It was a job that offered her big cash to afford the things she wanted from life: a home, a vehicle, food, expensive clothing, lotions, and hair care products. She was her own boss, and it gave her a feeling of empowerment to be the center of men's fantasies and desires. She gave twenty percent of her earnings to the club, the rest was hers. And when she left her shift, she was done.

Work stayed at work. And it afforded her the ability to care for her brother and father.

Gunshots and the smack of a door startled Shelby from her narcoleptic state. She'd blanked out while waiting for her brother. She leaped from the car, feeling as though she was trapped in a tunnel, heartbeat flaring. She glared at the house's rotted deck behind her. Leaves crumbled beneath her footing, meshed with similar footfalls from around the back of the house. There was the hint of gunpowder in the late-night air. Walking to the rear she yelled, "Wylie? You back around here? Thought I heard gunshots."

From the incline of trees came the rustle of feet rushing over the ground. All at once her brother formed from the dark, a thick hooded sweatshirt, a face of moonlit pigment, one hand grasping a Walmart sack and a pistol, in the other was a Walmart sack that rattled. "The hell did you do?" Shelby shouted with anger. Paying her no mind, he wobbled madly toward her. Panted for air. The rattling of pills and his rushed inhale blistered toward her and she asked, "Why are you coming from the woods?"

Offering her the two Walmart sacks, one weighted with bottles of pills and the other weighted with stacks of crumpled cash, ignoring her questions, he directed her, "Take these. Get in the car!"

Her mind was rattled, bouncing with heated nerves, and her vision waved and wrinkled. She wasn't doing shit until Wylie explained his actions.

In the trace of light from the moon, his face was ghouled with veins throbbing at the temples. Twins by birth. Same height, thin but muscular, his features were being more and more informed by addiction. His eyes recessed into his brainpan like slick black marbles. He'd moved in with Shelby after losing his job on a construction crew for stealing wire and pipe to sell at a salvage yard, needing more coin for his craving to feel warm and fuzzy. After that he'd disappear for days. Squatting in abandoned houses. Shooting the cotton with other scrapes of life. Then showing up strung out at her home or their father, Whitey's. Beating on their doors for a place to shower, settle, and sleep off the days of being strung out. Always promising he'd get clean tomorrow.

This week, he'd said his car wouldn't start. He'd been waiting at George Savage's lawn shack after her shift. Phoned her for a lift to Bedford's place to pick up some cotton. She'd run him on this errand from time to time. But now she'd this buzzing in her ears. A twisted ache in her forehead. She lashed back with, "Not until you tell me—"

Then it was as if she was hit with an oak slab, as that was all of the sentence she could spew before the pistol butt jarred above her vision, at her forehead's peak. Splitting and spiraling a pain from her brunette head of hair like a migraine. Shooting down her torso until she was weightless, numb, and traveling like an incapacitated drunk. The next thing she was aware of, she was driving with Wylie down a country back road.

Overhead streetlights canvased shadows around the young mothers leading baby strollers down the sidewalks that ran in front of the shotgun houses constructed of brick, wood, and shingle near the intersection of Portland Avenue and Twenty-Second Street, just down past the Outlaws' Motorcycle Gang clubhouse. Desperate for his gear, Miles navigated the Ranger, with Kimball's hulking mass riding shotgun, his complexion swollen and busted. Miles crossed under the rusted railroad trestle, navigated down the historical area where old homes stood like relics with monstrous elms and oaks decorating the yards and busted walks of the working, the Ohio River behind them, smelling of fish, fuel, and river stench. Lights opened to a driveway, as Kimball pointed: "There." Miles steered right. Braked to a stop, shifted to park. Killed the engine. Kimball sat massaging his jowl.

Childers's outline sat between them. Half his face a wreck of dismembered flesh. "Feed this fuck some more pain, he's getting ready to spear you with lies."

Glaring at Miles, Kimball said, "Know what you are? A son of a bitch. If you'd have waited just one—"

"Told you!" Childers spouted.

"Shut the fuck up!" Miles spit, shot a right jab into Kimball's left jowl. Cut him off with, "If I'd waited one more day, you'd come back with the same horseshit you're feeding me now, same as you do every goddamned night. I'll bet your dealer don't turn me away."

"Fuck you, man, fuck you! Warden Bush don't like company in the middle of the night," Kimball ranted.

Miles pulled the truck keys from the ignition. "Maybe you shoulda considered that earlier, gotten my juice to me two weeks before now!"

Opening the driver's-side door, Miles walked around to the passenger's side, Kimball still exercising his tonsils. Miles opened the door. "You getting out or do I gotta drag your ass out?"

Unanswering, Kimball shrugged his shoulders upward. Miles was beyond sarcasm now. Scooped a handful of locks, tugged Kimball from the truck. "Motherfucker, that shit's attached!" Miles released his locks and Kimball shrieked, "I should put a beatin' on you, ole man!"

"You gonna take this lip from him, Turtle?" Childers asked.

"Back the fuck off," Miles told Childers, while looking at Kimball. "Wanna go another round just flinch, I know what you got," he spat.

Looking at Miles, Kimball mumbled, "If Warden's pissed off for us paying an unannounced visit, he'll wax you."

"Think I'm afraid of a biker after the hell I've lived through?"

Kimball went crickets as they walked toward the diminutive home. A light on in the rear illuminated panes of flaked paint. Miles started to the front door until Kimball told him, "No. Only strangers track to the front. Common visitors and iron heads, as he calls them, trail to the back. This late he ain't gonna be happy, regardless. On top of he don't know you."

"He knows my buddy Benjamin Franklin. Known him for several years now," Miles said, shutting Kimball up.

They walked over the rippled concrete ruts with grass spitting up between the cracks, beneath the yellow glow of an overhead motion light attached to the side of the house. A neighboring home stood twenty feet to the left; in the rear of their destination, a garage light burned hazy with moths swarming its rays, a video camera watched them. Several Harleys sat beneath it shimmering, with skulls and flames painted over the gas tanks, their chrome catching the moonlight through the trees. Kimball stepped up onto a concrete step, knocked on the door to the kitchen that sat like a greenhouse with blinds pulled down on every window of the squared construction, panes rattling to the thump of death metal music from the home's interior. Then came the muffled bark of dogs. Miles's heart ramped a few notches. Pit bulls. The music thump went dead. Clomp of heavy feet. Several mechanisms clanked down the door, locks being unbolted, a crack of light fed onto Kimball's features from the kitchen. Exhaust of cigarette smoke, whiskey poured and swallowed. From teeth and beard words came: "The fuck happen to you, princess?"

"Fuck you. It was a disagreement. Need me some gear."

Jimmy Suicide snickered. "You lick your mama's happy spot with that mouth before or after you talk filthy to her like that?" His laugh got serious when he eyed Miles and asked, "Who's the fuckin' Mickey Rourke look-alike lurching over you?"

Kimball sucked up his pride and said, "Enraged client that patterned this *princess's* face. I owe him gear."

Suicide shook his head when, from behind him, came the words of Warden Bush. "Goddamned tool, Kimball, you's told no more holding out on customers. Let the decomposed carcass in."

The door swung wide. Light embered like a bonfire. A table sat in the center; a Desert Eagle .45, matte black, lay within hand's reach next to Warden's tenderloin forearm of ink. Shaved dome. Beard to the center of his pectorals. Sleeveless black Motörhead T-shirt. Arms and shoulders like a silverback gorilla, ears run with steel piercings, rings on every digit. Two pits, gray and white with silky fur, sat at his feet, mowing the lawn with their growls, each adorned with spiked leather collars, unmoving.

"Hush," Warden said. His eyes metered in on Miles. "An ole-timer needin' gear. How damn ripe is that," he said, with a deep carburetor voice.

Miles told him, "Just a grunt battling age."

"Let me guess, a marine?"

"Yeah."

"You look like a jarhead. Where'd you serve?"

"Combat engineer, Third Platoon, First Engineer Battalion, stationed in Da Nang. '67 tuh '70, finished my time guarding an ammo dump in Puerto Rico and boxing."

"Hmmm. You saw some shit?"

"Witnessed casualties on both sides."

"Looked for ordnances and deconstructed ordnances?"

"Yeah. Disorganized bridges, ammo caches, villages, and whatever else needed it, was in a recon unit my last few months in the jungle."

Warden's eyes went to razor wire, he rotated his neck, zeroed in on Kimball. His arms and chest flexed with fiber and vein. Rage spit from his pores. "How the fuck could you do this to a veteran? A man who fought for our country, our civil liberties, the red, white, and fucking blue?"

"Fuck," Kimball spat under his breath with sarcasm. "My mistake."

"Goddamn right your mistake." Warden's glare went from Kimball back to Miles. "From now on, you need gear, you come to the source. To me. Don't fuck with this mutated Baby Ruth–eatin' son of a bitch. Day or night, any hour."

"Sounds like a deal," Miles said.

"What's he owe you?"

"Ten-week supply of Deca, a twelve-week supply of test and T3, Nolvadex, and HCG."

"Need pins?"

"Yeah."

Warden shook his head, looked back to Kimball, nodded at Suicide. "Cough up his green. Know you got it or you're gonna take some more licks."

Suicide snatched Kimball's wallet from his back pocket. Split it open to Warden. Thick wad of hundred-dollar bills resided.

"How many motherfuckers you been holding out on, you worthless son of a bitch?"

"Look, they was a big race at the Downs."

"Clamp your fucking gate." Warden looked again to Suicide. "Grab the fuckin' mallet and the mole trap. He won't never hold out on no motherfuckers again."

Unlike the sour village skin that fertilized the rice fields of Da Nang, Miles longed for Shelby's scent of fresh cocoa butter spritzed over her toned curves of butterflies, daggers, and flowers that swirled into an ink collage, along with the stainless steel piercings about navel, vagina, and tongue.

Her Camaro wasn't in his drive when he got home at 6:30 a.m., after working the graveyard shift. Her voice wasn't on the machine. For weeks she'd been acting strung out, worn down from a combination of zero sleep, working her job at the Vu, and taking on the responsibilities of dealing with her brother. Holing up inside of herself. Miles

couldn't place a finger on it. Going to group at the VA, sharing with others the trauma he'd endured on top of listening
to the damage of other war vets, he knew something wasn't
right with Shelby. But he wasn't one to pry, even though
deep down Miles knew she wasn't herself. He'd noticed it
more and more over the past few weeks. Unlike the usual,
after his night shift in the dirt plant, when she'd be at his
home, waiting. Hunkered and spread across his mattress
like fresh cotton, displaying herself. Laying firm and clean,
locks fanning, her blades indenting the cushioned springs.
Welcoming his aging heft. Her elder by twenty-seven years,
Miles'd met her one night down at the VFW club. She'd
come in to pick up her father, Whitey, who'd been a heli-
copter pilot in 'Nam, then flew for the DEA after the war,
searching for pot fields around the counties, and who had
recently retired. Stayed drunk at the club every evening after his shift. Always wore a red, white, and blue bandana
around his head like a pirate. Miles'd helped her get Whitey
to her car one night. Whitey'd raised his voice with her,
tried to cop a feel from her breast when Shelby was helping
him into the open door. She'd released him, absolved his
weight from her, and he bumped his head on the door's
frame. Reached at her length of hair. Called her a useless
cunt. Miles rolled Whitey's hairy wrist till it popped with
pain. Ironed his face into the car's dash. Warned him if he
ever spoke to Shelby or any woman in such a tongue again,
or laid a squeeze to her, he'd beat the breath from his soured
soul until there was nothing more to beat.

Whitey cringed and mumbled, "That any way to treat a fellow brother? Another vet who served same as yourself? Shit ain't right, man, you're gonna get yours, Knox. Just you wait."

Afterward, Shelby thanked Miles. Told him, Daddy don't mean nothing by it. Used to talk down to her and her brother, and a lot worse.

Her mother left Whitey when he started drinking more heavily than usual, talking a lot of carnage to her; he'd spit on Shelby and her brother, call them names. Her mother left him when they were around twelve or thirteen. She couldn't take no more of it. Wanted Wylie and Shelby to live with her, but Shelby wouldn't leave her father, felt like she was abandoning him.

Leaning on the rear of Shelby's car, Miles told her, "That ain't no way for him to treat you, regardless of what war he fought."

That night they shared their lives with Whitey passed out in the front seat of Shelby's Camaro. Miles told her he'd been born and raised in Pennsylvania, lost his father, Claude William, when he was thirteen to lung cancer. He'd slaved in the steel mills of A. M. Byers, out in Ambridge, PA. Miles's mother had moved him back to Corydon, Indiana, months after his father's death. She was a strong-willed woman, and Miles held a grudge against her. It started just before he left for the marines. Miles questioned his mother as to why he held her maiden name on his birth certificate and she wouldn't explain why, why he'd been brought into this world under her name, Knox, and not his father's, William. For the longest he convinced himself that he was a bastard child. Thought maybe the father who raised him wasn't his real father. But his mother had left her first husband without a proper divorce, fled the state of Indiana with Claude. Didn't get her divorce settled until years after Miles's birth. He discovered this after sorting through old letters and paperwork.

After clearing out her home and rifling through the old black-and-white gloss of family pictorials of his father, he could see his resemblance to his old man. He found his mother's diary, and read it; she was ashamed of bringing Miles into this world out of wedlock, using her name instead of his father's, she'd just never explained the how and why she did what she did, but by then it was too late. She was gone.

"Finding out such a secret, holding that spite," Shelby said. "That must've been horrible."

"No worse than the violence I encountered overseas," he told her. Explaining, he told her he'd been kicked out of school when he was seventeen because of fistfights; he was smaller in stature, didn't take much lip, he had a chip on his shoulder. Something to prove. Tough-guy attitude. Wanted to be an NYPD officer, but he didn't meet the height requirement. So he chose the next best thing. Enlisted into the Corps. "Life either makes you or breaks you," Miles told Shelby.

"Yes it does." Shelby smiled. "Yes it does." She paused before asking, "Your mother ever remarry?"

"No. She dated men. She worked hard. Was a big card player. Loved poker and euchre. There was one guy though, I believe had he lived, and asked her, she'd have married him."

"Really? How long was she with him?"

"Yeah, they was together ten or fifteen years, he was retired from the railroad. Served in the navy. Nicknamed Seabug. They traveled to Pensacola every winter. Couple of snowbirds. Enjoyed all the same things: playing cards, drinking beer, eating fried seafood. But his smoking, drinking, and eating whatever he desired, and never paying a visit to the doctor for a physical, caught up with him, just keeled over one day unexpectedly."

"That's really sad."

"It was. He was good to her," Miles said. "All right, enough of the sappy shit, tell me this: Why would you even consider picking Whitey up when he's stone-cold drunk like this, unable to drive? He's so damn abusive and disrespectful, especially toward women; I mean, why even bother dealing with the SOB's bullshit, why not let him walk home or get pulled over?" Miles questioned.

"'Cause if he called and I didn't show up and he wrecked, died behind the wheel or even worse, took another person's life, I'd never forgive myself. Knowing I could've prevented it, no way could I live with that," Shelby told Miles. She continued with, "There was a time when Wylie and me was kids, when he'd been a good man. Then, as we got to our teens, started to mature, something changed in him, he started to view us differently."

"War ruins people," Miles told her. "Why I never married. Too many bad dreams, demons and ghosts, the faces and the evils that rampage in my mind. Only things that tame it are the iron."

Her tissue-soft digits reached over and squeezed his biceps. Chuckling, she said, "I thought you's in too good of shape for an old Vietnam War vet."

With a flushed face beneath the glow of overhead lighting, Miles told her, "The weights I push help with the anger, the adrenaline I rear from a pump, it's energizing, even if short-lived, it works all that rage and bad mojo from the memories of war. It keeps me going. Keeps me sane."

What Miles didn't tell her about was the booze. How it soothed the ghosts he lived with when he couldn't shake the images of battle, and his anger redlined, bared its teeth, when those voices and images of Childers, Nafus, and the other dead soldiers wouldn't keep quiet. When Childers reared his ugly head and fed that fire, angered him with his words when a conflict arose, readied him to stomp someone's ass.

Shelby smiled with her delicate brown eyes and said, "You're an interesting man, Mr. Miles Knox."

"I'm all man, not really all that interesting. More *simple* than anything else."

"Like the song?"

"Just like the song. You don't strike me as a Skynyrd fan."

"They're some of my favorite songs to dance to when the club's not bouncing C and C Music Factory or Prodigy or Lords of Acid." Shelby smiled.

"Dance?" Miles chuckled.

"Yeah, I'm a—"

He cut her off. "—Stripper. I know. Hell, the whole bar down here knows 'cause your daddy bitches about his only daughter baring and flaunting for other men."

"It's a job that earns me whatever I desire for little to no effort to a bunch of suckers."

Raising his hands, palms facing away, Miles told her, "I ain't judging."

Growing silent, Shelby chewed on something. Miles lifted his heft from leaning back against Shelby's vehicle and told her, "I'll let you get Whitey home. It's probably getting past your bedtime."

"Wait a damn minute," Shelby said, grabbing his arm. "You don't keep a girl out past curfew and not offer to buy her a drink sometime."

"Damn, girl, I's old enough to be your daddy."

"Yeah, well, you're not my daddy and I'm old enough to make my own decisions."

Smirking, that was one thing that attracted Miles to Shelby: she never judged him and he never judged her. She never treated him like an aging man. She was forward. Respectful. Kind. After that first encounter, there were drinks down along the Ohio at the Dock Restaurant. Margaritas for her, Maker's for him. After weeks of phone tag, more drinks that turned into mornings after his shift, where she'd surprise him with bourbon. Grilled rib eyes and sweet potatoes with cinnamon and real butter. Nights she was off from dancing and he was off his shift from the factory were spent around his firepit with a bottle of red wine and some Chris Knight tunes, Miles talking about the war, her talking about her brother, his addiction that he couldn't kick. She wanted to get him help but knew he'd never commit. Sometimes, Miles would take the two of them fishing at his camp. Talk about which bait to use for which fish. Shelby helped Miles forget about being in Vietnam when they were together. Made him feel youthful. And he guessed he maybe did the same for her, and at least kept her brother clean for the amount of time they passed fishing.

Miles now missed those mornings when Shelby'd press the aches from his knees, thighs, hamstrings, shoulders, and back, work the tension and creaks from his hitting the garage where he pressed, squatted, and deadlifted for multiple sets every other day before work. The other days he walked, jogged, and hiked his property or the gravel back roads. Sweating out all the booze he drank, cigarettes he smoked. Fighting to keep muscle mass. His heart pumping. His body fit for movement. He wanted to stay strong and attuned even with the booze he consumed. But work was where he watched one night drift into the next for twenty-plus years. In between batch alarms for material to be rung of moisture and pressed into Play-Doh. Dropped and fed to a spray dryer. Bagged out like cooking flour. It was a brainless endeavor.

Raking his hand over his head, through his hair, he was tired. Tired of missing Shelby. Tired of wondering why after all these months Shelby just stopped calling. Stopped coming over. What Miles wondered most was, where *was* Shelby? He missed her. He'd not seen nor heard from her in over a week. It was unlike her.

Laying the sack of gear on his kitchen table, he wasn't gonna call her again, go to her place like some dopey, zit-cheeked adolescent with cooing eyes and an upset stomach of puppy fuckin' love and a hard dick. He was too old for that shit. He went to the cabinet instead, reached for a nightcap, the bourbon. Poured a few fingers' worth. Removed a fresh lemon from the countertop, a paring knife from a drawer, sliced the lemon in half, squeezed both halves into the glass, walked to the bathroom. Sat the three or four swallows on the talcum-colored walk-in shower. Shed his clothing. Viewed himself in the mirror. Veined and bulging leathery flesh. Thick thighs, softball shoulders. Faded tattoos of Ka-Bar knives, dogs with devil heads, camo military helmets, and the bold script of SEMPER FI: always faithful.

Twisting the hot water, listening to it bounce from the shower stall, he thought of what Shelby always said to him, that he reminded her of the actor Stephen Lang. Maybe he did, he thought, stepping into the aged fiberglass shower. Inhaling the steam, twisting the cold water on, just enough to cut a little scald from the hot. Feeling the burn harden over his reddening flesh, he felt his tensions numb, and he thought about Warden Bush's place, how he'd set the steel mole trap on Kimball, had rigged clamps into the floor to hold the trap in place. There was a lot of blood. Miles clamped his eyes, let the water bead down his frame, and he thought it was sick that that was their form of amusement, their way of righting another man's wrongs. He thought about the lever that kept the spring release locked. Warden had made Kimball slide his foot beneath it, and if Kimball tried to pull his foot free, the surface leveler would be disrupted and the three steel spikes would spring down through Kimball's boot.

Kimball's left hand had sat palm-down on the table. Suicide kept slamming the mallet onto the tips of Kimball's digits. Mashing them. Trying to make him twitch. Make him jerk his foot. Move. They timed Kimball. If he could sit ten minutes, they'd release him. It was a lesson for his holding out.

Kimball's breathing was deep lung-sagging gulps on the ride back to the factory. Miles thought he sounded as though he'd punctured a lung, lucky Warden hadn't left him drowning within himself, flooding his lungs with fluid, gagging like he was gargling, give him something to really whine about. What they'd done to him was mental, they were breaking him down, forcing him to rebuild. Endure one type of pain to overcome a worse pain if he gave in.

Miles cut the hot water off. Twisted the cold full blast.

Slid the door open just enough to reach outside, grip his glass. Lifted it to lips, took a sip. Sat it back down, inhaled the frosty air from the cold water. Slid the door shut. Tilted his head back, let the water soothe his neck. His back. Creating goosebumps all over his body, killing any inflammation in his joints as he recalled the fifty-gallon drum that hung outside his hooch in Da Nang. Filling it in the mornings from a stream. Letting it sit till evening so it'd be warm. Otherwise it was cold. They used a mule to haul it, which was nothing more than a flatbed four-wheeler. The drum held near enough water for eight to ten men to shower with. And sometimes, that cold hurt more than freezer burn. You just had to grin and bear it.

Miles killed the water. Opened the curtain. Reached for his towel. Dried off. And that was when the screams of men came racing through his mind. Turning to the toilet, he held his shriveled dick in his hand, aimed for the porcelain bowl's center, and watched the molten stream foam and splash. Listened to Childers's voice shudder through his mind in splashes. Asking him, "Remember that 105 round?"

Yeah, Miles remembered it. "You tripped it."

"Naw, quit laying that on me."

"Clumsy-footed fuck, you was born with two left pigeon feet. You about took out the lot of us."

"Asshole. It blew my shit to heaven."

"Let me piss," Miles told Childers.

Over there, they shit and pissed into cut-in-half steel drums. Used diesel fuel to keep the flies at bay. When a tub was full, they paid a Vietnamese, or as some called them, *a gook*, to pull it out the back, light the fuel, and stir it with a long stick of wood. They called them shit burners or shit stirrers. The vats were to be burned and emptied daily. Long before they were full. The Vietnamese had to load the halved steel on the rear of the mule. If the shit-filled drum didn't get burned, it'd be spilling out, and they'd need help loading it. Meaning a marine's assistance. God help the Vietnamese who splashed shit on a jarhead. 'Cause his skin would get pounded to the shade of a beet or darker than onyx. Miles had helped more than a few times, and he'd bite his temper, keep it in check. Always placed himself in the other's skin. A shit job was a shit job, regardless of the continent. It wasn't as if these men woke up every morning wanting to spill human feces on a GI to commandeer a good ass beating.

"Miles, always holding a soft spot for his fellow man," he heard Childers say.

"Way I was raised, no one in my family judged others by skin color," Miles replied. "Wasn't in my parents' DNA. Then I joined the service and heard every racial slur known to man."

Miles thought about how the Marines broke you down and built you back up. Everyone got their heads peeled, was issued the same fatigues, boots, linen, and bed. Slept together, ate together, showered and shit together and trained together. The Marine Corps made you hard. Everyone was equal in war. You bled together and sometimes you died together. And there were no luxuries. Luxury wasn't something a man held over there. That was something others couldn't fathom when you explained your service, your time in battle. You just did what was necessary to survive another day.

Flushing the toilet, Miles wrapped the towel around his waist. Reached for the glass of bourbon, wanting to block out the war, he longed for Shelby as he pushed the glass to his lips. Thought of her lips, warm, tangy, and moist as a sponge saturated by heated honey. Exiting his bathroom, walking down the hallway, where black-and-white photos hung of men lounging in fatigues. Some on tanks. Others in the bush. Along rutted roads or posing with *mamasans* or *papasans*. Wet feet slapped again the cold scuffed hardwood, leading him onto the living room of cracked and chipped ceramic. He'd remodeled this home ten years ago. Ripping up floors of carpet and tearing out walls of old Sheetrock. Laying new flooring, rewiring and hanging fresh drywall. And now he sunk into the leather couch and rested the sweaty glass on a table. Looked over everything with bloodshot eyes, realizing all the new had rubbed off.

Reaching for the cordless, beside him he felt the shifty shadow of a patched complexion and saw Childers, who said, "Musta got tired of your ole cob."

Miles had given up not trying to call Shelby, to act like a puberty-stricken adolescent, he thought, as he told Childers, "I'm giving in to my fucking puppy love. So eat a dick, with you and your birth control glasses." Childers had worn specs and the Corps issued him a pair of thick black-framed glasses with Coke-bottle lenses. There was no damn way a chick was gonna bang him when they were on R and R over in 'Nam. Hence calling them birth control glasses.

Punching in Shelby's number, Miles waited, let the phone ring until her machine picked up and he said, "Shelby? Miles. It's early a.m., call me, baby, call me."

Clasping his eyes, Miles started to drift into a world where the earth was helmed by flames, the roads covered in shrapnel. Jarheads screamed and fought against the unholy communist rule of the North Vietnamese Army. Gave their being for territory. For simple farmers. Some marines were wounded and pinned down. The midday sun scorched the dead hides to the bone till reinforcements were called in from above or naval ships were radioed with coordinates and shelled rounds from the seas. Miles and other marines kept their heads buried. Crawled about the land of foreign timber. Dodging and returning rifle fire, mortar rounds, and grenades. Explosions and combustion. Scavenging through the fall of the dead for provisions of unused ammo. Compared shoe sizes, traded their boots if they'd fit and were in better condition. Same with their pants or flak jackets. It was what war did to a soldier, taught them continuance. Survival.

Shaking his mind from the drift of scar tissue cutouts, Miles pried his eyes open. Traded the cordless phone for the glass of remaining liquid, killed the last inch of Maker's, reflected on those memories of darker times, of hunting an enemy with a similar military background, as he longed for Shelby. Her tips brushing bumps over his hide. Her warm kindling his. He wondered where in the hell she was at.

Early-morning sun caused the land to lay as though ravaged by flame when Shadrack crossed Moberly Road's patched travel of pavement. He'd slept in a homemade hunting blind constructed of cut cedar trees, laying crisscrossed, keeping him hidden from sight. Waking now, he had waited till dark began to clear from the woods. Listened for heavy trots over the ground. Wondered if the man had followed, had tracked him through the wilderness. Most of all, he wondered if his father and mother had really been shot, if they were really dead or if it had all been a bad dream.

Frail arms and legs burned with briar and twig engravings. His feet did not bleed when trouncing over thorns and broken limbs. The bottoms had been toughened by calluses from running barefoot outdoors around the burned-out house where he lived near Blue River Village. Toughened from wading into the river, walking over the rough, jagged, and slimy rock bottoms. Sometimes wade fishing, other times swimming.

Walking down Harrison Springs Road, fields ran along the right and left flanks. Hay sat rolled into round bales.

Tall as rear tractor tires with a sign that read in black letters
FOR SALE. To his right a deer lay dead and rotted. The smell
fermented and insect luring.

When he reached Devil's Elbow Road, he turned his
back, started walking along the busted blacktop, when
from behind tread cut the distance as a vehicle approached.
Shock drizzled up Shadrack's spine, his heart thumping in
his ears, he wasn't sure if he should stop and wait for the
vehicle to pass or start to run, believing it could be the outline called Coyote who'd shot his father and mother. An
off-balance rumble honked its horn. Slowed beside him. A
voice came from the truck's rolled-down window. "Shad?
What in thee Sam hell are you doing out here at this time
of morning?"

It wasn't the man called Coyote. It was a familiar face.
A friend of Shadrack's uncle. A man he'd met maybe a
handful of times over his young years. Shadrack's fear less-
ened upon seeing the familiar face, though he stayed silent
at first, as he slowed his breath and found some comfort.
The truck door screeched. Boots clomped over the road.

Shadrack looked at the man and said, "Will . . . will you
take me to Uncle Nathaniel's?"

Thick farmer's arms reached down from the whisker-
faced man who answered to the moniker of Tacker. Scooped
Shadrack up. Opened his driver's-side door. Said, "Son,
you're colder than my ex—ole lady's heart. Hang on, I'll get
you to your uncle Nate's." And slammed the door.

Shadrack lay in the seat. Mute and trembling beneath a worn navy-blue hooded sweatshirt Tacker had placed over him. Knees like two aged baseballs where the leather was no longer white but rimmed by dirty prints and scuffed by turf beneath. Screams and gunshots rifled through Shadrack's memory. Tacker ground the gears of his Chevy. Turned down the road where Shadrack's uncle lived in a cottage-style home with the wood siding painted black. Shutters around the windows squared gray. Tacker drove beyond the potholed road. Ruby and Ring, two walker hounds, stood with their white coats patched by tan and raven. The hounds bellowed as the Chevy stopped. Tacker walked to the driver's side. Cradled Shadrack from the front seat. Carried him to the house, where he was met on the back porch by the click of a .45's hammer. The barrel pointed at him. Tacker stood stunned and Nathaniel asked, "The hell you holding my nephew for at seven in the damn morning?"

"Came up on him walking along Harrison Springs Road, boss. Was on my way to open the gun shop. Only words he rifled was your name."

Hands thumbed the trigger. Pushed the pistol down his waist, took the sweatshirt from the boy, gave it back to Tacker, took Shadrack, wrapped his arms around him. Smelled the mineral of his sweaty skin. Scents of wood, foliage, and earth. Scooped him up and carried him into the house. He hadn't held the boy in this manner since his birth at the hospital, cradling him in the hospital room with his smiling brother and tired sister-in-law, everyone proud and at peace.

Walking through the kitchen where a woodstove sat, past a hand-planed cedar table, hints of fresh-brewed coffee accompanied them through the dining area and into a living room, which lay immaculate. Devoid of dust. Decorated by squared framed photos that hung from the wall of Shadrack's school pictures over the years. Of Bedford and Judy from various family gatherings before Bedford hurt his back. Shad sunk into the worn sofa, Nathaniel wrapped a handmade quilt around him, tried to confirm what was in the boy's weary eyes, his fear, his slight shake and blink. Shad stared at his uncle, took in the lengths of growth matted over his head like fresh driveway seal, blue-eyed, shirt buttoned to the top, lean faced, whiskerless and smelling of aftershave. So different from his father, Bedford. Nathaniel was clean and strong, Shad thought, like Bruce Wayne, like Batman.

Nathaniel prepared for the worst, knew his brother sold pills. Oxycodone that he received for his back pains. It was something he held little comfort for. Had warned his older brother to abandon company with opioids. Like most drugs, it was something Nathaniel'd been educated about and dealt with from his time in law enforcement. But he knew the deal. What Shad was to do if an exchange went south at the run-down house, and so he asked, "Hell happened, Shad? Bedford and Judy in the thick of it?"

Shadrack wanted to cry till tears rinsed the night from his cheeks. Replayed the memories in his mind, he searched for words that would explain the screams and the gunshots. His teeth rattled and he mustered words that were direct in their delivery. "Regular. Come. Shot them both—" The soft skin of the child's lids took shape over his eyes to calm the wet and he said, "—Dead."

Nathaniel grasped Shad's arms, thumbs nervously applying pressure.

Tacker touched Nathaniel's grip. "Ease up, boss." And Nathaniel did. Told Shadrack, "Sorry, buddy." Then asked, already knowing the answer. But needing it confirmed. "Shot who dead?"

Tears warmed the hems below the child's eyes before he got choked up and said, "Dad and Mom."

The echo of kids hollering and splashing chlorinated water from the wading pool couldn't drown out Becca's telling of her ex-husband crapping under her parents' Christmas tree when she and her ex had been dating years and years ago. Shelby laughed as they sat in their bikinis, Shelby wondering if she'd ever tie the knot herself while the sun beat down on their toned flesh, the rubber straps of support from the lounging chairs beneath their spines, asses, and legs.

"You're kidding me?" Shelby questioned.

"Hell no, Kev and I had been drinking bourbon with my folks, got a little drunk. I slept in my old bedroom, he passed out on the couch. His ass wakes up in the middle of the night, thinks he's in the bathroom, and squats under the tree."

Pool water glistened its blue tint beyond the distance of their pedicured toes, bright lime-green polish, and Shelby was fighting tears of hysterics. "God, that sounds awful."

With her Ray-Ban sunglasses over her nose, just below her vision, Becca fingered her damp pecan-colored locks over her ear and said, "You ain't shitting. No pun intended, my dad wakes up to Kev passed out under the tree, laying on his side, pants around his ankles with a big old pile of you-know-what behind him. It. Was. Horrible."

Sweat began to moisten and bead upon Shelby's skin, and she wondered again if she'd ever be married as she planted her feet on the heated concrete, maneuvered her body to standing up, walked to the pool's edge, wanting to take a dip, to cool off. Getting to the pool, she thought about Miles; regardless of age, she'd marry him, even though they'd only known one another a short time. Kneeling to slide into the water, she thought about her brother and her father, their addictions, her responsibility to care for them, and then she slipped, her legs hit the water, and the rear of her skull hit the concrete lip around the pool, next thing she heard was the ringing in her head, the bells sounding in her ears from the black cloth that swelled and dispersed like dye within her mind's eye and she fell into the pool. Blinking her eyes, her fluttering vision grasped back onto the color of day, blue skies overhead, the cough and belch of water from her lungs and out of her mouth, the sounds of kids playing and splashing water found quiet as hands gripped and tugged her back to the pool's lip. Her head swiveled upon her neck like a Barbie doll or an action figure. Mouths were moving but she heard zero. She could only feel and what she felt was cold. Cold as what she drove around with in the trunk of her Camaro.

Now, she lay on a creek rock floor. Hands strung behind her back with shoelaces from her shoes. Sweat dribbled down her forehead, mixed with the crust of blood that lined her cheekbone and the hammer of gunfire rollercoastering through her mind. Blinking her eyes open, she focused on unlaced boots in front of her. Worked her way up over a pair of lime-green polyester pants. Arms inked with tribal vines and thorns. Infected black and purple boils, limbs hung from the sleeves of a wrinkled black T-shirt with a huge white skeleton head and MISFITS across its forehead.

It was her brother, her fraternal twin, Wylie. He sat with a trucker cap upon his head, eyes sunken, rimmed with black from no sleep, lips a plum color, and he said to her, "Sleeping Beauty awakes."

Hints of pulpy skin and woodsmoke lined Shelby's nostrils and she asked, "Why'd you tie me up?"

Last she remembered, she was driving, then things went pitch-black.

Wylie chuckled, pulled a blue hanky from his pocket. Knotted his left arm off, his sleeve rolled up, two-fingered a swat against his skin but couldn't get a good vein. Removed his right boot. Acted as though he hadn't heard Shelby's question. Pulled free his hole-pocked sock, which was browning. To his left sat a black ceramic mug and a bottle of prescription pills. A loaded shot was in the mug. Wylie spread his first two toes apart, found the bright pink sour-skin he needed, grabbed the needle, stabbed it between the toes, unloaded the rig.

His every movement she felt, or recalled from walking in on him when he was doing these actions in her home, it was as though she were his shadow or vice versa; she felt his numbness line her insides, watched him lay the needle down. He grabbed his open beer, took a swig. That slurping sound he made turned her stomach. Always did. Then he slid his sock over his foot and back into the boot. Fondled her with his expression, just as he'd done when they were kids, in front of their father. Smiled and said, "'Cause you ask too damn many questions. Always have."

An ache traveled from her fingertips to her neck. Felt like tiny pieces of iron flake floating up and down the insides of her limbs. Jabbing her nerves to a discomforting state, spewing lava. She tried wiggling her hands. Worming them little by little to create a gap, but couldn't tell if she was doing anything. She wondered where she was. Studied the wood-paneled walls devoid of any decoration. The room was a blister of heat, ready to ignite, as if taking up residence on the sun.

Beneath her form-fitting T-shirt, her flesh was damp, and she could smell the mildew perspiration. She wanted her hands free, free of restraint, wherever restraint was. She wanted to be home, showered, and wrapped in Miles's hulking warm arms. She missed him. Realized she'd not seen nor spoken with him in some time.

It was September, that in-between season in the Midwest that would bring the cooler weather, so Wylie had a fire going. He sat jerking his head, his arms a bit unsteady. Shelby watched Wylie create another round of what he called his fix, as he dumped a handful of pills onto a sandblasted plate with white flecks of paint. Crushed them with a spoon into a chalky powder. Then diced the powder with a butcher knife. Dumped the white into a ceramic mug. Dissolved them just as she'd caught him doing at her home. She eyed the fireplace he sat beside, wondering how many fixes he'd already prepared and shot into his bloodstream, over and over, again and again. The fireplace was familiar. So damn familiar. She was drawing blanks, gaps in time, places.

Above the fireplace sat a faded color photo. Two young men. One Black. One white. Each dressed in green military fatigues. Boots unlaced. The Black man wore a jungle hat, the sides rolled up like a tongue, rested his hand on his crotch. The white man didn't wear a hat. Had his hair slicked over his skull. Held a smoke in his right hand. She couldn't see the cigarette from where she lay, but she knew he was smoking a Marlboro red in the photo. He'd smoked them since he was sixteen. Pumped iron three or four days a week. Ran and walked the other days. Sucked down Maker's Mark. It was Miles and one of the men he'd served with. One of the many men who made it back to the States in a body bag.

Wylie had brought her to Miles's camp. A place Miles inherited from his uncle Bud after he'd passed. Miles told Shelby his uncle Bud had been a Korean War vet who often joked of the girlfriends who'd kept him company. The skinny ones he dated in the daylight, garden-eating gals, he called them. The big-boned gals he took out at night to the all-you-can-eat steak and shrimp eateries. He didn't discriminate, he loved females of all shapes and sizes, that was what he told Miles. His uncle had been a cutup, a peaceful man who saw a lot of bad shit. But he drank like a fish to saturate all that bad from his memory.

Miles had taken Wylie and Shelby fishing and camping here a few times. It was peaceful. A hundred and fifty acres of seclusion, devoid of interruption. Of people. It reminded Shelby of where her brother and she had grown up. Their father and mother had bought a three-bedroom ranch home out off Corydon Ramsey Road, with ten acres, a two-car garage, and a fishing pond. That was when her parents got along. When her father wasn't a vile and rude drunk. They taught Wylie and she how to line their fishing poles, how to bait their hooks with thick nightcrawlers, how to attach bobbers. Seemed like a made-up past now. That home was slowly rotting away with her daddy inside it, just as her childhood had.

Flames popped from the fireplace. Shadows danced in the room. Lifting her head from the floor to look up, her neck, shoulders, and hands throbbed.

Searching her mind for points of reference, of how she'd gotten here, she recalled getting off from work at the Vu several days ago, where she danced nude for any and all shade of suckers, swine, suits, and grease monkeys. Men who'd come sip on ten-dollar Cokes, near beers and gaze at shapely flesh as it bounced, rubbed, caressed, pinched, and teased, fleshy assets for currency that enticed others to lay folds of green down. Men with desires and fetishes not met at home, thinking they'd be a sugar daddy. Thinking one day they'd take a girl away from the life of dancing and earning, give her a new life in a nice home or townhouse, keep her all to himself, his personal infatuation of lust.

Suckers, Shelby always thought, suckers and pigs. It was just a way for her to earn a living, nothing more, nothing less.

Reflecting, the last thing Shelby remembered after leaving work at the Vu a few days ago was taking Wylie to Bedford's place to get a fix. Then things got foggy, went dark, flashes of an argument, gunfire, and then she was driving and she could remember nothing beyond that.

She did recall she'd planned to drop Wylie at her place, then surprise Miles at his home, as she'd not spoken with him all week, maybe get some steaks and a bottle of wine and crash at his house. But the more she thought about it, that seemed like days ago, she felt there was an entire section of time that had been omitted from her mind. Somewhere there had been a divide. A shift of self, and now here she was tied up. She didn't trust Wylie, knowing how he was, that he was an addict, couldn't hold a job, would steal for his addiction. Laying here on the floor, she knew he had done something, as his actions suddenly seemed like her actions. She could feel them embedded beneath her layers of skin and thought. But the harder she tried to figure out how she'd ended up here at Miles's cabin, the more she was drawing a blank. Missing moments of her life, finding gaps in time, her head pulsed with a migraine.

Looking around the room for a clue, something to rustle a memory, on the floor, at Wylie, she saw two Walmart sacks lay to his left. Empty cans of Pabst Blue Ribbon beer were tossed about the rock floor.

"What did you go and do?"

Wylie reached for one of the beers that sat to his right. Shelby noticed the pistol handle hanging from his pocket. His back pressed into the wall, he took a hard swig of the PBR. Laid the can on the floor between his legs. From the sack Wylie pulled out and held a bottle of pills. Shook it. Sounded like a rattlesnake.

Told Shelby, "There you go with your damn questions. Bedford and his ole lady Judy got all that cotton. All that money from the cotton. Told them they sold me bad shit, I wanted a hundred more pills. They say no-go. Can only offer forty or some such shit. The rest is spoken for. Say they'd have more Monday. I'm thinking, why I gotta wait. I'm here now. They ain't. And I got that feeling, that yearn in my bones. Want all I can eat and shoot. Cut out the middleman. Decided fuck it! Fired a bullet in them each. Merry Christmas, motherfuckers!"

Shelby remembered the echo of gunshots. She felt the air in the room contract. The only word she could form was *Why?*

"Just told you, cut out the middleman. Hell, I might start doing it full-time. Rob the dealer."

Shelby twisted her hands, tried to keep the blood flowing. The restraint of the shoelaces was too tight. Cutting into her wrists. The bends in her arms itched with burn.

Wylie's mental state had deteriorated. He was in the negative. She should've seen this coming, the taking of another's life for his addiction. What she hoped was that Bedford and Judy weren't really dead. She hoped to God they weren't. She had to get free and so she told him, "They were people, human beings just like you and me and . . . they have a kid. A son."

"Man's only as good as his word."

"His word? He had forty pills for you."

"He could've told the other person to wait, can't tell me I can't have the other bottles, that's a load of shit."

Pausing, Wylie reached for one of the Walmart sacks. Dumped it to the floor.

"Look here at how many bottles they got full of the cotton. *Tell me to wait until Monday.* No matter now they won't be no more Mondays for nobody."

Wylie had gone mad. Off the deep end. And she thought about the boy and asked, "What about Shadrack?"

Downing a PBR, Wylie smashed the can in its center. Skipped it across the floor. He'd a hint of craziness hanging in his eyes just as he always did when he drank, the flames from the fireplace bouncing within them, and he told Shelby, "That rodent got his stomp out the back door before I could get a round in him."

Thank God! Shelby told herself.

Wylie reached for another beer, grabbed one from the box. Opened it. Took a hard gulp. Told Shelby, "Gotta think on this for a bit. Figure out what to do. So silence your chatter!"

You got to turn yourself in, Shelby thought. But telling him that might anger him more, set off something she couldn't protect herself against. She thought about something Miles told her when he was in Da Nang: you had to think like the enemy to understand the enemy, and she thought she needed to pretend to work with Wylie, to think like Wylie; she had to convince him she was on his side, he had to trust her in order to get free, so she asked, "Can I have one of them?"

"A beer?"

"I'm thirsty."

"How you gonna drink it?"

"Untie me."

Wylie chuckled. "Think I'm an idiot. Can't do that, sis, not at this stage of the game."

"Why the hell not?"

"'Cause I ain't decided what I'm gonna do with you yet."

The initial response was shock, tainting his memories of Bedford and Judy. Over and over, he told himself, *This can't be*. But Nathaniel had worked it all out in his head, put the trauma of what Shad had told him somewhere far away. Turned his loss to anger and came with thoughts. Thoughts on how things would be handled. But first, Shadrack's demeanor had to be nailed down. Every tiny action and word choice had to be rehearsed with not much time to spare.

Nathaniel was close to the boy. Had bought him the things Bedford would not. Spent time with him fishing, hunting, and telling him stories of his father and him as kids. Nathaniel knew Shad held a strong affinity for Batman comic books and action figures. And reruns of the animated series. He'd always felt bad knowing how the boy lived. How his brother and sister-in-law lived. Living off the government. Taking handouts. And being addicted to opiates. He'd thought of bringing in social services and trying to get custody of the boy. But it was his brother. His family. That was a hard line to cross. He'd recommended getting help, therapy, someplace to dry out. But neither of them wanted anything to do with getting off chemical dependency or the government's tit.

Instead of beating a dead horse, Nathaniel tried to keep an eye on Shadrack from a distance. Stayed out of Bedford's affairs.

Looking Shadrack in the eyes now, Nathaniel explained, "Shad, listen to my words: yesterday, after school, I got you from your home, you stayed here with me. You got it?"

The boy had a confused stare in the hilts of his orbs, like a schizophrenic lost in the medication of their numbing, lifting his chin up then down, deciphering the meaning of Nathaniel's language.

"Repeat it back to me."

"You picked me up from home yesterday to stay with you," Shad told him in an uncertain tone.

"Good. And Bedford and Judy had some things they needed tending. So we sat about shelling .22 rounds at cans till dark. Hit the stream catfishing 'cause that's what I did. Then I was to drop you off this morning."

Nathaniel nodded for Shadrack to repeat his words back to him, once more.

"Dad and Mom had stuff to do so we shot at cans and went fishing."

Nathaniel felt Shad had the nuts and bolts and began questioning him again about what had happened. About the short, lean man who'd entered. Face hidden by a hooded sweatshirt tarped over the bill of a cap. Raspy chords that bore the nickname *Coyote*. And Nathaniel told Shad, "What your daddy called him, *Coyote*, what we just spoke here, it stays between you, me, and the dead air that fills my home, you hear me?"

Hunkered on the couch, the rifling of AC air streamed from floor vents. A comforter was draped over Shad's shoulders. His face tracked by briars and branches. His soot-colored locks going every which way, he looked from the corner of his hound-pup eyes and said, "Okay. Yeah, I hear you."

When he felt Shad had a good learning on all they'd discussed, Nathaniel asked him, "You ready to go back home?"

Looking afraid he questioned, "To stay? What about the bad man Daddy called Coyote?"

Taking a deep breath, keeping his composure, seeing the fear in his nephew's eyes, he realized now, at this very moment, what he should've done years ago: he should've stepped in, fought to take custody of Shad. He couldn't make up for that mistake but that was exactly what he would do now. "Not to stay. You're with me from now on. That bad man is gone. Don't worry about him. I'll find him. But I need you to be strong, like Batman, but to do that we gotta go over there and figure out who this bad man is."

Shad sat thinking. Looked Nathaniel in the eyes and told him, "Okay. I can do that, I can be like Batman, as long as you're with me, like Nightwing or Robin."

Gathering some of Shadrack's clothing, he loaded them into a black Osprey pack, slung it over his shoulder, and

Nathaniel loaded Shad into the black Dodge Dually 4x4 with the belongings he kept for the boy when he stayed with him. He had to make it appear convincing even if no one paid mind to it.

Taking Devil's Elbow, Nathaniel thought about a call he'd taken one night, a case he'd helped Detective Thurman work. Where a man had violated a woman by fist, foot, and ball bat. Leaving her unable to speak 'cause her lips were ballooned, dental chinked, and eyes thin as thread to hem pants. He'd taken her statement and snapped glossies in the ER. The savage had struck at the Carefree truck stop in Leavenworth, had his way with this female, what some referred to as a local lot lizard, but the predator had left bite marks upon her breasts, thighs, and ass. Hands printing her arms from squeezing, then throwing her to the gravel like an empty Coke can and left for the garbage collector.

In Nathaniel's eyes, force should get returned to the violator by stringing, burning, or beating; for him fair was fair. Eye for an eye, tooth for a tooth.

Glancing over at Shad, who sat quiet and looked up at Nathaniel. "What?"

Exhaling hard, Nathaniel said to him, "I wish you'd not have seen what you saw, that you'd not have to do any of this. A boy your age is supposed to be learning things and having fun. Your family is supposed to protect you."

"Well, I'm okay now. You'll protect me, right?"

"Yes I will, buddy, yes I will."

Hanging a left at the stop sign, Nathaniel fell back into deep thought, knowing head prosecutors were supposed to be protectors but in the end, they were the worst. Throwing tickets out. Giving probation for long-term offenders, to milk money from offenders or their families, the more money they gave the less the offense regardless of the laws they broke. As a cop, he couldn't do a damn thing about it. Nathaniel called them Monty Hall's Let's Make a Deal. Unable to do what he felt was right in favor of bending for other men's agendas. Months before the woman was attacked, the county had thrown out a case on a teenage boy who'd been raped by a truck driver at the same truck stop. The boy'd been attacked from behind when he went into a bathroom stall. Only evidence was the boy's word against the truck driver's. There was no DNA, fucker used a condom, and there were no witnesses or cameras. If something like that happened to Shad, there wouldn't be a court. Nathaniel would be the judge with a nine-millimeter jury.

Reflecting back, when the lot lizard got into a trucker's cab, it was the driver from months before. This time he'd gotten careless. Left evidence. Semen and bite marks. It reopened the boy's case. Identifying the same pattern of teeth, bite marks. It shined a light on why the case had really been thrown out: The driver was a brother-in-law to a local attorney. Was married to the sister. It wasn't about right and wrong, it was about image. Saving face in the public's eye. Keeping the dirty family secret buried.

Beside Nathaniel, Shadrack asked, "Think we can get something to eat after this?"

Food. Shit, he hadn't even thought about Shad being hungry. "Yes we can. How about steak? That sound good?"

Shadrack's eyes lit up along with something like a glow in his cheeks. "You mean deer?"

"Is there any other type of steak?"

Shad smiled and chuckled. "No."

After the rapist got off, Nathaniel had had enough. Felt being a county cop had become nothing more than a puppet show for the small-town cliques and county clowns. He'd slogged through ten years, couldn't take another day once the word was out about his older brother peddling pills. It was something Nathaniel never confronted him with head-on.

In the end, Nathaniel'd taken his 401(k), his savings, applied for his gun dealer license, a Type 7, meaning he could sell nearly everything from machine guns to silencers. He'd opened a gun shop. Dealt it out of a small restored historic cabin outside of town, had Tacker run it for him, giving him a percentage from each sell. For Nathaniel, America had slipped into a sewer of false hopes and consumerism. A government that used working men's and women's tax dollars for their pet projects but did little to help the working class. In his mind they just wanted citizens to work and to keep their mouths shut. Seemed there was a select group of people who paid more attention to a movie star's private life than they did to the people who were running their own country into the ground. Men and women who pushed values onto other continents that weren't even values; these politicians would get the backing of their constituents, start a war, and destroy a country, make some backroom deals, waste tax dollars rebuilding that country, and leave the citizens of their own country, the same ones who voted them into office, to bleed out in the streets, slowly creating an American wasteland.

The values Nathaniel had been trained to enforce were nothing more than disregarded words on a document. Were there good cops? Yes there were. Were there bad cops? Bet your ass there were. But there were virtuous and unvirtuous people in all walks of life regardless of profession, all creed and color, everywhere, and he'd been acquainted with each. From Nathaniel's point of thinking, when it came down to politics, the truth never mattered, it only depended on what the narrative being pushed was to disgrace and divide one side from the other. And it angered him because in the end it was the innocent who were getting hurt.

When he resigned from the force, he acquainted himself with like-minded men and women. People he could trust and count on when the shit hit the fan. Factory workers, carpenters, welders, farmers, owners of restaurants, bartenders, barbers, feed store owners, and war veterans and mechanics.

These people had become the artery of his life. In his mind they were the backbone of America. They were blue-collar, working-class people. All denominations and colors. With them he'd formed a herd of similar opinions and views. They could see where the world was headed. They began to plan for their future. Stored barrels of drinking water that they filtered and purified. Crates of dry goods. Hunted wild game every season. Processed it themselves. Kept gardens. Canned their food. They became less and less dependent on the supply chain, on their government and its dictation of handouts and oversight. They collected gold and silver, anything of weight in case paper failed. Invested in American-owned companies, what few were left. They target practiced on the weekends. Reloaded their own ammunition. Anything their ancestors once did, they were following in their footsteps.

Everyone was a voracious reader. They shared and swapped books. Studied and read the Old Testament, the Foxfire series, survival manuals, *The Gulag Archipelago*, *Ordinary Men*, *Man's Search for Meaning*, the Constitution, which the government didn't seem to understand nor did they follow or read, *The Communist Manifesto*, *The Autobiography of Malcolm X*, *The Fourth Turning*, *The Idiot*, *Animal Farm*, *1984*, *Atlas Shrugged*, and too many more to name. They met several times a month at a country church, discussed their readings. Their struggles. Where they came from. There were families who'd escaped communist rule; one family had opened a restaurant while another opened a nail salon. They talked of their ancestors who died during the Cultural Revolution during Mao's reign. There was a family of color who lived in the Delta area of Mississippi, heard of a good-paying factory hiring in Louisville, Kentucky, and made roots in Corydon. All of these people shared family histories. Struggles and wrongdoings. But they found middle ground on common issues. Understanding. Reached out and bonded with one another, they worked jobs and lived from the land just as their ancestors had done. These were men and women who had grown tired of giving and losing, never gaining ground. They were tired of being looked down upon, judged, told what and how to think; they were a group of constitutionalists. They discussed their governments that had come before them and failed. And why they failed. Because they took from the people who worked. Sold them out and lived on their blood, their sweat, and their tears.

Hanging a left at the next stop, the trees rooted straight, curved, and broken. Leaves fumbled the land with the arc of sun delivering early-morning heat. When a vehicle came barreling toward them, Nathaniel swerved off the road, and Shad's expression expanded like a helium-filled balloon as Nate yelled, "Look out!" His right hand reached across Shadrack's body, protecting him as his left controlled the steering, the truck frame rattled through weeds and dirt. Shad asked, "Who was that?"

The quick view of the driver's complexion didn't escape Nathaniel's mind; it told Nathaniel who it was, the rear of his vehicle already gone. "Carney Dillman."

Nathaniel got a bad taste in his mouth. A lump in his throat. His pulse raced, quickly turning to irritation, then anger. He'd be placing Carney on his list of persons of interest.

Turning down the worn road, Bedford's place sat lone and morphing into rot. Separated from other homes by country miles of trees, hills, and fields. Nathaniel turned to Shadrack with the rhythmic chug of the diesel's engine rumbling beneath him. "Stay seated. Remember what I told you. We angled the greasy cats last night. Caught us some whoppers."

Half smiling but still a little shook up from Carney running them off the road, Shadrack held up his left and right hands, spread apart twelve to sixteen inches, palms facing one another, and said, "They was this big."

"Yes they were, buddy. Yes they were."

Stepping from the truck, Nathaniel surveyed the yard with his eyes, Shadrack's toys spread about the dirt, a Big Wheel, a bicycle turned upside down, some plastic guns he'd bought the boy for a birthday gift, everything covered by droplets of dew.

His heavy-footed steps made the dilapidated porch creak and give. The front door was ajar. Nathaniel took a deep breath before entering, pictured his own kin laid out like monuments of the dead.

Inside, Bedford lay on his back, black-blood-speckled arms at his sides stringing out from under one of the many concert shirts he always wore. Only resembling his birth name by the shape of his body. The prints of his bloating digits.

His complexion was smeared like a dream one couldn't recollect, being delivered in fragments and knots of bone and red to a parched mind. Judy was maybe a foot away from him, her chest ripped by a nickel-sized hole, a busted main line drained of self. Anxiety moistened Nathaniel's throat, bringing back images of a downed officer from a call he'd answered for a domestic dispute. The officer hadn't worn his vest. Knocked on a door that had splintered open with buckshot, took two rounds of balls and pellets from a madman blistering his wife with rights and lefts. Why was it always the women getting the brunt of the men? A repeat offender whose wife wouldn't press charges. That was why. Always believing their male counterparts would see the light. Change their actions of domestic violence. It never happened.

When Nathaniel arrived as the only available backup, because the other officers didn't answer their radios right away, the madman sat weeping, hands raised, kneeling beside the officer, the sawed-off he used laying on the officer's chest. His wife lay unconscious on the living room floor, her face appearing like spoiled fruit that'd been dropped and mashed across pavement, her chest barely rising. The madman looked up at Nathaniel, said, "I fucked up, I really fucked up bad this time." Nathaniel told him, "You sure the shit did. Now pick up the shotgun."

"What?"

Nathaniel heard the other cruiser pull up outside, knew what he was about to do was a sin. But so was letting this man live to do the evil he did. "Don't *what* me, you expiration-dated piece of shit, pick up the shotgun."

Shaking, the man grasped the shotgun.

Nathaniel hollered, "Put down your weapon!"

Listened to the footfalls of the approaching officer outside. His pistol trained on the repeat abuser. Nathaniel screamed, "No!" And pulled the trigger. Finished him.

Was it wrong? Yes it was. Was it ethical? No it was not. But when a person sees himself dealt a bad hand by another, sees a woman beat to a pulp over and over, retribution emerges. Takes over. Every man and woman has it within them. They just don't always act upon it.

Now, he studied the outlines on the floor. His brother. His sister-in-law. Blood had ponded around each, a pool of unfinished life. Deep down he knew they were no good. You play with fire eventually you get burned. But Shadrack didn't see them in that light. To him they were his mother and father. That was all he knew.

What Nathaniel didn't have time for was sadness. There were things that needed to be done. A killer to be found. Though he felt the urge to tear up, he didn't know if they were for his brother and sister-in-law or for Shadrack. This was the only life he'd ever known. One thing was certain: there was no time for victim mode. It was time to reflect on what he knew how to do, which was hunt and start putting pieces together.

Shadrack had said they argued over how much cotton Bedford had. That was what had gotten this started. Looked as if Nathaniel would have to finish it.

From the kitchen, where dishes lay smeared with egg yolk, bacon grease, and a counter of bread crumbs, he reached for a cordless phone sitting next to a half pot of molasses coffee. Dialed 911. Told the operator he'd been a county cop for ten years, needed to be connected with the Harrison County PD. Told the Harrison County dispatch the same. That his eight-year-old nephew had stayed with him last night, he was to bring him back home this morning to his brother and sister-in-law's home. That he'd showed up to an open front door and found them each shot dead in their home. Nathaniel gave her the address of Bedford and Judy. Told dispatch, send Detective Thurman, he's the best you got. And hung up.

They'd have nothing now. Nathaniel had infected the crime scene. But he had the perfect alibi. There were no witnesses. Nothing. All he had to do was speak with the detective and be on his way, begin his recon of the county for a man who went by the name Coyote.

When Thurman pulled up in his unmarked cruiser, the strobe of red and blue from the grille, Nathaniel could read what he thought within the age creases of his pigment. Thurman couldn't believe Nathaniel's kin had been taken from this world. He was a big barn-headed bastard. Attired in jeans and a navy-blue T-shirt, his chest and arms were lumberjack thick, country boy strong. He kept his hair squared like a military man. Shook Nathaniel's hand, grimaced and said, "Real sorry, Nate."

"We been fishing last night, got up a while ago to bring Shad back home, pulled up, got out of the truck, saw the door open, thought something wasn't chiming, told Shad to stay put."

"Damn," Thurman said. Already taking notes on a small spiraled notepad. "You told the boy yet?"

"Not yet. But seeing you here, he ain't no dummy."

Thurman finished taking Nathaniel's statement while waiting on the coroner and the ambulance. Then told Nathaniel if he needed anything to phone him and he cut him loose. Told him he'd be in contact later.

Back at his home, Nathaniel needed to piece things together. He glanced at a picture of Bedford and he on the fridge before the back accident, before the drugs had weakened him into an addict, as he pulled several packages of deer steak from his freezer. Placed them in the microwave to defrost and asked Shadrack if he wanted to get a shower. Get cleaned up.

"Yeah, I do."

Nathaniel set out a thick brown towel and wash rag for Shad. Told him to get some clean Levi's and a T-shirt, socks, and underwear from the backpack he'd brought along, and to just leave his dirty clothes on the bathroom floor, he'd wash them later. He was gonna get the steaks going in the cast iron for them.

Shadrack looked at Nathaniel, his eyes began to bubble up. Nathaniel walked toward him, knowing the answer but trying his best at compassion. "What's wrong, buddy?"

"What's gonna happen now? Mom and Dad are . . . dead, where . . . am I gonna go? Where am I gonna live?"

On a bent knee, wrapping his arms around Nathaniel's waist, the sobs came pouring out, Nathaniel rubbed Shad's back and told him, "With me, buddy, you're gonna live with me. The one thing your mom and dad took care of when you's born was custody issues. That's something we got in writing. I'll always take care of you and I'm gonna find who caused this."

With his face buried into Nathaniel's shoulder, Shadrack asked, "You promise?"

"I promise."

Walking into his den, anger fired through Nathaniel's vision as he eyed several books on a shelf. *Soldier's Manual of Common Tasks* and *The U.S. Armed Forces Nuclear, Biological and Chemical Survival Manual*, the Old Testament, and Winston S. Churchill's *Memoirs of the Second World War*. He turned on the stereo. Fingered the volume on his CD player. Bluesy rhythms with the yawn of an underlying groove grew from a low level. "Gimme Shelter" by the Rolling Stones. The tension building until Mick's voice kicked in. Turning the volume up, Nathaniel walked back into the kitchen, Shadrack's words echoing over and over in his mind, the one who'd shot Bedford and Judy had once been a regular, seemed sick, went by the moniker Coyote. The name didn't register.

The microwave beeped. The steaks were thawed. He grabbed the warm white chunk of freezer-paper-wrapped meat. Laid them on the marble counter, they felt softened up.

Nathaniel needed to pay Carney Dillman a visit. He had the suspicion that other than running him off the road, he'd been at his brother's house. He knew they grew up as friends, but Nate always warned his brother of associating with him, which he more than likely did behind his back. Nate wondered what Carney knew; he hoped he wasn't tied to the murders.

But first, Nathaniel thought, he still had connections from his police days, knew an old CI, Leonard, who he could ask about this Coyote and about Carney so he'd be informed, a step ahead; he'd have ammunition if needed before he paid Carney a visit, in case Carney was involved and tried to lie. One thing was certain: that bastard Carney was in a hurry when he ran him off the road. He did recall Carney ran guns. And Bedford ran pills. Nathaniel kept out of his brother's affairs, not wanting to associate with anything illegal. But as it looked now, he'd have to ring some bells to open some doors to uncover some answers.

Bending down in front of the stove, he pulled the bottom drawer open, removing a black cast-iron skillet. Placed it on a burner. Grabbed a stick of butter from the fridge. Unwrapped it and put it in the skillet. Twisted the knob for heat, the click-click to ignite a blue-orange flame that circled beneath. He unwrapped the steaks. Watched the skillet heat up. The butter transforming from a solid yellow rectangled length to a slobbery liquid while he removed a butcher knife from a hunk of wood that sheathed several lengths of steel.

Glancing at a picture of he and his brother on the fridge, remembering how much he loved deer steak, Nathaniel grabbed a large wooden cutting board, laid the length of tenderloin out, began slicing one-inch chunks of the beet-colored meat, placed the hunks into the skillet. Listened to them fry for two minutes on each side.

Removing two clay-colored plates from the cherry-stained cabinet, Nathaniel set two places at his oak kitchen table, thinking a boy without a father was a horrid thing to have. But Nathaniel was the boy's blood, his uncle, his god-parent. He'd have a good life. A future. Nathaniel would make certain of that.

When all the meat was cooked and forked from the cast iron, he heard the shower was no longer running and be-hind him came Shadrack, black reeds of wet hair, locks pushed off to the side of his pale-fired pigment, wearing a gray T-shirt with Batman on his chest, a pair of faded denim Levi's and Smartwool socks. The boy was a perfect image of Nathaniel at the same age.

"Feel better?"

"Yeah."

"Still hungry?"

"Heck yeah. Smells good."

"You want any sides, potatoes or maybe some mushrooms, corn?"

"No, steak's fine."

Setting the huge bowl of steaming steaks between them on the kitchen table, Nathaniel told Shadrack, "Go ahead, sit down, I'll get some knives and forks. You want salt or pepper?"

"Maybe salt."

Out the window trees curved and swayed in a wind that was picking up, beyond that fields of cornstalks were changing color. Pulling silverware from the drawer, Nathaniel wanted to remember his brother the way he'd once been before his disability and drug addiction. Hardworking with a strong-minded opinion until he'd hurt his back and waited on disability checks in the mail like a child waited to open Christmas presents. When Nathaniel thought about it, it was sad. Our government creating this weakness. A dependency. A welfare state. That was what drugs did, they robbed a working person of their worth, wilted their mind with a weakness for dependency, regardless of color or origin. And all the government did was create more programs that did little to instill skills or values back into a person's well-being, to build a foundation so they could help themselves and get better. Nathaniel had viewed all of it firsthand. Day in, day out as a county cop.

Walking to the table, he gave Shadrack his steak knife

and fork. Sat down across from him. "Dig in, don't gotta wait on me. This is your home now."

Watching Shadrack fork three steaks about the size of a belt buckle onto his plate, Nathaniel smiled. Watched Shad cut a chunk from the first one, placing it into his mouth, teeth working the meat like augers in soil. The boy was hungry. He seemed calmer now than before he'd showered, but Nathaniel wondered what was dancing in his mind; it'd be tough, he told himself, but he'd provide for him. He'd no longer have that freedom anymore to chase tail or have an evening drink whenever he felt like it; he'd have to raise the boy right. Teach him things. Understand him about hunting, fishing, and gardening. Morals. Stability. Respect, how it was earned, not given. Work ethic. History. Books. Carpentry. Wiring. Give him some skills, some common sense.

Chewing his food, Shadrack looked Nathaniel in the eyes and asked, "You gonna eat?"

Lost in thought, he snapped back. Forked a steak and smiled. "Yeah, I was letting you get a head start."

Cutting his steak, forking it into his mouth, what Nathaniel knew from being a cop was that the first forty-eight hours were the most important. He didn't have time to be soft. What he had to do was find this Coyote.

In basic, the DIs weren't allowed to touch you—they'd still lay a thump upon a marine's peach-fuzz head, bat an elbow to a forehead, or bust a knee into a gut or groin behind tin walls away from the higher-rankings' eyes—but out in the bush or on a search-and-destroy mission there were no rules. The VC sometimes got the butt of an M16 splitting their saffron hides when the villagers, the *mamasans* and *papasans* of Da Nang, showed disrespect, launched an un-opened can of beans, hit a jarhead in his face. Miles would lead a tank division down the road, eyeing the shrapnel soil as they passed villages. Marines tearing open the four-inch squares of C rations. Villagers dumping out and scattering the contents of crackers, a can of beans or soup, ground coffee and an opener no bigger than an index finger. Grip-ping them. Smelling them. Shaking them next to their ears and hollering, "No want, no want."

Some grunts scalded them: "Unappreciative gook fucks!"

Other marines tried to ignore their discontent, kept walking alongside the tank. After all, the marines were there to help, regardless of frustration; in Miles's mind he was there to fight communist takeover, to help the weak, starved, and violated. When Vega and he swept the dirt roads for land mines, eye-fucking the ground for any mal-formation that stuck out, and when an unrecognized for-mation did rear its ugly head, they'd scream, *ORDNANCE!* Halt the tank. Study the area, tread lightly to disarm and disengage the threat.

Now, in his garage gym, Miles tongued the regurgi-tated taste of bourbon he'd spit into a bucket after his fifth set of 475-pound squats for three reps a set. Rear of his neck, shoulders sore, he showered his mouth with water. Laid his back flat on the Olympic bench. His hands spread outside shoulder width. He gripped the weighted bar, roughed metal making contact with callused palms, he flared his back out, arched his spine, pressed his feet into the concrete, and lifted the circles of iron from the pegs. All 350 pounds of it. Lowered it slowly to the bottoms of his pecs. Held it for a count of two. Then exploded upward. The burn and pump of blood flamed through tissue as he grunted. His face dotted with beads of burning perspiration. Childers stood over him, barking, "Pussy! Come on, you fucking pussy. One more fucking rep!"

After seven sets of three to five reps, Miles stood in his kitchen gulping down a protein shake of casein, whey, milk, and eggs blended with berries and dextrose. His torso hard and bloated with the pump of something similar to ichor into his muscles, but his mind was stuck in 1968, like a film projector showing his own life's documentary on the kitchen's gray walls, walking that patch of road every day, sometimes matted down by patches of black oil, the cast of vegetation lining the sides of the road, the tank tracks digging in behind him and Vega, seeing the toll of death oscillate in his brain when they came upon the greening tree lines and brush in the distance, knowing an ambush was in wait, a firefight that always delivered bullet-torn bodies on both sides, scenes that he and other marines never got used to. They just expected it, anticipated carbine to their skulls, brains painting the air, gunfire or detonations dispersing their short-lived existence about the foreign territory, ending their lives long before they'd even had a chance to really live. Like the air they inhaled and exhaled, they expected death upon every mission, every outing into the villages they swept for enemy trespass. Finding food caches buried in the ground, under hooches, questioning the villagers, they'd lie to save their skin, get a marine killed. That was when marines set the village to flame with the flip of a cigarette, sent the VC to town; the marines walked back to their base camp, fires canvasing orange with black smoke behind them. Knowing they'd live to see another day.

At the dirt plant, Miles lit a smoke. Listened to the whine of a mangy mixed breed from the front seat of a Lincoln that sat out by the beaten and flaked shit-green dumpster. Thought about the barking yelp that sirened behind him while walking in front of a tank. Coming to a halt. Turning around, seeing the navy corpsman kneeling to the injured. The sound was equal parts razor whittling bone and sixteen-penny nails jabbing one's eardrums. A dog had been clipped by the tank. The corpsman checked the damage, was gonna take the canine back to his hooch, set its hind leg, when young kids came running from a village. Some in ragged tops, no pants. Others with pants, no shirts, sandals cut from Michelin tires, yelling, "No take number one chop chop. Give, give." Offering their hands, showing their palms.

They wanted cat or dog, it made no difference as long as it was some form, cut, or flank of meat. Villagers starved because of the communist conflict. Something the media or the protestors like the actress Jane Fonda knew nothing about, never ventured out into the war zones, out into the bush, the villages and the gunfights, and bore witness to the real conflicts and horrors. The other side of a conflict.

Sad-eyed, the dog's neck lay over one of the kids' arms, looking back at the marines as the kids rustled it from the corpsman's grip.

Crazy, Miles thought now, as he watched an emaciated Black man who stood nearly seven foot tall. He went by the name Pie; he'd worked down the street, had once played college ball back in the sixties for U of L or U of K, Miles couldn't recall, until he found the bottle, then a job in the chemical plant nearby, and these days he hustled pallets. Wearing ragged dress slacks he dug through a few stacks of wooden pallets piled next to the dumpster. Searching for those that still held form. Boards intact that could be refurbished to fetch a profit of three to five bucks depending on the condition and who the buyer was.

Stopping his salvage, the old man glanced at Miles and said, "Shit you looking at, cracker-ass motherfucker?"

Miles's knees twitched with an arthritic burn as he leaned against a railcar marred by the soot of travel from

South Dakota to Kentucky. The metal housing was engraved by stick-figure consonants and vows of Latino gang graffiti with a three-pronged crown above them.

Exhaling smoke, Miles laughed and said, "Lay your frustrations on the tracks, ole-timer, I'm on your side. Have been all my life."

Here was a man living in the land of the free, struggling to survive in 2001, not the 1950s. Living on the fringe to make ends meet or ends meat, depending on how one viewed it, either way the man was giving Miles a rash of shit. But who could blame him.

Pie straightened up, twisted his head sideways, his eyes were fogged over with cataracts, and he said, "Fuck you, peckerwood."

Miles shook his head, took a drag off his smoke, watched the Black man turn back to the pallets, mumbling and grumbling, *honky-assed son of a bitch*, as he dragged several skids to his vehicle's trunk. Sliding his feet more than stepping. Struggling to lift and stack each into a prune-colored vehicle that was crunched and rusted. The car's ass end nearly rubbing the ground. Then he bungeed the trunk down. Pulled a seven- or eight-dollar bottle of Jim Beam from his back pocket. Twisted the cap off and tilted it up. Killed it.

Earning his way in this crummy existence as he'd done for God knew how long, Miles thought, as Pie's dog barked, poked its head from the rolled-down car window, sniffing, its eyes identical to its owner's, fogged with white. One chewed ear stuck straight up, the other flopped down as though it were broken. Its head was like a large mallet. It was an old pit, keeping watch for its owner, its provider.

Reminding Miles of the curly-haired rescue Shelby had when he'd first went to her home, the dog was older, on its last days, but she'd fostered it from a shelter, wanting to offer it some semblance of happiness before it passed. Gertie, she called it. It lay snuggled like a teardrop in its cushioned bed while Shelby worked, taking her clothing off in a dive for cash. Using her assets. Look but don't touch. She'd done it since she'd turned eighteen. Wanted a job that paid well. Tried out on amateur night. Made six hundred bucks in three hours. She was thirty now, still held the form of a twenty-year-old. Gertie had passed some weeks ago, but she died happily in her sleep. Like that ole dog, Miles wondered what she saw in his old ass. Some leathery-skinned, steroid-infused man. Maybe she was offering him some semblance of happiness in his final days. Regardless, he knew what he saw in her, other than she was beautiful beyond belief, she was someone who didn't judge him for what he'd done overseas. Killing other men. She was nurturing. Caring. Didn't care how he earned his living. Working in a factory for a good check, each worked a job with no real sense of fulfillment, only that they earned a healthy wage to provide a simple but comfortable existence. But there was something he'd recently caught sight of, her staring off into nothing, or her mumbling to herself, in a different tone or voice, almost like a low-level whining of sorts, but when he questioned her, she'd snap out of it, act as if she was just thinking, and he ignored it, wrote it off as nothing more than sorting out issues with her father or her brother, knowing those two men could take a toll on anyone.

Inhaling a final drag from his smoke, Miles flipped the butt out into the sooty gravel that spread around the rusted tracks. Wondered where she'd been at this week. He'd phoned her again before stepping out the door for work. And still there was no answer. He was really missing her smell, her touch, the sound of her voice, but most of all her company and the words they shared.

Watching the ole hustler twist the cap back on the empty bottle of Beam, he made eye contact with Miles again, held a pissed-off Rottweiler expression, and winged the bottle at him.

Reflexes were knees bending downward, Miles's cartilage knotted with pain, creaked and popped. Stiff from squatting 475 pounds. The bottle exploded glass off the railcar. Tiny shards rained down all around him. "You fermented ole cocksucker," Miles muttered as he stood up. Worse than trying to help the villagers in Vietnam, where you never knew your enemy from a VC civilian.

"If I didn't like you I'd break your bony toothpick ass into two parts and use you to pick my teeth," Miles said.

Behind him, a deep, gargling rasp hollered, "Knox, don't finger a curve on that useless street coon!"

Pie swiveled his head sideways at the man and yelled,

"Who you be calling coon? You Humpty-Dumpty fat fuck? We worked together back in the day, watched your lard ass sleep on shift."

"Put the feet to the street, Pie, 'fore I call the po-po to escort your ass off the property."

"Fuck you, butterball, probably ain't seen your dick since you's born. No wonder your old lady left you for a real man like me."

Miles turned to the thump of steel-toed boots, was met by a swath of obesity, a man with a scouring-pad beard peppered by years; he wore a red hard hat over graying locks, a blue short-sleeved button-up over a hard gut with dark circles beneath the pits. It was Conrad McNabb, his foreman. He was an old-school racist with legs so fat and curved, what some called bowlegged, if they were straightened by surgery he'd be two feet taller.

Miles knew the aged bastard was gone by 4:00 p.m. every day, down at Steve's bar by 4:15; it was near 6:00 p.m. now and he asked Conrad, "The hell's up your two-ton ass?"

Blister-faced he said, "A size ten from that Ron Jeremy–looking shit of a plant manager we got, he reamed my ass real good about you handing Kimball a beating last night, and to make it worse I done viewed your handiwork."

"Prick had an unpaid debt, no concern of yours or the company."

"You know the company policy on fighting. I tried to turn a blind eye, said I'd give you a verbal warning, but someone went over my head. They want a sit-down. They'll let you finish your work tonight. Then have you come back Tuesday morning, let the manager and human resources hear both sides. You'll be needing your union rep."

A tracer round was heating up inside Miles. He thought that rotten hunk of shit Kimball couldn't take his medicine like a man. Had to snitch. Miles stood hulked and festering from the inside out, his hands curved into meteor balls; he was gonna lay hurt down on someone. And that someone was Kimball, again.

Conrad was steamed and said, "I got forty hours of hand-to-hand combat from when I's in the US Army. Never lost my cool on the job one damn time, don't test me."

A burning fizzed in Miles's ears, twisted with the volume of shelled rounds and clipped limbs decorating the villages that mapped out of the recesses of his memory with a recon unit.

"I got four years in the US Marine Corps, ate army fellator fucks like you for trail mix. Spent nearly three years in 'Nam, finished up in Puerto Rico guarding an ammo dump, boxing with the Ricans for cash on the weekends and the rest was spent on a barstool of human condition."

Conrad told him, "Know all your stories. Get moving, punch in before I have to write your hotheaded ass up for being late—"

"Hell you say," Miles interrupted as he brushed past Conrad. Nearly knocked him on his ass.

Feeling undermined, Conrad reached for Miles's shoulder, grasped the thick, rounded trap meat, and said, "Look, hard-ass, just 'cause you're bigger than a Texas long horn don't mean I can't slap the piss and vinegar outta you."

Miles's left arm swung around. Circled over, come up under Conrad's, used his forearm to place pressure on Conrad's elbow till it creaked and cracked. Conrad screamed, "Son of a bitch!" Miles released his arm, shut him up, slapped a right palm through the air, and knocked Conrad's hard hat off his head. Conrad moaned and cursed, "You son of a—"

"—Save it." He was a radiator running on its last vapors of engine coolant just before the smoke started beneath the hood. Entering the bay door to the dirt plant, Miles clomped across the floor in a rush. To his right, the sound of spray dryers was a deafening rumble of heated air. To his left, the smell of soil being washed wafted within the butter-thick heat of the factory. The corrugated-tin walls were decorated by webs of insects recessed into the corners. Industrial fans whisked air up out of the building walls and through the roof. Iron stairs climbed angles to upper landings, detailed in chipped grays, yellows, and reds.

Kimball stood with his back turned, getting the lowdown from Towers Chumbley about what was going on for the shift change. Miles didn't give him a snowball's chance in hell to react. Landed a left jab into the bend of Kimball's neck. Doubled a right hook to his ribs and another left hook to his kidney. Kimball's hard hat scuffed to the floor and he followed.

Towers moved his ass from the scene. Miles's knees clanked as he came down on top of Kimball, who squirmed and whined. Miles rolled him onto his back and shouted, "Knew you'd wanna take it like a little bitch. Lay face-down. I wanna see your eyes, maggot. First you try to rip me off, then you cry wolf to management."

Kimball's purple-mashed fingers pawed over the flour-like dust from the marred floor. Sweat and shower gel shot-gunned from his pores. He'd a fresh hunk of Red Man in his mouth, could taste the tobacco juice inching a burn down his throat. Wanted to spit or cough but couldn't breathe. He shouted. But the only words that came were garbled red juicy tobacco.

Miles rooted his left hand into Kimball's hair, the first right splintered the plastic of Kimball's safety glasses. Slapping them from his complexion, blood leaked from Kimball's face, his eyes watered, and Miles kept peppering his vision with knuckles. It was the only sound Kimball could hear, bone drumming his skull like an engine with a thrown rod. He wanted Miles off him. Struggled but was overpowered by the old man's strength.

With Kimball's locks in his left, Miles released his grip and quit punching him. Felt gritty fingers and hands wrap around both shoulders like meat hooks, tugging and swaying him back and forth with a voice rattling him back to the present. "Miles? Told your ass to punch in 'fore you's late, not to ground and pound and punch an operator."

Miles blinked, he'd been zoned out, gotten lost in his

own roid-rage madness. Standing up, the juice was searing his nerves. Creating a stone-cold craziness to river through his veins. "Screw you!" he told Conrad as he left Kimball on the concrete and bumped past him and the other operators on shift, thinking to himself, none of it added up, Kimball squealing to management. As he headed up the metal steps into the upper rung of heat in the building and to the break room to punch in, he knew Kimball was a tool but he wasn't a fucking narc, wouldn't have said shit about their dispute, considering it was over his selling illegal drugs. Steroids. And getting his ass kicked by an old man, Miles's anger had gotten the best of him, he thought to himself, maybe he had handed an ass beating to the wrong sheep, hell, he might actually lose his job for whipping the same guy's ass twice.

The slow crunch and give of gravel came like the pops of kernels, like those evenings she spent with her girlfriends on her nights off when Miles was working. Movie nights. Monica and Becca would come over, they'd camp out on the couch and floor, pop open some beers or bottles of wine, Shelby would place some popcorn in the microwave, and they'd watch old flicks like *Top Gun*, *Pretty in Pink*, *St. Elmo's Fire*, or *Sixteen Candles*. Laughing and reminiscing about school and the cool kids who came from the privileged families. From money, those who judged others based upon what they wore, where they lived, and how they looked. The good-looking guys who wouldn't give them a second glance were the same guys who now came into the strip club to push cash at them because what they had at home was no longer appealing. Funny how once a person graduated, where they came from, how they dressed, their stature in life, no longer mattered. But now, all those thoughts, those memories, that judgment, it was replaced by the chug and knock of a worn engine that played tricks on Shelby's mind. Flipped her internal switch from happy memories with friends to now, with one ear pressed against the wood-planked wall, the other ear was opened to sounds. She was tired and twisted into a pretzel of cramps. Stopping every now and again, glancing at the empty cans of Pabst ornamenting the misshapen stones around Wylie like oil splotches staining a garage floor. Drool strung from the corner of his mouth in one long saliva stringer; she wanted to wipe it as it expanded into a dark circle on his shirt.

Shelby wiggled her wrists, tried to free her restraint from the shoestrings that cut into the meridians like steel cuffs. What she wanted was to be free. From Wylie. Clasping her eyes shut she tried to focus on something positive in her life, something less restraining and stress-filled than her brother or her father and so she thought of Miles. Of his being an older man. Appreciative of her, of others and of life in general. Finding pleasure in exercise, whether it was hefting his weights or taking long walks or jogging down the country back roads; sometimes he took her hiking on the Adventure

Trail in the Harrison-Crawford Forest, a twenty-five-mile loop. Packing plenty of nuts, seeds, jerky, and water. Going out maybe five or six miles, then turning around and coming back. Then getting back to his place and grilling rib eyes or boneless chicken thighs or wings for them on the grill, he immersed himself in it. If she drew a hot bath or started the shower, he'd wash her hair for her without asking, rub lotion on her back and her feet when she was finished. For a beast of a man, he had a sentimental side. Leaving fresh-cut daisies on her pillow when she'd sleep over at his place, as he was always up before her, with hot coffee and breakfast ready.

Laying on the floor, she realized she'd not spoken to nor seen him in near a week. She missed his large, muscular arms wrapped around her. Comforting and protecting her.

Opening her eyes, that thought of feeling safe and secure drifted as she watched the sudden convulsing of Wylie's body; it halted her dead as a skunk baked by the sun. Bolting his head from his shoulder but never opening his eyes, then slowly bending his neck, she watched as his cheek made contact with his shoulder once again.

His hat had fallen to the floor among the cans. The fire had died down. Cutting back on the heat of the already-chilled room. She knew Miles kept a .20-gauge Mossberg and a .22 survival rifle in the back bedroom on a shelf in the closet. She remembered Miles explaining to her the history of the .22 long rifle. Created by some man named J. Stevens and the Arm & Tool Company in 1887. Miles was a history buff on guns and wars. Had taken her to the site of the Battle of Corydon Park; it was the only Civil War battle fought on Indiana soil. Taking place on July 9, 1863. Four hundred and fifty members of the Harrison County home guard tried to defend against General John Hunt Morgan's 2,400 Confederate troops, holding out for Union soldiers to come help and stop Morgan's push through southern Indiana. Now it was nothing more than a pull-off of acreage with a cabin that offered a glimpse of what homes looked like in that era. What Shelby wished was, she was there now with Miles, and if she was she'd hold his hand, walk the green landscape, take in the wooded area, or sit in her Camaro, share a bottle of red wine. Something expensive, Opus One or Duckhorn.

Then the dread shifted, set back in. She'd have to get free first. But if she did, if she could, she'd go straight to the back bedroom. Find the rifle or the shotgun. She hoped she'd not be forced to use either firearm . . . Then a drift of images swarmed her mind like fireflies in the dark. She saw emaciated skin, the zip of insects, and that odor that only comes with the decomposition of a dead body.

Out here, there was no phone, no form of communication in the cabin. Neighbors were down the road, across a field, or through the woods. She'd a cell phone in her purse. But that was in her car, she'd no idea where her car was. *Outside the cabin*, she thought, *it has to be.*

She knew tricks weren't being played on her when an engine killed from outside. A vehicle's door slammed. She thought of Miles at first. His slow gait of bulk shuffling his worn soles across the ground outside the cabin, tromping around where there was a thirty-acre spring-fed lake full of bass, crappie, bluegill, catfish, and snappers. She wanted to scream, "In here!" Words barked under someone's breath: "Who in thee hell?"

It wasn't Miles.

Wylie bucked from his disoriented comatose state. Eyed Shelby. The front porch gave with a creak, one step became another followed by the drum of a fist again the wooden door that echoed through the cabin and Shelby's brain. Wylie dead-eyed her, one mirroring the other, each in a state of panic. Shuffling across the floor, raising an index to his lips, the drool hung like an unspoken testament to his madness. He forearmed the slobbering goo from his lip, from his passing out and drooling all over himself, pulled the pistol from his pocket, held it at the ready in his left hand.

Knowing Miles would pluck that pistol from Wylie and stuff it up his backside, she wished he was here, would show up and rescue her from this state of craziness. Wanting to scream, Shelby knew better. Didn't want a chunk of lead in her frontal lobe. The thump of the fist bucked the door again and a voice questioned, "Miles, you in there?"

Shelby recognized the tongue, it was Katz, an Indian with long streaks of gray. Drove a truck for Kentucky Container. Lived down the road in a small brick house, he came by and fished, drank bourbon with she and Miles several evenings. Told jokes about the women who had tornadoed through his life. The seeds he'd planted in them. The child support he paid. The three houses he'd built and lost in divorces. He never had much luck with the ladies. But he was good at keeping an eye on Miles's land.

When an answer did not yield from inside, Katz pounded the door once more, offered, "Look, I know someone's in there. Your Camaro is out yonder ways and I can hear breathing. Shit, I believe I can smell your sour ass."

Wylie was already standing, shuffling the .38 to his right hand, stumbling to the door in an OxyContin stupor. Swiveling his head around on his shoulders, in a quick motion he unbolted the brass deadbolt, the pistol between the door and Katz. He cracked the door to the daylight that was blocked by curtains and blinds, and Wylie squealed, "What you want?"

Katz said, "Miles out here with you?"

Anger and fear streaked Wylie's mind. Shelby screamed, "Run, he's got a gun!"

Katz's face pinched in confusion. His eyes metered wide as if Wylie was crazed and he said, "The hell you talking about?"

Wylie stepped back in one motion and ripped the door open. Buried the .38 upon Katz's veined, cauliflowered sniffer and said, "Step your antique ass in here."

Nathaniel didn't want trouble, he only wanted to find his brother and sister-in-law's killer. That was what he told himself as he looked out to a circle of tracked soil, where a child in a bulbous diaper watched a crooked-knee female, her strands of hair tied back, attired in ragged threads and sorting items of paper for burning from a faded red plastic trash can. The girl pulled out shreds and wads of newspapers, magazines, greasy food packaging, tossed them into a corrosive orange burn barrel beside a green-and-black wood-paneled house with a silver tin roof. They were about twenty feet from the road as Nathaniel passed by.

Standards of hard living. No trash pickup, you burned or buried what you used. Some would call it the ways of decay, or the wash, rinse, repeat of society. Nathaniel knew these roads and hollers and the people who congregated within them. This was where he started. And where Leonard resided. Surrounded himself with what some unfairly viewed as the lowest rung of human, those who were born and bred into a life of struggle. Always working to pay last month's bills with this month's grocery money. Nathaniel knew Leonard would have an answer as to who this son of a bitch who was monikered Coyote was. And if he didn't he'd know someone who did.

Leonard was a dealer-turned-CI, an informant for the county. He was a wannabe revolutionary, parading around the valleys in his dirty moth-holed red fist shirt, praising Che Guevara and the heavy-headed propaganda tunes of Rage Against the Machine. But he didn't know the first thing about Guevara or the wealth he grew up in, how he went to school to become a physician, or about the people he'd killed in Cuba, taking wealthy farmers' land from them and redistributing it to the poor. After helping to take over Cuba, he headed to the Soviet Union, where he found solace, made a deal to fight back against the US, having Russia invest into Cuba's sugarcane in exchange for fuel and weapons for the Cuban army. Nathaniel had questioned Leonard about this small piece of history once and the guy stumbled with words, telling Nathaniel *them peeps needed to die, fuck capitalism.* Yet he wore the shorts and shoes and listened to the music that capitalism helped buy and distribute from workers, on top of that he sold drugs.

Nathaniel argued this to Leonard years ago—that he was reaping the benefits of capitalism, even though it was illegal to sell drugs, he was the private owner, earning and living off the profits with his own free enterprise—when he'd crossed paths with him as a county cop following leads for missing persons. People who were linked back to Leonard. Dropouts. Deadheads. Squatters. Freight hoppers. Young men and women Leonard would come into contact with, selling them drugs, offering them a roof over their heads. Basically anyone who'd buy into his rhetoric about how horrible capitalism was, even though he was selling drugs, illegally, yes. But he was profiting off them and on top of being a home owner and a landowner that he worked to pay for by selling drugs. He was part of a free but illegal market while buying from other free markets. Nathaniel laughed at his monologues condemning oppression when he himself was busted for slinging dope, black tar, H, Night

Train, and the marijuana that he grew in undisclosed locations, paid others to care for and cut. Law enforcement, the dirty under-the-table guys, recognized him as a dealer but took a twenty percent payout from what he earned along with his answering questions about the local crud when needed. He basically weeded out his competition, no pun intended.

Leonard wasn't so smart that he couldn't get busted. But he was smart enough to take a deal when it was offered. That was how he kept his freedom, by giving names and connections, cutting under-the-table arrangements with detectives who owned him. Detective Thurman was one of them. Nathaniel could trust the guy, but only so far.

Leonard knew who did what drug, where they bought it, and where they laid their heads. It was how he earned his keep.

Nathaniel eyed Shadrack, who sat in the passenger's seat holding a comic book with Batman and the Joker on the cover. "When we get to this place you keep the doors locked, got it?"

Was it the right decision to bring Shadrack? Probably not. But he wasn't leaving the boy with Tacker after all he'd been through.

"We going to the bad man's house?"

"Well, this is a bad man, just not the one we're looking for."

"But he might know where the bad man we want is?"

"He might. You're a fast learner."

In the rearview, hills, trees, and fields came and went outside the truck's diesel roar. Time was dissipating quick. The autopsy would take another day. Nathaniel had spoken with the funeral home briefly. Bedford and Judy had their last rights prearranged at Cesar's in Harrison County years before they'd started peddling pills. They were to be burned. Their urns already picked out. The thought of loss fueled Nathaniel's rage as he hung a right onto a gravel-and-dirt drive. Pulling to a stop. Shifting to park, Shadrack's eyes widened at the sight of a buggy that sat off beside the trailer. Dirt-spattered metal frame with flaking red-white-green paint, large circular lights mounted from the top-row bar, knobbed tires and busted red vinyl seats patched by gray duct tape.

"Cool," he said.

"People who own it aren't none too cool."

Next to it a wrecker was parked, its chipped hook dangling from a thick chain in the heated breeze.

Customers, Nathaniel thought. Men or women chasing that punch to heating their veins, turning their minds to warm dough while soaking up Leonard's commie rhetoric.

Opening his door, he looked at Shadrack. "Remember what I told you: lock the doors when I get out. Be back as soon as I get some answers."

Shutting the door, listening to the locks click, Nathaniel waded through weeds that scraped his denim-covered knees. Stepped on Red Stripe beer bottles, Big Red soda bottles, and wrappers for stolen medical needles. A tire hung from a tree limb off to the right of the trailer. A bar-nacled push mower sat lost in the yard. Windows that re-cessed into untreated plywood additions were mildewed and covered by yellowing newspapers and faded magazines, blocking out daylight. A satellite dish was stapled to the roof. Nathaniel thought it was a shame Leonard wouldn't fix the place up considering how much cash he made from dealing drugs. Instead he lived in a state of decay.

Facing the ragged mesh of screen, Nathaniel pounded the scuffed and split door.

The sound of music was a muffled thump from within; bass jarred the rotted lumber beneath Nathaniel's boots with Zack de la Rocha's vocals screaming, "Killing in the name of!" Then the screech of heavy feet. The door swung open slow. Nathaniel slid his left boot to chalk it. A silhou-ette stooped in the haze of the trailer. Words came from the open door, almost shouting.

"You lost, mister?"

"Looking for Leonard."

The kid was young, twenty to twenty-two. Faded stoplight-yellow T-shirt, military-green cap with the bill pushed up, safety pin dangling from his left earlobe, smiley face tattoo on his right cheek looked to be drawn by a third grader in art class, he'd a pair of fatigues cut off below the knee. Was bone thin, vanilla-cream pale, biceps were plas-tic ice tray bumps covered by more kindergarten tattoos of skulls, stars, and pot leaves. He'd a small amount of peach fuzz spreading over his chin. Trying to play badass, the boy said, "Get in line. Everybody and their damn brother comes here looking for Leon. You got a name?"

"Nathaniel. You got a name?" he asked, trying to offer respect even though he held zero.

"Acre, Acre Coy."

This kid is barely a half acre, Nathaniel thought to himself, and said, "Well, Acre, Leonard worked for me years back as a CI. Got a few questions that I need to find answers for."

Why all the fucking questions, this isn't a shakedown, just need to connect some dots, Nathaniel thought.

Acre chuckled, pushed his hand down the side of his cutoffs, scratched his crotch, said, "CI? You don't look like no pork belly I ever knowed, 'sides that, Leon don't work for no po-po, only works for Leon. Might wanna move on, you're on private property," Acre told Nathaniel, waving his hand to motion him away.

Acre tried reaching and pulling the screen door closed but couldn't. Looked down at Nathaniel's boot blocking his action. Before he could look back up and breathe a word, Nathaniel had thumbed his .45-caliber Kimber free from behind his back with one hand while his other had reached out and twisted Acre's left ear like a titty twister. Gripping part of the lobe and part of the safety pin. Acre's eyes found moisture and his mouth squealed. Nathaniel forced Acre's neck to his shoulder. Pressed the Kimber tight below Acre's jawline and told him, "No more asking, you dumb son of a bitch, I'm in no mood for your hillbilly revolutionary bullshit!"

Pushing forward, Nathaniel led Acre backward by his ear into the trailer. Rage Against the Machine still blared from the speakers. Two pieces of malformed crud sat on a broke-down sofa with necks bent backward, eyes like cue balls sunk back into their skulls, their mouths trapped somewhere between an inhale and a yawn, either snoring or gagging.

Nathaniel canvased his odds. He didn't come here to die. Only to interrogate for answers. He had Shadrack in the truck.

The count was three to one so far. Not great odds. But considering the IQs he was surrounded by, he wasn't outnumbered yet.

Of the two men on the couch, one had half an arm, and each rested their dirt-covered bare feet on a glass coffee table graffitied with handprints, a tarnished spoon, cotton balls, an empty rig, a lighter, and a wadded Ziploc. Bob Marley, Peter Tosh, and Cro-Mags CDs lay scratched and scattered. Walls were covered with Rage Against the Machine and System of a Down and Che Guevara posters.

With watering eyes, Acre stuttered and slobbered, "You stupid son of a bitch, you—you can't do—do this, this—this is trespassing, know who you're fucking with?"

Gritting his teeth, Nathaniel told the kid, "We just had

a meet and greet, Rain Man, discussed introductions at the door." The stupidity of the ordeal clawed the walls of his gut. He only wanted to ask some questions. Garner answers. Move on. Add to that the odor in the room was a decomposed-body air freshener combined with unwashed feet mixed with a pile of stupidity. Pins and needles sprinted up his spine. Trolled his anger. He needed to speak with Leonard. Nathaniel's time was being wasted by this kid.

He'd never met Leonard inside his home. Looking around, to his right, down a hallway of fisted wood-paneled walls, Nathaniel saw a bedroom door with a red, white, and green sign that read NO ENTRY UNLESS YOU BROUGHT WEED. The door was closed.

Bingo!

Bringing his focus back to Acre he said, "Leonard in the bedroom at the end of the hallway?"

"Fuck you!"

Nathaniel needed to make this Acre know he meant business. He released Acre's ear with his left. Keeping the pistol pressed under his chin with his right, he slid his hand into the front pocket of his carpenter pants. Nathaniel told himself, *Sometimes a farmer uses a cattle prod on stubborn cattle to get their attention, make them find movement.* Digits slid into circular openings of metal. Pulling his left hand from his pocket, he lowered the pistol. Acre held a confused expression until the side of his face got lit up with a tight left rabbit punch of weighted brass knuckles. Not enough to put him down but enough to rattle the bone of his jaw. Wean his balance. Followed by a left uppercut between chin and neck. Enamel met enamel. Bit down and chipped.

"Son of a bitch!" Acre spit. "Chipped my fucking tooth."

Acre's green eyes teared up. He tried to shake it off. Nathaniel pressed the Kimber into the peak of the young man's skull. "Turn around. Walk down the hallway, before I spread you like warm jam to baked dough, decorate the carpet."

Nathaniel glanced at the two men on the couch, expected movement, but they were lost in H-ville. Nathaniel never did get the appeal. Blacking out, losing half your day. Destroying your body. Your mind. He could do that on a fishing bank with a bottle of Maker's. And at a much slower pace.

With Acre turned around, Nathaniel told him, "Raise your fucking hands, place one foot in front of the other, and walk." Nathaniel led the young man down the hallway as his shield. At the hallway's end, from behind, Rage went quiet on the stereo, then came the jamming of a guitar and the picking of bass, pounding of drums, "Bulls on Parade." Nathaniel nudged Acre, heard Leonard's voice pedaling loud with adrenaline. "Look, ain't fucking around, this is grade A shit!"

The door was cracked. Scents of soured pigment, soiled cotton, and gingivitis swam into Nathaniel's nostrils as he pushed Acre forward, the boy's body opening the door slowly. Nathaniel felt his heart stomping in his temples.

The room came into view. Grids of wire over windows with ripped shirts for curtains. A bare mattress atop a box spring in the left corner surrounded by water-stained walls. Two men stood with a large foldout card table and balloons knotted at the top, golf-balling out with drugs.

Leonard stood with blond dreads hanging down like clumps of gummy marijuana. Pale, chapped, fleshy complexion boiled by sweat and tattoos of faded puzzle pieces, squids, and black ravens. A bloated man stood with his back to Nathaniel. Blue cotton work pants hung off his ass below a red sleeveless flannel shirt. Hair in long greasy slivers.

An oscillating fan hummed, circulating thick, putrid air in the room as Leonard wheeled out his expectations. "Yeah, yeah, look, motherfucker, you gotta earn my respect. I don't just hand out this kind of H to any fold of skin that wants to earn a place in my legion of comrades."

Pushing Acre into the room, Nathaniel's boots sunk into the matted carpet of half-eaten donuts with pissants, pizza boxes, and empty bags of Grippo's potato chips.

Leonard made eye contact with Acre.

"What the shit? I'm in mid-employee pitch here!" Then noticed Nathaniel. His fogged-over eyes widened when he viewed the pistol Nathaniel was training on Acre. "Why are you holding a wad cutter on my boy Acre, thought I had an understanding with the county, you call before you show up?"

"Lost your number and your housekeeper got mouthy

after the introductions. Had to pepper his ass, was ready to leave him in the smokehouse to cure if he didn't settle."

To Nathaniel, Leonard said, "You gonna holster that piece so we can trade consonants and vows, get to why you're offering me a fucking unannounced visit?"

"If everyone can keep their hands at eye level, I'll ask, you answer, and be out of your hair."

"Answer? Wait, wait, you gonna have to get in line, can't just come onto my property waving high-caliber luger, and wait—wait a sec, you, you're not even po-po no more."

Nathaniel was losing his cool. Raised and drove the Kimber's butt down into the rear of Acre's skull. "Ahh! Shit!" Acre screamed, his hands grabbing his head, his body losing its tough-boy swagger, getting weak-kneed and planting into the carpet.

"Up off the floor. Get against the fucking wall," Nathaniel demanded.

Wobbly, Acre took his place next to the future employee in the red flannel.

Nathaniel pointed the pistol at Leonard's head as the man in the red flannel raised his hands, stepped backward until he bumped into a wall. Nathaniel said, "Enough small talk. I'm looking for a man goes by the moniker of *Coyote*, what do you know about him?"

Nathaniel's words didn't make an impression upon Leonard, who mashed his lips in a shit-eating smirk and said, "Lower the fucking gun."

"You know him or not?"

The fan pimpled Leonard's paper-towel skin. "What's in it for me?"

Nathaniel wasn't in the mood for favors. "How about I allow you to keep wasting space. Not in the mood for reach arounds today. Know him or not?" Nathaniel stepped forward, pressed the .45 between Leonard's unibrowed eyes.

"Why you looking for him?"

"Believe he murdered my brother Bedford and his wife Judy over drugs."

Leonard's eyes got razor thin. "The man you need to be paying a visit to is Carney Dillman."

There was a look on Nathaniel's face that wasn't for poker. He had a flashback to getting run off the road by Carney; his blood pressure was reaming his arteries and he questioned Leonard, "Why would Carney Dillman murder my brother and sister-in-law?"

"How could you not know that Carney is the one who gets your brother his lists of doctors to visit, lines up his clientele? Way I hear it, they got a fifty-fifty split, and I've been told this by more than one fiend in the valley."

There was a numbness that crisscrossed through Nathaniel's body. Feeling like an idiot—Carney Dillman, man who ran him off the road. He'd done time in Oldham County, Kentucky. Gritting his teeth, Nathaniel still didn't believe Carney would murder his brother and sister-in-law.

"How long?"

"Done answered enough of your Q and A."

Like spontaneous combustion, Acre came from the

wall, swinging his arms like a combative octopus let out of its underwater restraints, reaching and swatting at Nathaniel's pistol. Nathaniel backhanded Acre across his complexion with the pistol. Knocked him into the future prospect of an employee, the obese man in the red flannel shirt, who caught him and stood shocked at what was transpiring. Leonard came forward, reaching for Nathaniel's throat. Taking him by surprise, channel-locking and squeezing around the cartilage, pushing and pressing Nathaniel, driving him backward into the wall. Shaking and rattling the trailer floor and walls.

Crimson faced and slobbering, Leonard said, "Son of a bitch, come up in my fucking home, waving a gun at my people, interrupting my business!"

Leonard's teeth glowed fluorescent yellow. Eyes white and veined. Nathaniel swam in a sea of red. Carney fucking Dillman. Lungs huffed for wind. Gritting his teeth, he swiveled from Leonard's weak-ass throat grab, swiped an elbow across Leonard's temple. Drew blood. Followed by the side of his pistol rapping him on the other side of his head. Brought a knee up to his groin, into the balls, dropping him to his knees, then he brought his left foot down onto Leonard's hand, crushing it, Leonard squealed, and Nathaniel brought his boot up into Leonard's face, kicked him backward onto the card table. Balloons scattered everywhere.

This wasn't what Nathaniel wanted. With Shadrack

waiting in the truck. He needed to get the fuck out of here. One thing he didn't miss was being a cop.

Rubbing his swollen face, Acre was coming back at Nathaniel again when he raised his pistol. "Park it, motherfucker."

Leonard struggled from the floor like a Slinky and palmed his mouth, wiping blood.

Nathaniel stepped backward, keeping his pistol raised, bore down on Leonard and Acre, told them, "Enough. I got what I came for." Foot pedaling backward into the hallway. Knowing he was headed to his truck, back to Shadrack. Leonard raised an arm to Acre, eyed Nathaniel, and said, "Remove yourself from my sight but remember, this ain't over, hear me, this ain't over!"

Hours had passed after attacking Kimball. No one had mentioned anything else about the assault. Everyone started their shift, offering Miles space as he fumed. Time to cool down.

But then came the combustion.

The sound started with a loud burst of air releasing, a pop, traveling down into the housed feed screw, Miles didn't think much of it as the sound traveled up the metal housed bucket elevator and into the squared metal storage bin about the size of a large tree house mounted twenty feet in the air but ten feet across the concrete floor. Another large metal-circle halon ball popped. From inside the masonry structure of the downstairs office window, Miles gripped the phone from the desk, looked out the chicken-wire between glass, anger ripening his blood to a hard pump, swelling his muscles as he watched Kimball standing below the feed at the machine that filled bags with dirt. Miles knew Kimball hadn't ratted his ass out for the beating and the belittling. The question remained, who did it?

Dialing Shelby's number, he waited. Listened to the ringing tone while Kimball dropped a fifty-pound bag on the scale to his right, viewing the weight for correctness. Scooping it up, Kimball stacked it onto the wooden pallet behind him. Shelby's answering machine answered, and Miles hung up just as another pressurized gray circular halon ball sounded off from the spark that turned into a flame within the spray drying system. The basic setup was that dry organoclay was pumped into the factory through three-inch-diameter pipes using an aeration system, where it was combined with water and steam in one tank, entered another tank, where sand was separated from the clay, the clay was then centrifuged, shot to another tank of water, combined with another raw material, then filtered into a cake, mixed, and fed to a spray dryer. It was dried by 350 degrees of heat and fed from the dryer to a bagging system using stainless steel feed screws and bucket elevators.

The halon balls were placed at certain areas of the feed screws and bucket elevators that delivered the powder to the bagging system to extinguish and suffocate any spark within the operation caused by metal rubbing against metal, such as a bolt or nut that had worked its way loose unknowingly, falling into the system, where it could rub, causing friction. The dust particles from the clay, once dried, were highly flammable and explosive if introduced to a spark; in theory, the halon ball would recognize a spark, release a chemical agent that removed any oxygen from that area to kill the reaction, i.e., prevent an explosion.

But then came the combustion. A combustion that would carry down the rounded steel chamber of the iron spray dryer that stood over sixty feet tall, similar to a grain silo, only chopped in half, honed of solid metal surrounded by insulation with steel legs of support running up to the sky. Now, the large gray ball emitted a powder to suffocate the air, chased the flame like an oncoming train, choo-chooing down the rails. Traveling through the system, another halon ball went off, still chasing the flame, and Kimball was walking toward the office when a long encased feed screw, about the width of a narrow workbench, blew its steel sample door off and a blue circular flame ignited straight up like a Roman candle produced for the Jolly Green Giant. It was over four feet in diameter and twelve tall. Miles's heart redlined his sternum. He bent his knees. Rolled beneath Conrad's desk and then a sonic boom came.

Something slammed the metal entrance door hard, tee-ing off like a ball bat to a car hood. Then silence. Miles came from beneath the desk, stood, and looked out the splintered window. All he viewed was black and the sound of air escaping. A leak. Gas line that fed the spray dryer was all he could think. The lights were out in the building. Dryer alarms from the upper floor rang out. In Miles's mind, he was tossed back to artillery being batted about the tree lines, severed twigs and surrounding foliage. Pinned down by an unseen enemy, and then came the mortar rounds. Earth metered into the specks of granite. Ears rang and Miles blinked hard.

Standing in the office, he realized there'd been an explosion. Something he'd never experienced during his twenty-some years of employment. Panic drew in his limbs. He reached for the phone to call someone. A shift foreman, 911. The phone was dial-tone dead. His brain was a blot of chalky Wite-Out. Then he remembered Kimball. Dropped the phone. Began pulling desk drawers open. Searching for a flashlight to open the darkness of the building. He found nothing, only a box of goggles and a respirator for the dusty organic environment. Reached for the office's doorknob, cracked the door, looked to the floor for Kimball but was overtaken by the smell of burned clay and a thick haze of gritty smoke thick enough to be cut like cold Jell-O. The air was pudding-thick with ignited clay dust. Closing the door, he began to shake; regardless of how big of a peckerwood Kimball was, he had to find him or what was left of him. He started to pull a hanky from his pocket, then grabbed the goggles and the respirator, secured the goggles over his eyes, the respirator over his nose and mouth, cracked the door, crawled out into a void. Unable to see a damn thing, he felt the sheen of grit against his flesh, the heat and taste of granule. Leaving his foot between the door and the jamb, stretching his body over the concrete, his digits passed over what felt like rough edges of skin that held a pulse. Miles locked his hand down around what he thought was a wrist, came up on his knee, heard the door close behind him, and heaved the deadweight. Dragged the heft. Maneuvered backward. Little by little. Hit what felt like a wall, turned, reached, and felt the door, found a tiny sliver of space between jamb and door, patted it up to the knob, opened the door, dragged the body into the office.

He extended his knees to standing, removed the goggles and respirator, coughed and wheezed for air, wiped at his features with a hanky pulled from his back pocket, took on a fit of coughing with his mind in a collapse, words stamping his drums with, *Shitbird, scumbag, numbnuts!* And then the rush of chaos overtook him, enemy fire cascaded in a circle, marines being pelted by gunfire. The tatter and ping of helmets. Faces spraying loss over the battlegrounds. Miles reached at the scourge of lips blistering his drums, his hands palming the mouth to silence and calm the shrieks, screams of pain, he bore down on a private, his upper body black with sweat and fluid; Miles's eyes worked their way over the marine, his legs were two rips of skin laying over sheared bones and fiber. *Help me!* He shuddered. *Help me!* All Miles could think about were the private's jungle boots—what size were they? Where *were* they, 'cause once he was no more, he'd no longer hold any use for them.

Time lapsed and Miles blinked, he was staring down at Kimball on the floor, face smudged by the organo soot of flamed dirt. Smoke was seeping into the room. The panic knob in Miles's mind hit the upper limits of stress as he wanted out. Stood upon a desk against the back wall, palmed and pushed at the ceiling panel that held the pattern of bacteria beneath a microscope, but there was no other way to the upper floor's level, where he knew a window was cut into the sheet metal. The ceiling was boarded over by treated two-by-sixes. "Motherfuckers!" he shouted. "Ain't gonna off me that goddamned easy!"

Looking to the wall with a squared opening of duct work where a large AC unit was bolted in, he grabbed the unit, knowing on the other side of the opening, the outer wall of the building exited to the alleyway. In one swift motion, Miles gripped, tugged, and ripped the AC from the wall, tossed it onto the floor above Kimball's head, glanced down the aluminum duct that'd been cut through the concrete blocks, could see darkness from the outside, felt fresh air leaking in but the ending was covered by a screen. Pulling himself up, he went feetfirst into the duct, dust and dirt rifling his inhale as he worked his thick body to the ending, kicking the screen loose, and a voice shouted, "Knox, that you?"

"It ain't the fucking Easter bunny," he huffed.

Not wanting to move Kimball anymore, unknown as

to what his injuries were, Miles didn't wanna risk lifting him and dragging him through the duct work, he waited on EMS and the fire department as they came with sirens ablaze. Getting the bay doors open, the smoke had begun to feed up into the outside air, clear from the building, the black particles of scorched clay dissipated into the darkness, the overhead lighting from within the plant slowly reappeared. Once the smoke was cleared, the fire department wanted the MSDS book, wanted to know what hazards and harm they could possibly be dealing with. Once it was established there was no harm, EMTs came in, got Kimball secure, lifted him onto a stretcher, and wheeled him out to an ambulance and rushed him to the University Hospital. Miles waved his hand at an EMS worker wanting to take his blood pressure, listen to his insides while he breathed. "I'm fine. My nerves have just been sucker punched is all."

When the plant manager arrived, an overweight man in his forties with thinning gray hair, magnifying specs, and a Zorro mustache, bringing his penny loafer–wearing swagger toward Miles, Miles thought how he sometimes talked too much about himself and his accomplishments; many employees thought he was arrogant and ripe with BS, he'd a chemistry degree and bragged about it every time he stepped into the plant. But Miles figured, that's all the man knew, so that's all he spoke about. He wasn't a bad guy but he just wasn't that damn interesting. His name was Barney Wagner and he rushed the local TV crews away, telling them everything was under control, no one had been seriously injured, it was just an explosion. That they'd know more over the next few days after an extensive investigation. He pulled Knox off to the side, told him, "Be sure you're here prompt by eight a.m. Tuesday morning with your union rep, 'cause regardless of your saving Kimball, I won't tolerate fighting on company property, nor will I stand for your short-fused temperament. We got standards around here, rules. This is not a place that employs barbarian or Spartan attitudes."

And Miles heard Childers say, "Waste this softy son of a bitch." He wanted Miles to stomp Barney's silver-spooned mouth into a stuttering paste. Instead, Miles nodded and told him, "Bet your paper-pushing ass I'll be here."

The aged and round silver gas can, stained by spilled fuel and the collection of dust, sat within Rob's father's woodshed. Rob had grabbed it to dump upon a brush pile, but being a twelve-year-old kid, he'd horse assed around, pouring it on the lengths of sticks and rotted limbs, spilling quarter- and dime-sized droplets upon his denim overalls and the ground on which he stood, not paying much attention to his carelessness. He and Miles had run around in the hills of Pennsylvania, fishing in a nearby pond or stream, building forts with loose branches and fallen hunks of tree, creating roofs with mud and leaves, their fathers working with one another at the steel mill and owning large swaths of acreage. The boys were almost like blood-related offspring. When Rob struck the match to the sandy pad to create the spark that turned to flame, Miles watched as he tossed it onto the brush. It ignited but also quickly followed the droplets across the ground that trailed all the way up Rob's leg. Next thing he knew, he was engulfed by orange heat and then the sensation of a stabbing burn stung his flesh. He was on fire. And in a panic. He screamed and screamed. Miles did the only thing he knew to do from school, what the firemen had taught the kids upon their visit: Stop. Drop. And roll. Miles didn't hesitate, pulled his T-shirt over his head, pressed it against the flames as he tackled Rob to the ground, and began to roll him over the dirt and dead grass and didn't stop until the flames were smothered.

Now they were seated upon the red vinyl barstools that lined the thick wood-grained oak bar like mushrooms in the wild at the VFW. Miles's nerves were vibrating at four hundred amps of electric current. He sat reflecting, knowing he'd saved Rob's life all those years ago, knowing he'd done the same for Kimball. But he wondered what would eventually happen to his job, regardless of his saving Kimball's life. Deep down Miles knew: they wanted his job. Twenty years of seniority. Topped out on his pay. 401(k) matching. Insurance. Getting rid of him they'd save over a 100K a year. Could rehire someone for less money.

Cigarette smoke ghosted from the metal tray as he

thought, come Tuesday when he met with management about his beating Kimball's ass in the street, he knew they'd explain how they frowned on fighting in the workplace. Even though he'd technically not fought on work property. He'd done his business in the middle of Thirteenth Street's pavement and on his own time. It'd be his word against theirs. He'd call it disrespect, an unpaid debt. Kimball owed him money, though he couldn't say what the money was for. He could lie, say it was for a house payment, a car payment, anything but steroids. Wasn't like Kimball would admit to dealing roids. There had been a time when that meant something, when men settled their obligations by manly means without outside interference.

Truth be told, Miles had had a short fuse since he was a teenager. Fighting with anyone who'd give him lip, who picked on him 'cause he was smaller in stature but bigger in attitude. His father had taught him how to box when he was ten. Taught him the open stance. The southpaw stance. How to make a fist. Keep the hands up to guard the head, the elbows tucked to guard the body. How to clench, throw a jab to keep the other fighter at bay and set up the cross, the hook, the uppercut. How to work the opponent's body in order to find the face. His father had been a good man until the cancer gnawed him from existence.

Seated at the bar, Miles took a swig of his bourbon, closed his eyes, and thought about the men he'd served with; flashed back to over there, he was haunted by the shifting memories of faces cracking jokes, rodding their weapons. Smoking Luckys and playing mumbly-peg with their knives, a game of tossing Ka-Bars at one another's feet. Only to be disrupted by the bark of an AK, or the shake of mortar rounds, or memories of the dead, laid out, the warmth within the bodies not from their souls but from the sun. They were lifeless and rotted.

Maybe losing his job was what he needed.

Opening his eyes, to his left was a walnut-paneled wall that opened into the kitchen, where a thick batter of fried fish heated the air above, with the swap of laughter behind him from Whitey McCutchen and Bill Shivers, as Bill barked, "Don't you know I got this hog-headed heifer on two bad knees and a weak wrist. This gal was worse than a three-legged dog with fleas and every time it tried to scratch it fell over, only she'd all of her legs, problem was, she'd no damn balance."

Miles tried to block out the vulgarity that was always spewing from Bill's tongue. Stared at himself in the mirror.

On the opposite side of the oak bar, bottles of Jack, Jim, Turkey, Early Times, Southern Comfort, and Evan Williams lined the bottom of the mirror below his reflection. The sheet metal screw of smoke twisted in reverse. He made eye contact with the man's image that suddenly appeared in the mirror, seated on the stool beside him. Lifted his Maker's and said, "Appreciate the round."

The man was carved-up scars. His left arm had been

chewed up by an explosion that gashed his flesh to thick textures of putty pink. Had he lived, Miles imagined he'd have a metal plate in his head; staple scars erased some of the fine blond hairs that used to bloom over his skull. He'd seen action with Miles on the roads of Da Nang as an engineer. Sweeping the grounds they trespassed daily. Miles believed he would've endured countless skin grafts to sit here with him. Hidden within the cave-like basement atmosphere of the fluorescent lights of the local VFW, his name was Childers. And he haunted him daily.

Like Miles, Childers would have forever been scarred by the trauma of war. Unlike Miles, he wouldn't carry a reserve of it to unleash what he'd endured upon every soul he encountered from day to day. At least that was how Miles imagined his demeanor.

Childers sipped his bourbon, smiled, and said, "You've already spit that to me four times, Miles, I'd appreciate the deed being returned."

Behind them, Bill continued. "I got a pint bottle of JB in my left. A prick that could drive railroad spikes in my right and this saddlebag honey says she's gonna blow the beets."

Miles sipped his Maker's and told Childers, "Know what the problem is, I'm surviving in a time and place where the working man gets disrespected at every turn, can't even collect his due from some faced young feeder that supplies him with juice, who instead wants to bet it on horse races. Who bets on horse races in this day and age, Bukowski?"

"I hear that. All take, no give. Expected to sit there and take it up the ass, dry and no Kentucky Jelly."

Miles chuckled. "Hell has happened to this country. We give our humanity to it and pansy-ass shit birds like Kimball take all we fought for. Parasite took my money, was gonna wager it to fend a profit. Then the goddamned building blows up and I save his filching ass after I done beat it. And my plant manager threatens my employment."

"Politicians do the same damn shit, tell us what we wanna hear so we'll vote for them, then they do the exact opposite once they get in office, fuck us over using our money," Childers said. "I hear they wanna cut into social security, put it in the stock market."

"Stock market?"

"Yeah. Ain't no more pride. Everything is stamped by a foreign territory. We don't even make shit here no more, keep getting sold out to China."

"Yeah, we got bought out back in '96."

"I remember you talking about that."

"Voted a union in just before the deal was sealed. Only thing it done was save our pay and maybe our benefits. Us older types was trying to help the younger ones."

"Trying to keep what you all'd earned."

"Right, after all them years." Miles paused. "Hell, the younger ones didn't even vote for the fucking union."

"Ain't fighters."

"They give two shits about what the older types have done."

"Either born with it or you—"

Bill's tone bellowed louder. Interrupted Childers with, "And this gal has got girth. A double-wide of stretch marks, smells like talcum powder and sorghum. I had to butter my doorjambs down with Lucas bearing grease to get her through the damn door. Then she goes and tosses her lung butter all over my goddamn carpet."

Whitey giggles and asks, "So what'd you do?"

"Hell you think I did, banged her while she's dry heaving, didn't give her a chance to back out after I done been through all that."

Both men busted up laughing. Slapping the blue Formica of the tables, rattling ashtrays and beer bottles. From the kitchen, Sue, the bartender, came out with her faded pavement perm, specs over her Wicked Witch of the East nose and a dish towel over her shoulder. Folds of skin rallied from her arms as she pointed and yelled, "Bill, can you tame that repugnant tongue you got sifting from them lips? Shit fire and save matches, you and Whitey sound like a couple of twelve-year-olds whacking they puds to they daddy's cock books."

Childers cleared his throat and finished. "—Or you ain't. Problem is that all the younger generation, all most of them wanna do is talk on the phone and play video games. Don't have much interest in learning a trade or a skill set.

Shit, they don't even wanna exercise. Then they go to college and get brainwashed and can't afford to pay back their loans they earned a shit degree in."

Childers had been born and bred in Kentucky. Miles hadn't known him long. Like Miles, he was demolition. Walked some of the same roads daily. In war a friendship could end just as quickly as it began. Miles had known him longer in his mind than he had in battle. In his head they still argued over who set off the box mine along the roadside. The mine that had blown Childers into fleshy puzzle pieces. But it had also created a human shield. Saved Miles's life.

Bill yelled back at Sue, "Got something you can whack." And his chair scuffed across the tile as he stood up.

Miles took a drag from his smoke. Disregarded the outline of Bill behind him that reflected in the mirror in front of him, behind the bar. He thought of the men he'd met at the VA for group therapy once a week, where he discussed Childers and the others he served with, or when he went for his yearly physical. Young men. There were a lot of them. Men who thought they were prepared. Thought war would be like *Full Metal Jacket*, *Platoon*, or *Apocalypse Now*, or in Miles's day, they romanticized about the DI or *Sands of Iwo Jima*. Believing they'd drink, kill, fuck, and come home unafflicted. Become heroes. Instead they came home without appendages, sight, or right mind. Broke down and barren. Their lives scattered. They were unable to be reimbursed for what they'd lost for a roomful of gray scalped suits forcing their agendas onto others while the media made a mockery of it all. Everyone seemed to envision that freedom was garnered with hugs and handshakes. Not blood, body parts, and death regardless of innocence.

Miles tasted the enamel of his teeth biting down and rubbing. Seeing outlines frail as fence posts. Kids without limbs. Men and women chewed by artillery, dancing like puppets maneuvered by serpentine wire, and he told Childers, "Like that for every soldier. Before I's shipped to 'Nam, I got thirty days of survival training at Camp Pendleton. Threw me and a few other leathernecks out in the boonies, taught us how to use a compass, lived in tents, ate by campfire like a couple Boy Scouts. We had fighting simulations for taking a hill, map reading, worked in three-man teams. Killed rabbits for nourishment. Some guys had never been camping or hunting so they got taught how to skin, gut, and cook a hare. Here's the kicker: there were no fucking rabbits in Vietnam."

Childers chuckled. "Dealt with the same thing during my training and they wasn't many dogs nor cats over there either."

"No they wasn't." Miles laughed. Sipped his bourbon and said, "Other thing was land mine training. Mines we was trained to detect and dismantle were conventional, they'd been used in World War Two for German tanks. In Da Nang, the VC made their own mines using the undetonated explosives we'd used on them."

"Like an IED in today's wars?"

"Yeah, and they'd rig it with their own detonating mechanism. Stored them in caves and underground bunkers till they were ready to use them, though if they drew moisture, they wouldn't spark. Became useless. Saved our asses a handful of times."

Childers nodded his head. "Yeah, you know, it's a wonder anyone ever makes it back from a war. On the one hand, you might die, and it's a rush, on the other hand you make these connections with others, a real brotherhood, and you just want to disappear with them if *they* die."

"No one really makes it back. Sitting here now, we're still living it in our heads," Miles said. "Faces and places. Sounds and movements. Only takes a trigger to joggle a memory or moment. It never leaves us."

Childers raised his bourbon to the air, and Miles raised his glass of Maker's.

Miles grinned. "Semper fi, brother, semper fi."

Childers took a drink. Miles tossed back the remaining swallow of his Maker's. Miles's mind quieted. He sat in the wash of his flashback knowledge. Miles closed his eyes, chewed on Childers's words—born fighters. Same words and conversations he had in group with other soldiers. Feeling a good buzz soaking into his body from the Maker's, Miles drifted and remembered bearing down on Kimball in the factory, only he replayed the details *differently*, imagining when he'd attacked Kimball, metered out his sockets for a twinge, then rolled him onto his belly. Facedown. Knowing the man wasn't combat material. He looked big and brutal but was soft and brittle, like a dried Play-Doh action figure. Miles could smell his ignorance. The waft of his hygiene pouring into the air. There'd be yelling from operators on the upper mezzanine, combined with the howl of heat and motors and spray-dried clay. Then a few workers would rip him from Kimball, but not before he'd plant a whisper into his ear: "I know you wasn't the one who ran their tongue to management, but you still got a good ass handing coming down from me again, you swindler."

Then a voice would shout, "Dammit, Knox, get the fuck off of him!"

He'd release his arthritic hold only to have other hands governing and restraining him. Force him across the slick and dusted factory floor. Kimball would be left wilted. Rubbery. And shaken. His lungs starved of air until someone would have to hammer a fist down into his center. Create a cough. And Miles would laugh and tell him, "For a big wad of a human you sure are pussified."

Then came the splash of vapor, bouncing somewhere on the floor behind Miles, pulling out of his reimagining of events at the factory. He opened his eyes. Followed by anger on the other side of Miles's empty glass that was smudged by prints. "You son of a bitch. You filthy, rotten son of a bitch! Put that up. Put your goddamned dick up! Stop that nonsense! Stop that shit right now!"

It was Sue, her cheeks were a strawberry beyond its ripening, ready for picking.

Miles and Childers twisted around on their barstools, saw the backside of Bill. His denim bib unbuckled, the metal clanging the floor, and his half-moon hairy ass crack poking out as he staggered toward the bathroom with a trail of liquid rivering between his walk. Childers started to step down but Miles said, "I got it, finish your bourbon."

Childers said, "All right, goddammit. All right."

Miles planted both feet on the tiled blue floor and walked toward Bill.

Whitey sat laughing. A Pabst in his right. "Bill, believe you've pissed someone off."

Miles reached for Bill's right arm, U'ed it up and into his back. Bone and cartilage darted. One thing was certain— Miles was older, but his grip was that of an alligator. Urine was still streaming over the floor in spurts. Bill tried to turn into the pain that Miles offered him. But he met the hefty wall of Miles's body. His strength. Bill slobbered, "Who the hell?" Jerking as Miles guided him toward the entrance/exit door of the VFW, telling him, "You got little respect for them that support you, Bill. Serving you booze, giving you a place to swap tongue with like-minded folk regardless of how repulsive the topic. All you do is make a mess of yourself for others to clean up. The sun has set. Time to saddle and ride your broke-down ass home before I hand it to you."

Bill nearly tripped over the jeans material that hugged

his knees, telling Miles, "Best let go of me. I beat you where you stand."

The retch and tang of Bill's breath could've dropped a swarm of hornets and Miles said to him, "I've dealt with gas pain that hurt worse than you'd deliver. Believe your days of pugilism are wrung out." Miles slammed Bill's face into the metal door. Reached around at the same time with his right. Unlatched the door, swung it open into the night. The floor dropped to the concrete outside and Miles released Bill's appendage. Gave him a shove while raising his right knee up and extended his boot, kicked Bill in his ass. Watched him stumble forward to the ground, where he went palms to pavement. Piss warmed him as he rolled around, belching and cursing, "Rotten . . . cock . . . suckin'—" And the door closed.

Back inside, Whitey hollered, "You're about a bastard, Knox."

Miles eyed him. "You want some of what you gave over the years?"

Whitey shook his head. "Ain't right. We's all been down in the shit. Just having a few laughs. Think 'cause you hunted your own you can get all Billy Jack on us?"

"You need to help your buddy home before I serve your ragged ass walking papers, too."

Whitey stood up, said, "Don't think for a second 'cause you're fucking my daughter that I won't stomp your ass. You're gonna get yours, Knox."

Miles stared. "I might, but it won't be by you, so when you're ready, I'll be waiting to rick your ass like timber."

Wylie trained the chromed .38 revolver on Katz, who stood with long wires of a positive and negative mien, his eyes stuck on the pistol, and Wylie said, "Get your Tonto ass in here, plug that hole up 'fore I close it for good."

"Wait a damn minute," Katz said.

"I got your damn minute, told you to plug that hole!" Wylie brought the pistol across Katz's complexion. Dragged him through the cabin door and onto the floor, right cheek down, blood warming his lips the shade of rusted mud.

"Spread them arms, wanna see fingernails," Wylie barked.

Katz glanced around in confused horror, said, "Calm the fuck down with that steel, I's just checking on the place for Miles."

With his arms spread, face turned, he spoke at Shelby. "I don't understand what the fuck is going on here."

Bent down on his knee, Wylie hammered Katz's skull with the pistol butt. Shelby screamed, "No. No! He didn't do nothing! I-I don't wanna be a part of this anymore."

Wylie came off a single knee and stood above Katz. Shelby squirmed and jerked. Contorted her body. Katz lay in front of her. Wylie laughed.

"Think you're so smart, don't you, bitch. I know what you're thinking, that I'm weak. Who's weak now, huh?"

"I've never thought you was weak, Wylie. When we was growing up, you were always the strong one. Reading your Conan comic books, you wanted to be like him, this hulking figure that stood up to bad people and bad things, what happened to you?"

"Shut up, I don't wanna hear your words." Looking down at Katz, Wylie said, "You best stay put!" He disappeared into the kitchen and came back with a nylon stringer.

"Put your nose to floor, don't wanna see no whites of your eyes."

Wylie slid the pistol down his front, then harnessed himself over Katz like he was riding a horse, grabbed one arm, then the other, looped the stringer around his wrists, pulling it tight, then knotting it even tighter. Stood up, left Katz laid out in front of Shelby.

That was when something inside his head shifted and Shelby smarted, "What are you gonna do? Some person has to know he come here. When he don't go back they gonna come looking for him."

Angered, Wylie walked out the door, slammed it shut. Walked from the cabin down the gravel drive, off to the left over the embankment to the lake that looked like a reservoir of nicotined glass. Something wasn't right in his head. He pulled a crumbled pack of smokes from his sweatshirt pocket, and a Bic lighter; thumbing a flame, smoke spewed from his pigeonholed nostrils. Warm wind grazed his features. What he needed was a beer. Something more to take the edge off. Watching something out in the darkness of the lake, water splashed. Must be a bass. Maybe he could use a rod, do some night fishing. That'd calm him down. Help him get his head straight. Thinking about Miles, coming out here, the man knew a lot about fishing. Knew about fishing from the top of the water, using a jig with the metal reflectors, crappie and bluegill loved them, he also knew about fishing in the deeper waters too, using a sinker to weight the line, a bobber on top, thick nightcrawler or chicken liver soaked in garlic, bait the hook, wait for a cat or bass to hit, let them play, pull that bobber beneath the water. Then jerk that sucker hard and fast, all in one motion. Set that hook and the fight was on. This reservoir was loaded with some monster fish. Miles knew all about them, was full of stories. He was a kind but brutal soul. He was reminiscent of what Shelby and Wylie's father Whitey once was, before Shelby and Wylie found age, then everything changed. Their father got cruel and complicated. He used to take them wade fishing down on Blue River, in their green rubber boots with the yellow shoestrings. A bucketful of minnows bought from Smitty's Bait Shop. Or a coffee can of nightcrawlers found at night with flashlights in the yard. They'd load their stringers with fish, then Whitey would drive the orange Chevy down to the Idlewild restaurant in the Harrison County forestry, get them some cheeseburgers and french fries from Mary, the owner, and listen to ole salty-headed John Bussabarger with his Ward Cleaver–slicked hair tell stories about racoon hunting and horseback riding.

Shelby had always been tomboyish, could do anything Wylie could do; it was how she was raised. Fishing. Hunting. Playing baseball, Matchbox cars, learning how to use hammers, wrenches, and screwdrivers when Whitey fixed things around the house or changed the oil in the vehicles.

Then he changed. Somewhere along the line he became vindictive toward their mother, started taking it out on them. Never wanted their mother to work, but she did, and Whitey hated that she had independence and didn't need his money. But he was also dealing with mood swings from the war. The shit he'd seen. And the things he done. Followed by all the excessive bouts of drinking. He quit doing things with them, instead forced them to do things to one another.

It was wrong.

Miles understood Shelby and Wylie. Their trauma. What he wished was that Miles were here now.

Those are my memories, not your memories!

"Shut up!" Wylie yelled. "Get out of my head!"

Guilt was setting in. Guilt from attacking Bedford and Judy. For attacking Katz.

No, no! You killed, you murdered Bedford and Judy.

"What are you saying?"

There was a stinging pain in his head, something like a migraine.

You're a murderer!

"Shut up! You're not out here, you're inside," Wylie told her.

No, you're inside. Inside of my damn head! I want you out! Gone!

Bringing his hands to his head, digging and clawing into his hair, or was it her hair? He needed that beer and one of Miles's fishing rods from beside the fridge out in the small shack. He'd gotten sidetracked by all the thinking. He needed to find a task to focus on, make sense of what was happening in his head.

He walked up the bank, across the gravel drive, off to the side of the cabin. The shack had electricity. A fridge on a concrete floor. Creosol boards and a rusted roof with leak holes covered by tar. Sliding the door open, as it was attached to a corroded track that needed a good greasing, he reached and tugged the string attached to the ceramic fixture, and the bright bulb lit the area. Opening the barnacled fridge he found a six-pack of Miller High Life. Grabbed it and a container of past-due chicken livers. On the wall leaning beside the fridge were several fishing rods. He took one and walked back to the lake, trying to remove Shelby from his head. Popping a beer open, ice-cold foam floated and oozed from the can. He sucked a quick guzzle down his throat to wash away the bitter that mashed his insides with confusion, wash away her voice. Swallowing, feeling the drawl of skin around his jaws and throat tighten, his mouth burning with the chilled beer, laying the can down, looking around at the grass, dirt, and rock, he realized he was seated along the bank . . . he was drawing a blank, didn't even remember walking from the shack to the bank. A cigarette burned on the ground beside him. He didn't recall lighting it. Reaching for it, bringing it to his lips, he took a hard drag from the smoke.

"What the fuck is wrong with my head?"

It's not your head, that's what's wrong, it's my head and you've streamlined it full of junk, you're puttying it up with your damn cotton.

"Hearing you, your voice, it's gridlocked my temperament on crazy, my addiction, my wants and needs, bleeding my desire for more cotton. Making me wanna get fucked up and stay fucked up," he mumbled.

He pressed his palms into his eyes. His mind could hold not a single stream of thought. It was pained. Words and images jumped from one bandwidth of information to another. And he wondered how he'd gotten here to this lowered existence, after working ten years in construction. Started out of high school as a gopher for a local builder. Learned framing, roofing, insulating, and drywalling. He'd picked up on the wiring and even the plumbing.

You told me that one day you'd have your own crew, you even lifted weights, took care of yourself, but then you began drinking after work with the others, went from a few beers, adding a joint here and there and I told you, it's gotta stop. But you wouldn't listen, said you had control of it. Next thing

you're no longer working out, no longer taking care of yourself,
you're trying some meth, then popping pills, and shooting the
cotton. That's how you got to that lowered existence!

Taking a hard gulp from the can of Miller, talking to
himself, removing the plastic lid from the slimy chicken
livers, the smell stronger than spoiled milk and rotted fish,
he worked them onto the fishing hook.

"You always looked out for me."

I looked out for everybody.

"You was like Mother, worked hard, made good money,
saved what you made, and when someone needed help,
you'd help."

Warned you to quit the drugs or you'd get addicted. Then
I couldn't help you.

He stood up, casting the line out into the lake, hearing
the loud splash, and sat back down.

"You were right, more drugs I used, the more money I
needed to buy them."

And you kept coming to me to borrow money, more and
more until I cut you off.

"Addiction wasn't cheap."

You started stealing copper wire and pipe from building
sites for scrapping. Got caught and tarnished your name, your
credibility. Started getting credit from dealers.

When the tug came from the lake it nearly jerked the
fishing rod from his grip. Rearing back, the pole curved
down, Wylie stood up and walked closer to the water, his

line zigzagged back and forth, the reel buzzed, and he hoped
Miles had at least a thirty-pound test on this line 'cause the
weight felt somewhere around a twenty-pound cat.

A rush of excitement waxed his insides, knowing he
couldn't just reel this bastard in. Catfish liked to fight; you
had to wear them down, reel them in little by little. What
he didn't have was a damn dip net, so he could wade out
and scoop the bastard up once he was close enough. Swiveling left, the fish went right. Tugging right and the fish
went left. Forearms stiffened and pained, he spit the spent
cigarette from his mouth. Body was coated in a glaze of
sweat. He reeled the line in slower, just like their daddy,
Whitey, had taught them when he and Shelby was kids.
Wylie gave the bastard some slack, pulled left, the fish went
right. Wylie played this back-and-forth opera for near
twenty minutes. Giving and taking, slowly working the
weight toward him, closer to the bank, waiting for the cat
to tire. When the line slugged to a deadweight, pedaling
backward, he drug it, walked backward up the bank.

Winded, lungs flamed for oxygen, seeing this malformed shape on the water's edge, just the remnants of a
head, he reeled in some line, giving it no slack, walked toward the mucky scent of slop and mud; it didn't flop but
came straight at him on four clawed feet, piss nearly
squeezed from his insides and run down his inner thigh.
He jumped back, yelled, "Shit!" Couldn't believe what he'd
hooked.

A damned snappin' turtle.

Walking through the cabin door, out of breath, everything changed, viewing Katz facedown, arms behind his back, wrist over wrist drawn tight by the fishing stringer. Shelby's heart fluttered and her forearms ached, her grip hurt. And a pain lay heavy on her eyelids, bending down, her body was stiff, brittle, and she laid a hand to Katz's neck. He was still breathing.

Behind her, out the open door, wind was picking up, Shelby's insides felt like a worn scouring pad, rough and weightless, knowing something was wrong with her, this swapping of persons from herself to her brother. She had finally lost it. Had she murdered two people over drugs? Over a want, an addiction for something her brother's body craved more than air? Or was it hers?

Overcome by this knotted and compressed feeling that somehow she was tied up, her hands bound, she fumbled and worked her hands back and forth, feeling the raw burn of shoestrings, as if lathering them in soap, only her hands weren't constrained. And there was no shoestring.

What she feared was that she'd pass out or doze off. Only to awaken in a catatonic state, go mad, murder again. Kill Katz.

Distraught, she thought of Miles, trying to focus on something positive, *your protector*, that was how she viewed him, he was strong and caring and thoughtful, he had to know she was missing. He knew it wasn't normal for her to be out of contact with him for this amount of time. But how long had it really been? How long had it been since she worked a shift at the Vu? Days, weeks? Looking at her palms, twisting her hands, bringing them to her face, digging her palms into her eyes, rubbing. She wanted it to stop. She wanted control. Wanted Wylie out of her head. She could barely string a coherent thought together, let alone stutter a sentence, but she had argued with her brother when he took over her mind, her thoughts. *Calm down*, she told herself, *calm down*.

Slamming the cabin door, looking down at Katz, he didn't move; someone would come looking for him, they'd have to. But would they know to come here?

All at once, Wylie came toward Shelby like a hot coal from a firepit, seething and heated; he stepped over Katz, kneeled down to Shelby, rooted his left hand into her hair. His right held a cigarette centimeters from her retina. Orange-ash heat caused her eye to dampen and flick.

Cinching her eyes tight, she tried just as she had before to fight the hold Wylie had over her, unable to break his mental restraint and Shelby repeated to herself over and over: *You're not real. You're not real. You're not here.*

Seeing his turnip flesh laid out over the carpet, set with neon blue, not a twitch nor jerk, no movement, he haunted her thoughts as her left palm became a raw hunk of meat. Rubbing over the top of her right hand. Rinse. Repeat. Rinse. Repeat. It was a nervous tic. OCD. Shelby didn't quite understand the hold Wylie had over her or her mind, but something inside her finally clicked, a realization of sorts, and the pain she felt in her mind was somewhere between a migraine and a hammer smashing a fingertip as she fought to rid his control of her actions and perceptions.

Inhaling deep through her nose. Holding her breath. She counted to ten. Exhaled slow. When she felt the tension ease up, she slowed the mock washing of her right hand over her left. But when she stopped, her arms went stiff, her elbows locked up; it was as though she were restrained, and she pressed through, feeling bones and joints unhinge. Crack and pop. Was it real or was it her imagination getting the best of her, she didn't know. Something in her left shoulder cracked. Her elbows bent and her right hand was no longer rubbing her left, but then came a new pain delivering deformities of ache down her neck and traps. Inhaling deep through her nose again, she held her breath, counted to ten. She heard Wylie scream as she jerked and thrashed him away, balling her fists, fighting the stiffness from within her frame, feeling depleted of spirit but not beaten.

Dark settled from a low evening haze to a graying black unsettled cloud cover of cold and warm dampness in the air. The Dodge's dash lit up with numerals for speed and

RPMs. Tunes rattled from the door speakers with CCR's "Bad Moon Rising" and Shadrack looked up at Nathaniel with confusion. "Why you driving so fast?"

Snapping from his field of anger, nerves were anxious and on edge from the encounter at Leonard's home, lowering the music, Nathaniel told him, "I'm closer to finding this *Coyote*."

Looking lost at the answer, Shadrack asked, "What are you gonna do when you find him?"

Having Shadrack with him wasn't the best idea, creating an underaged accomplice, placing him in harm's way. Nathaniel hadn't thought that far ahead. "I'm gonna do my best to do what's right."

Nathaniel had the pedal to the floor. Diesel plumed sludge from the exhaust and the Dually roared down the back road. Nathaniel tried to gather control of his actions. His composure. He couldn't show up at Carney's half-cocked. He had to be on point.

Shadrack sat in thought as if contemplating, comic book closed in his lap, unable to read in the dark, and then he looked to Nathaniel and told him, "I can tell you if it's the man who kilt my parents."

Somewhat in shock, unexpected, Nathaniel asked, "You saw his face?"

"Not his full face, just how pale his skin was and everything else. His clothes and how big and tall he was."

Taking the curves with the Blue River to their right, the

two-lane road narrowed as a solid rock wall climbed up over twenty feet on their left, leading their navigation to the stop sign where they hung a right onto 62, headed down the road a mile to where they'd hang a left to White Cloud.

The open iron gates, specked with oxide, welcomed the mash of rubber down a drive peppered by blades of grass seeping through cracked rock. A weathered house sat with flaking paint and faded powder-blue shutters. From outside the truck, Nathaniel could hear the thump of "Hank, why do you drink?" Anxiety ran through his body about how he'd handle the interrogation with Carney. Questioning if he'd murdered his brother and sister-in-law—if so, it'd be tough to not end this man's life. He wouldn't be missed. Add to that his helping to acquire prescriptions for his brother to sell. The way Nathaniel figured it all in his head, Bedford had taken all the risk. Picking up the pills. Letting strangers enter his home. Around his wife and son. Taking the money. All Carney had to do was pick up his cut. With zero risk. But then, Carney and Bedford had been friends all through childhood. Would the man have murdered him? It was a question Nathaniel could soon uncover.

Glancing at Shad, Nathaniel had to think about the boy, who had no one else to raise and care for him, only

Nathaniel. Now before his every action he had to take Shadrack into consideration. There lay the question of morality. Right and wrong.

Looking at Shadrack, shifting to park, Nathaniel told him, "Same as last time, keep the doors locked."

Stepping from the truck, .45 tucked down his back in a clip holster, the music drowned out the sounds of the Blue River that streamed behind the home, crunching over the uneven pavement, stepping off, detouring over dirt and loose gravel toward raging orange skeletons of pallets and cedar logs that formed a teepee of flames from a bonfire that reared off to the side of the home where two outlines sat. One was male, the other female. Each had canine hides laid out beside their feet.

Studying the male known as Carney Dillman, Nathaniel knew all about his criminal activity, aside from running a prescription drug ring with Nathaniel's dead brother, Nathaniel had always referred to him as a river-rat hellhound. He'd served time for beating a man into stupidity during an armed robbery; once he was released, he used his connections from the pen. Garnered prospects with other militia groups throughout the surrounding counties to deal arms. AKs, AR-15s, M16s, pump-action and semiautomatic shotguns and handguns. He was always two steps beyond everyone else's thinking. He also scouted out rich gun collectors, those with prized collections. Burgled their homes when they were out of town with the help of the

Hubbard brothers. Only to resell the arms in other states to other collectors for a hefty price tag.

It didn't matter how Nathaniel played this scenario out in his head, because everything could go to shit at the bat of an eye. Carney sat off from the fire facing Nathaniel in a wooden rocker, its seat and backing weaved with baling twine. A mason jar of Maker's Mark rested between his legs. A knife sticking out from his creased and scuffed biker boot. From his slicked-back locks on top, with the sides burred to stubble, he looked like he was from the Capone era, only leaner. Harder. He'd inked skulls of a cannibal nature around his jugular, wavy black-and-white American flags expanded over his slug-shot shoulders, running down bricklayer biceps that were graffitied with obsidian flames and Old English lettering.

With bonfire flames casting the dance of shadowy fire over his outline, the one dog growled, its hackles spiked. Carney's chords sounded as though they'd been chiseled with a steel file. "Give it a rest, Luther." Making eye contact with Nathaniel he asked, "And to what do I owe the pleasure of this visit from one of Harrison County's finest?"

Beside him, the female, Ivy Stable, lounged with legs outstretched, her flesh the color of a cadaver. Branded a gearheaded tomboy because her grease monkey father raised her to know the mechanical ways of engines at his shade tree mechanic barn, she held the schematic prints to all engines, transmissions, carburetors, and the air, fuel, and spark needed to make them hum within the automotive den of her brain. She'd make men blush with her knowledge of vehicles from all makes and models.

Nathaniel surveyed the situation, took note of the boot knife, of Ivy seated beside him, the booze they were lounging with, and said, "Bit warm for a mound of flame, ain't it?"

Ivy smiled, her orbs lined with black, she said, "Good for the pores, sugar."

Nathaniel knew the love connection surrounding Ivy; she'd stalked Carney for days until she caught him weak-legged and circle-eight-eyed from no sleep one night at the K & H tavern in Lanesville. Out in the lot, she placed her footing one step behind his own. When his truck door creaked he turned into her embrace and swapped some groping; after she drove him back here and he awoke the next morning with the pop of bacon, the perk of caffeine, and the twist of his favorite bourbon, Pappy Van Winkle. Low and behold they had become an item.

Sipping from his jar of bourbon, the ice clattered as Carney lowered it. Spoke in a low-level rasp of jailhouse whit and country-boy philosophy. "You gonna lay me the reasoning for your visit or talk about the damn weather all night?"

"You had to know I'd pay a visit, you were in a hurry, ran me and my nephew off the road earlier, trailing away from my brother's place."

Carney chuckled. "I might've paid a visit to a man's

blood kin who owed me some coin earlier, but I don't recall running anyone from the road."

Heat was rising in Nathaniel's veins. "I'm calling you a liar. I paid a man a visit today who let the cat out of the bag, know you were in cahoots with my brother, running a prescription drug ring."

"That so, big ten-four, so you must've paid black-tar-peddlin' Leon a visit. Big fucking deal. Your brother needed to wean his pains and earn a living. I proffered the man some salvation, that's more than I can say for his ex–law enforcement brother."

Carney's words dug into Nathaniel and he came sharp and to the point. "Someone murdered my brother and sister-in-law, you ran me off the road driving away from the crime scene. Did you fucking kill them?"

Sides of Carney's hair was sandpaper-short. Looked like you could use it to scuff the paint from one's quarter panel as he indexed an itch. Kept his actions calm and collected, glanced at Ivy. "You believe this shit, guy shows up uninvited, accuses me of murdering his brother, of killing my best bud since birth." Twisting his gaze back to Nathaniel, he said, "Do you hear what it is you're accusing me of, killing one of my own partners? What would I gain from murdering Bedford and Judy?"

"You gonna dead-eye me and tell me you didn't run me off the road again, that it wasn't you?"

Unblinking, not a crease in his complexion, Carney told him, "Look, I've never had no beefs with you over the years, with me doing time, you being a pig. I'll level with you: I paid a visit to make my weekly collection, he never answered. I drive fast, so yeah, I probably ran you from the road, my fucking bad. That don't place a notch by my name for murder."

Half-truth, Nathaniel thought, *the son of a bitch could pass a lie detector.* The door was ajar when Nathaniel arrived. But he told the quiet part out loud—money, something Nathaniel hadn't considered. Not only were there no drugs on the scene, but there was also no money. There was only one other question to offer. "Answer me this. Shadrack was in the house when they were murdered, only name my nephew heard was *Coyote.* That name ring any familiarity?"

Pallet wood popped in the fire. The wind picked up. The stereo music went silent. Songs switching. Ice rattled in the mason that Carney raised to his lips, taking a swig, lowering the jar, and swallowing he said, "*Wylie Coyote.*"

Wanting for the real name, Nathaniel demanded, "Who the hell is it? Bugs Bunny?"

"Wylie McCutchen. Whitey's boy. Son of a bitch is a tool. Half-baked upstairs."

Nathaniel mumbled, "Shelby's brother." When he was a county cop he remembered seeing Wylie down at the Dock in Leavenworth or one of the Mexican restaurants in Corydon ordering beers alone or with Shelby. He was a loner. Never kept the company of friends. He was transparent. Never caused trouble with the law. He had a clean record.

"Now that's a sample I'd like to taste," Carney spat.

Ivy evil-eyed Carney. "Best watch your lip, sugar."

"That girl's all fire, thirty years young, she likes the older men like myself, shacked up with that old roid-raged war vet, Miles Knox. Man's old enough to be her daddy. That's the word down this curve of back road anyways."

Something like an ice bath traveled through Nathaniel's shape as he thought about Miles Knox, a man of respect. A damaged soul who'd seen everything go bloody and turn the rivers red. Fuck, he'd *swam* in them rivers and drank from them. Man was a fucking marine who had been down in the shit. Nathaniel and he had sat sipping the tides of shell shock down at the VFW after his shift patrolling the back roads of Harrison County many nights. Hell, they'd night fished together. And then he thought about his brother and sister-in-law, how Carney sat unfazed at the mention of their deaths and words fell from his lips without much thought. "Then McCutchen must've murdered Bedford and Judy."

"Afraid so. That's the prognosis for the nickname."

Ivy interrupted with, "Know they's fraternal?"

"Shelby and Wylie, they're twins?" Nathaniel questioned.

"Yeah. She takes care of Wylie. He's an addict. He's known to crash at her place when he's not using, them two is close."

Carney raised his jar, sipped his bourbon. Lowered it and barked, "Like a coyote who was caught in a snare, you got plenty of blood, a leg, but no coyote."

Wanting to get on the road, Nathaniel knew where he needed to pay a visit next, told Carney, "Appreciate the answers."

"What, no apology?"

"For what?"

"For accusing me of murdering Bedford and Judy."

"You might not have murdered them, but to grow up with my brother, you sure as shit show zero compassion."

Carney offered the stare down. Nathaniel turned and walked back to his truck, knowing he was headed to Shelby's home but not sure of what he would find.

He wanted to clear the anger from his mind after Whitey brought up what Miles fought to forget, of what he once hunted in Da Nang. He sat in his El Camino, remembering how he'd been dumped out in the middle of nowhere with a recon unit. No contact with the enemy. Pulling surveillance. Staying tucked in the jungle foliage to be a part of the decorations, taking a sniper with you in case you see a higher-ranking official. Taking an artillery officer, a radio man, an ordnance man, too. Radio air strikes to naval ships with coordinates when camps or outposts were found, where the enemy was dug in. Miles wanted to forget, not forever, just for a cluster of time.

What he really wanted was to see Shelby.

The thought of her was consuming him. Being with her

always helped him to dislodge from his past. Let him take a breather and savor the present.

Closing his eyes, inhaling, he recalled her scent, her fumy-flowered flesh. Clean and velvety. She held a vibrance, a glow that delivered something reminiscent to happiness. What he wondered was why she'd not contacted him. He thought about the passing weeks. Catching her staring off into nothing. Frying bacon and eggs over the stove, setting the smoke alarm off. Questioning her and she'd snap back to existence. Tell him nothing. Tired was all. He didn't press her. But looking back, he should've pressed more, something wasn't right and he wrote it off. He knew better. He had demons. Sat through group sessions at the VA, so he knew all about trauma. Now he was worried and missing everything about her.

He missed their mornings that drifted from the darkness and their evenings that slipped back into the dark. There were mornings and nights they'd curl up at his house, no TV, just words, conversations, building a fire, sipping bourbon, keeping some old honky-tonk turned down low, talk about the war he fought, the men he served with, where those men were from, raised on farms and by factory workers, and how most of them had not made it back. Shelby'd discuss her upbringing, being a tomboy, playing in the dirt with dump trucks, Matchbox cars, no Barbies; she had superhero dolls, G.I. Joe, Godzilla and Rambo movies. Her father would buy her and Wylie pocketknives, air rifles, and slingshots. Her mother worked in a factory. Earned good money. But as the teenage years found she and Wylie, abusive tools entered Whitey's skill set. Her mother wasn't around as much. Working. Running around with girl-friends. Her father was irritated, began verbally downing any and all women. Always belittling her. Yet when she moved out of the house, took work as a stripper, she was the one he relied upon, the one he had abused, calling her an idiot or brainless twit one day only to phone her the next day, demanding she stop by the house, cook for him. Clean his clothes, or pick him up from the bar when he was too drunk to navigate. The man was a condescending, abusive, womanizing waste of skin, from Miles's perspective.

Miles fired the engine of his El Camino, left the VFW, passed Whitman's used-car lot, where Chevys and Fords lined and curved light from their shined panels and hoods. He hung a right on North Oak Street, parked in front of the town hall's bricked structure. A police cruiser sat in the alley. Miles jaywalked across the street, hit Holiday Li-quors, left the ghostly image of Childers riding shotgun. He grabbed twenty-four sixteen-ounce Millers. Laid the cold weighted case on the counter. Kingsley manned the register, centipede-browed with a BE ALL YOU CAN BE camo hat rounding his head.

"Wanna fifth of Maker's, Knox?"

"You're all right, Robert, even with that army cap on your head."

Kingsley chuckled, grabbed a bottle for Miles. "And

you're all right for an ole jarheaded shit-for-brains. That'll be forty-five dollars even."

Miles sorted two twenties and a five from his wallet. "Appreciate it." Grabbed the case with the bottle on top.

"Hold up, got something you might find interest in."

Kingsley walked from behind the counter, off to a small fridge, kneeled down, opened it, pulled out a sheet of paper wrapped in plastic wrap. Came back, laid the cold sheet on the counter.

Miles eyed the shape that Kingsley lay on the counter; it was sectioned off by many squares like graph paper, only it wasn't geometry. Miles was curious. "Hell you got there?"

"Blotter acid."

"Hell's that?"

Kingsley chuckled. "Old jarhead fights in 'Nam and you don't know what acid is? It's LSD."

"You go hippy on me and get your nipples pierced? Look, I smoked my share of the wacky weed over in the jungles, it eased the nerves but I never did no mind benders."

"I didn't go hippy, got a connection that runs with the Grateful Dead, gives me a call every now and then when he has some acid or mushrooms, thought I'd offer you a sample, if you want some. Give it a test run."

"The fuck does it do?"

"Gives you a helluva buzz. Might cancel out your booze, give you a bit more energy and clarity. Makes music a bit more, uh, groovy. It'll last you anywhere from eight to twelve hours."

"How much you selling it for?"

"For you, it's free."

Miles considered the offer; he heard stories, even seen a few guys he'd ran with over the years say they'd taken it, some seen clowns chasing them or faces or body parts melting, mostly they just sat back staring into the air, listening to music, have a sudden outburst of laughter, get weirded out, but they never got out of hand, it couldn't make him any worse than he already was. "How do I take it?"

Peeling the wrap away from the top of the sheet, he told Miles, "These small squares here, about the size of a fingernail, you tear one or two of them off, place 'em on your tongue, and they'll dissolve."

"Then what?"

"Then you wait for your ticket to ride."

"Ticket to ride?"

"Your acid trip, takes about forty-five minutes to an hour."

Miles reached beneath the wrap, pulled on one of the corners, two squares stuck to his finger, he placed them on his tongue. "Bottoms up."

Sealing the plastic up, Kingsley smiled, took it back to the fridge. "Let me know what you think, like I said I get some every so often, just a change of pace from the booze."

"Like I said, you're all right for an army guy."

Chuckling, Kingsley asked, "'Fore I forget, you hear about Bedford and Judy Timberlake?"

Almost out the glass door framed by stainless, Miles turned and said, "Naw, they in some shit?"

"Word is they shits been decanned, they's murdered."

"Drugs?"

"No one knows. Word around town is Nathaniel had they boy, his nephew, out fishing all night, went to drop him off this morning, found them each shot dead."

"But the boy's alive?"

"Yeah."

"Damn, Nathaniel's good people, shared many pints with the man, got a lot of respect for him. That's one son of a bitch you don't wanna get in a pissing match with."

"Got that right."

Miles exited the store. Walked down the sidewalk. The old library across the street now stood as a red masonry relic, storage for old facts after the bank beside it was moved; the building then remodeled into a new library. He jaywalked back to the El Camino. Got in, sat the beer on Childers's lap in the passenger's seat. Rested the Maker's between his legs, against his crotch. Shifted into drive. Hung a right on West Chestnut, then Water Street, turned left onto 62, crossed over Indian Creek. Lurked away from the glare of town lights and through the navy shade of night, thought about the murder of innocents. But he couldn't be acquainted with it. Had enough of his own heavy shit to haul around. Wanted to pay Shelby a visit, surprise her, hold her in his arms; he needed that female warmth. Nothing sexual, just some companionship. Figured he'd trek the back roads, stay clean of the county fuzz all the way to her house.

Driving up the hill, Jim Morrison sang about Texas radio and the big beat. Miles thought about when Tuesday arrived, depending how the meeting with management at work swayed, he could be jobless. Have to sit staring at Conrad, maybe Kimball and the higher-ups. Miles figured if worse came to worse he'd roll his funds over from his 401(k) rather than wait until he was sixty or sixty-five. He was already drawing his pension from the company that sold the dirt business to the competitor, about eleven hundred bucks a month. Add that to his disability from the military for his ear damage that he'd been living from, tossing his weekly earnings into the bank. Been doing that for the past five or six years. Social security was still years away. His house was paid in full. The El Camino was paid off but was old; still, the 350 small block growled like a young walker hound. He'd been living on a little over two grand or less a month. He'd been drawing more than that but didn't spend it. Didn't use much electric, water, or gas 'less Shelby was around. Money he spent was on booze, smokes, roids, and red meat. Most of his meat he usually killed, like deer. He'd bag two or three a year. Then he'd buy half a cow from Dyan and Alan Feller. Sometimes he'd get a hog from them for some sausage and bacon.

Flipping cigarette ashes out the passenger's-side window, Childers's outline jutted his head, tilted a sixteen-ounce of Miller back as they turned left at the stoplight, swung onto 135 South, and said, "Ole Jim had the groove, was white-boy blues back in the day."

Miles was swimming in thought, thinking about jobs; there was a time when those were plentiful. When they meant something. Now, it was something more men and women was searching for and when they got one they usually hated the fuck out of it. Wasn't like anyone wanted to hire an over-the-hill war vet who drove the dead around in his front seat and would beat a man bloody over a renege for his steroids. Once a marine, always a marine.

As he sped through the cut of thick calcite and cedar decorating the right and left flanks of the road, he passed Hayswood Park, the yellow cast-iron gates locking off the entrance, teeter-totters and square-framed shelter houses sitting on the hillside beneath the full moon's glow. Miles crossed over Indian Creek once more. Climbed another hill through more carved stone and hung a right onto Heidelberg Road. To the left an ashen silo climbed into the sky. A brownstone sketched the right side of the road. Then came the farmland, fields and fence line, quickly twisted and shaped into the belly of wilderness as Miles pressed the gas.

Some of the land had been sold. New-construction plumbed-and-squared homes, mixed with old farmhouses. Then became distant, replaced by wilderness as Miles laid heavier on the gas pedal, speeding up, making the night come quicker. The darkness and the trees and foliage trailed outside his vehicle. It brought on those instincts of not knowing. Of those times when he left the dirt roads and their flanks peppered with rice fields, and hit the boonies, the jungles where the NVA came in at night. They'd demand shelter and nourishment from the farmers with the threat of death if they disobeyed. It was how the NVA hid and waited to ambush marines. Bringing the firefight. The loud explosions popping all around, sometimes you were unable to home in on the location of gunfire, all you could do was shoot in the direction of where instincts told you there was an enemy. And a crazy marine named Vega, always cracking the humor in a firefight, once screamed, "Hey, Knox, you're from Indiana, right?"

"Yeah, the hell's that got to do with the price of rice in Da Nang?"

"Nothin', but is it true John Dillinger's thirty-six-inch dick is in the Smithsonian Institute?"

And there all of the marines lay, returning gunfire at an unseen enemy, laughing, not knowing who was next on the waiting list for a body bag.

Miles snapped back to the road, glanced at Childers, whose outline flickered and fuzzed, said, "Sorry, wasn't talking to you."

"No need to apologize. Sure plenty of vets talk to their Evil Caspers."

Miles slowed down, hung a right on Mathis Road. Took a curve that was as sharp as a bent elbow.

"Evil Caspers?"

"The unfriendly ghosts of the dead."

Miles chuckled. "Even after thirty years?"

The crank of thunder spat off in the distance over the trees; climbing the hill of gravel, the El Camino's stereo speakers rattled with "Riders on the Storm" and Childers said, "Yes, sir, even after thirty years, maybe till the end. Fuck if I know."

Beat and barren structures lined the road as it snaked and dropped and rose. Houses sat distanced by acres from one another, nestled into hillsides or sitting roadside; some of the shapes began to slowly expand and contract, as if they were breathing, and Miles shook his head. Something was off. Told Childers, "Talking to vets at the VA that dealt with the dead for months, some for years, they all say you gotta figure out what they want."

And Childers said, "Gotta figure why they're storing their luggage in your room."

"You mean penance?"

"I mean peace. Maybe they need you to do something for them so you each can find peace."

Peace. Miles didn't know what the fuck that was. He'd tried more than a time or two over the first few years, to pick up the phone and dial Childers's parents, who still lived in Kentucky. Had even looked up their address. But he couldn't do it. Didn't know where to begin or what to say if he called and it was really his parents. That was when the tides of mash came on thick. He'd lost sight of making contact but not of the memories. And he told Childers, "Pass me one of them Millers."

"You sure your roid-shooting ass needs to be drinking and driving like this?"

Reaching over into the passenger's seat, Miles ripped one free. "Just give me the goddamned beer."

Miles thumbed the tab down, swallowed the golden pilsner, which was cold enough his tonsils felt like a walk-in freezer, thought of the three beers they got every month when in Da Nang. Two choices: Schlitz and Miller. Hot or cold, it made little difference. Over there it was a delicacy. They wore the same boots. Same uniforms. Were given seven magazines for their M16, held twenty rounds. Day in, day out. He broke his rifle down, his pistol down, kept them clean. He was a man of purpose, repetition. Discipline kept him breathing. Same as it did now, pressing the iron, pushing the pavement, sweating out the poison he saturated his liver with.

Ejecting the Doors from the CD player, he Frisbee'd the disc onto his dash. Grabbed Waylon Jennings's *Honky Tonk Heroes*, fed it into the player. There was a sunken, light-headed feeling flowing from his skull down to his shoulders and arms as he focused on the slow picking of strings that came with Waylon's words. Miles told Childers, "Worst part of being in Da Nang, monsoon season. Doing search-and-destroy missions in the rain and mud. Couldn't keep your smokes dry. Weapon'd get drenched, jam it up in a firefight. I'd be cleaning the son of a bitch first chance I got. There I'd be, checking villages for evidence of the NVA, knowing they'd been housing them and the villagers would lie about it. I always worried about my gun jamming. I couldn't tell a VC guerrilla from a fucking Vietnamese farmer. Never wanted to kill the farmers."

"They's living a double life."

"Living in fear. Playing sides. But when you found cleaning rods for AK-47s in their homes, it'd burn a marine's ass, you'd get your interpreter to grill them. Listen to their stuttering yik yak of half-assed mojo, you're soaked, fingertips morel-mushroomed, uncovering weapon caches wrapped and buried in the soil beneath their huts or in their chicken coops. It was tough, feeling that you was there to help them and all they wanted to do was break one off in your ass. Never knew who your enemy was. Always second-guessing yourself."

"Demolition. I never lived long enough to see what all you seen."

"When we found weapons, I'd rig up some C-4, pile that shit together, and blow it into shrapnel, give the farmers a ticket to town. Wasn't easy. I placed myself in their shoes, how would I feel if I was them, having foreign soldiers raid my home, my family, my farm, evacuate us, say they're helping but all they're doing is destroying my home, my livelihood, and what I grow, and if I help them the NVA will murder me, rape my daughters, and kill the rest of my kin. It was like walking on a razor-sharped axe over a pit of cobras."

Childers's voice all of a sudden slowed down, like a record being played on the wrong speed. He said, "A double-edged sword. Tell me something, Miles, what'd Whitey mean back at the VFW when he said *hunted your own*?"

Taking the road slow, Miles swigged his Miller. His head and body were getting cloudy and numb. He could hear the minutes ticking on a clock and he didn't even wear a watch. He told Childers, "I've only ever told Shelby about this. Some of it made the town paper. Some of it didn't. Most of it was classified, as in we never existed, nor did those that we hunted. But before that, when you and me was in front of the tank. I was sweeping for mines. You was walking up a ways from me. Believe it was Liberty Road. You gave the hand signal to stop 'cause you seen something. I did the same. For whatever reason I watched you kneel down. And you waved me over to step slowly. I did. Real easy. Watched you start to stab down into the dirt with your Ka-Bar. Probing, they called it. Then just as I was within a few feet, the world turned up the volume. Got so loud and heated, I went deaf with a ring in my drums. Face was on fire and welted by burn, stinging with red, like being coaled by a stove. You had hit the pressure release plate of a forty-pound box mine. That coulda been me. Between that and surviving Operation Allen Brook weeks before, I was like the Angel of Death or some shit. Blamed myself for what happened to you. So I volunteered to go out with Recon when they needed volunteers with demolition experience.

Me and Vega, we was what they called combat ready. No screening. All training would be hands-on, like an apprenticeship. Went hunting for something in the boonies. What no one knew was what was in season."

Coming to the bottom of the hill, Miles's entire frame was vibrating with energy and a wavy, heated-honey feeling; he crossed a newly constructed bridge in a stupor of silence except for Waylon Jennings, and the road took a hard left.

Childers sucked on the suds and said, "And what was in season?"

"It wasn't a yellow-skinned enemy like we thought," Miles said.

Childers went silent. Then said, "War rearranges a person's wires. See kids with nothing, playing in the dirt one minute, then they setting you up, blowing you and your buddies to shit the next. What that does in your mind, you no longer see them as kids, they're VC, the guerrilla forces, which makes they moms the foundries that spit them out. They're the fucking queen bees that need to be removed. That's how war rewires your mind, makes a soldier think in strategic terms of paranoia."

"Only person I trusted in the bush was the men in my unit. Never trusted the villagers or the ARVNs we fought beside."

"Army of the Republic of Vietnam."

"One and only, they was spineless."

"Yes they were."

"Would run out the door on you in a firefight. You knew you was safe if they wasn't running."

"Meant there was no NVA around."

"Was pissifying, we were there to help them battle the threat of communism from the north. Killed your morale especially when you're watching your own lose their lives for them and their people."

The El Camino barreled up a steep incline, came to a stop sign. Headlights outlined the flint-colored tombstones of the graveyard that sat on the other side of Old Forest Road. The air glowed like it was under a purple-black light. Shapes of unknown movement came and went like flares lighting up and burning out. Miles cut the wheel to the right. He'd drive down to Mount Solomon, hang a left on Walnut Valley to the dead end. Was feeling numb but powerful and said, "Seen so many bodies scattered and piled like a forest of trees that'd been timbered after an ambush. One fight lasted nearly eight hours. Lost nearly three units. No supplies could get to us. Watched men baking in the goddamn sun. When reinforcements finally arrived, the firefight quit and jarheads snapped pics of those without wind. Mangled, bloodied, and blackened. Some of them posed with the NVA corpses. Guess it was a release to say, *I got you, motherfucker.* 'Cause Vietnam wasn't a battle for territory so much as it became a battle for a body count, for how many NVA you killed."

"Get numb to it," Childers said.

"That's something they don't learn one in boot camp."

"What's that?"

"That to become a soldier, you gotta become something that's not much different than the enemies you're fighting; in reality you gotta become something much worse or you won't survive and that's not counting what you don't know about, the men in your government calling the shots, who have a financial interest in the war you're fighting. They don't care about you or even about peace. They just give you a medal, a piece of paper, a ceremony, and shake your hand."

Memories were beginning to tear at Miles's mind. There was something like anger roaring through his veins and he felt the pump of blood expanding and pressing the tissue of his body, a cold sweat moistened his forehead, his hands gripped the wheel tight, and pressing the gas pedal to the floor, the engine screamed with horsepower, gravel spit and clanked the rear end of the El Camino, and the world outside the car became one big blur as he barreled down the gravel driveway to Shelby's home.

In the bedroom, rumbling through the closet, throwing blankets, sheets, and quilts to the floor, Wylie was rummaging the shelves. Last he recalled, he was arguing with himself, with Shelby; he needed a nail and a hammer to tack the zinc through the snapper's rod-iron-hooked head. Secure his ass into a tree to cut the reptile skin from around its shell, just as Whitey had learned Shelby and he when they would go gigging for the bullfrogs at night, slogging through the warm slop and stink of farm ponds around the county, stepping on the hard-shelled backs. Reaching into the muck for the tail. Lifting it up, careful not to be bitten by the curved snout that would mulch through tendon and bone, not letting go. He'd found Miles's push mower and placed it on top of the turtle to weight it down, keep it from trailing off.

Now, stepping from the closet, coming from the bedroom, he was losing his mind, glancing to the rock floor, then the hearth wall of ivory and flint where the fireplace held orange coals that shadowed the room. He was an outline short. Didn't see Shelby, only Katz.

"Shelby?" he yelled.

There was the drop of his pulse. The ramming of blood-pumped muscle behind the marrow of Wylie's chest. Looking for the light switch on the wall to his left. Flipping it on. Katz twitched and moaned: "My head, my damn head."

"Shut your hole before I stomp you into stupid," Wylie threatened.

This how it's gonna be? I get you outta my head and you think you can come back?

Wylie pulled the .38 from his waist, from behind him, boots came in heavy footfalls. The hard-hitting bony-fisted knuckles to the rear of his head knocked him into the room's center. Wylie turned around to Shelby's painted-on jeans. Her torso bent and contorted. She came at Wylie once more, swatted at the weighted revolver with her open hand like a cat.

From the floor, Katz shouted, "What kind of crazy is going on with you?"

"You dumb bitch. Knew I couldn't trust you!" Wylie's voice shouted.

Wylie came at Shelby, reaching and clenched her outgrowth. Flung her across the room to the rectangular entrance. Before she could gain her bearings, Wylie punched her senseless. She swayed backward down the hall. Her digits patted the walls for balance. Turning toward the light of the front room she took in the open door to the outside.

Katz had worked his way up from lying flat on the floor, sat upright, hair matted by fluid, his face disheveled and pocked with confusion as he eyed Shelby like a confused pup.

Then she felt Wylie's hand prod her scalp. Twisted her into his facade, heated and mollusk. She raked her fingers downward. Skin gave and balled beneath her nails. Eyes metered wide and burned.

Wylie yelled, "Cunt! You fucking cunt!"

Get out of my head! Shelby screamed, and hammered his forehead with her fists. Their pain was breached and shared like two halves making a whole. Wylie drove her backward over a wooden pew that'd been cushioned with pillows for sitting.

Katz sat lost, watching a maze of two hands working as four. Unable to comprehend the back-and-forth madness of limbs and words. He pressed his back into the wall. He lengthened his way to height. Stood up. The room slanted to off-center. Dizzy, knees latched and unlatched, his body weaved. Something wasn't firing in his brain. He struggled to place one foot in front of the other as he looked out the open door. His truck sat parked out in the gravel driveway surrounded by the dark. A breeze sanded his face with flakes of dust, causing his eyes to bat and blink. The distant sound of branches rubbing and creaking stirred, this was his chance to escape, but he couldn't step out onto the slatted porch, take the steps downward to the yard. His knees didn't wanna bend, they were locked up. Stiff. Swiveling his head from side to side he wanted to rub the crazy from his eyes, all of it, the fighting, yelling, and attacking, but couldn't. His hands were still bound behind him. Then all at once a gunshot pierced the air, sent explosive waves through his head, and brought him back to the moment with a ringing combined with the sounds of a female screaming.

Taking the curves of Highway 62, trees appeared and disappeared in waves, blurring darkness and shadowing lights as truck tires screeched. Wind outside the truck hummed over the hood and cab; night danced with a strong wind. To Nathaniel's right lay a holler of flattened stone, sectioned out from years of rainwater flowing and washing over the earth, large limbs of broken trees lay scattered among decorations of rubber tires, washing machine doors, and the guts of a dryer or gas stove, all sorts of disregard from rural types who used the holler like a dumping ground for appliances when they quit working. Behind it a hillside expanded upward, the night saturated and soaked up all the in-between wilderness.

Shadrack looked to Nathaniel. "The wind is really loud."

Nathaniel hung a right down Walnut Valley Road, the holler half-circled down into the earth, running beside him, headlights sawed through the dark. He was skeptical about finding Wylie and when he did, how would he handle it? Glancing at Shadrack he told him, "There's a storm brewing."

There was the shadow of a haggard trailer cut into a hillside. The surrounding land was steep with trees and brush. Nathaniel slowed down for another curve and Shadrack told him, "I don't like storms."

Crossing a creosote-stained bridge, Nathaniel took a steep incline, remembering the bridge had once been a narrow slab of stone, only one vehicle at a time could cross, the other vehicle would have to yield. Then the years took a toll and it began to weather and crumble and tax dollars widened the valley road, built a newer, wider bridge that allowed two vehicles to cross at the same time. Getting to the top of the incline, he hauled ass down the other side, then went up another hill. What he hoped was Shelby wasn't a part of this mess; he knew she'd had a hard upbringing with Whitey, then her mother leaving, and he told Shadrack,

"Nothing to be afraid of. Little thunder, wind, rain, lightning. They'll pass through and things'll settle down."

Taking in the countryside, cornfields and houses sat off in the distance, some with a tiny glow, others camouflaged by brush and trees. "It's the big booms of lightning that I don't care too much for. Afraid they'll get me. Catch me on fire."

Passing the Hughes home, it sat off the road big like a plantation from further south; on past it he followed the flowing fields, until he saw the upside-down DEAD END sign in the distance. Nerves pulsed, he knew it was game time and he tapped his dash, telling Shadrack, "No lightning is gonna come through this vehicle and burn you up, I promise."

Shelby's home was brick on the bottom, powdered aluminum on the top. Windows were framed by black shutters. A zinc light opened up the perimeter, hanging next to a cryptic red barn that sat up on a hillside off to the right. Everything illuminated in an electric-glowing purple haze. Nathaniel killed the engine of his Dodge. "I gotta stay in here by myself again?" Shadrack questioned with a concerned tone.

"Lock the doors, nothing's gonna get you, I promise, I'll be right outside the truck. I can't have you alongside of me if something gets out of hand."

"You gonna hurry?"

"I'll hurry."

"Promise?"

Touching his head, thumbing his hair over his forehead, he said, "I promise."

Opening the door. Stepping out of the truck. Closing the door. The locks clicked. Nathaniel looked at the only vehicle in the drive, a bumperless burgundy Nissan truck. The wind whipped in waves. Slow, then fast, and then died down, the surrounding area desolate of any other movement. Opening the Nissan's passenger's-side door, he thumbed the glove box, removed the registration. Wylie McCutchen. Expired. From behind there was the approaching crunch of gravel, the loud rev of a 350 small-block engine. Stepping away from the Nissan, seeing the glare of headlights fast approaching, whoever it was wasn't backing off the gas. Lights came like an eclipse, blinding Nathaniel. He started to reach for his .45.

"Who in the shit?"

It's a dead-end road, he thought to himself. Only two choices, Wylie or Shelby, and Shelby could mean Wylie. Regardless, Nathaniel wanted fucking answers. He unholstered his .45 from his back, just in case.

The burning blur was hauling ass, turned to Nathaniel's right at the last minute. Retreated off the gnarled driveway and ran off into a mess of sycamore, walnut, and cedar.

The bark of the mad infested Miles's mind as NVA fighters ran out in front of the El Camino. Miles jerked the steering left, the bounce and thud of uneven field rattled the car frame beneath his boots, up his legs, body, and his teeth until a plot of trees came staggered and rooted. Booted feet stomped the brakes. Halted his passage, flung him into the steering wheel. Smashed air from his lungs. Marred his El Camino with the scrape of trees down the driver's side. Gathering his bearings, catching his breath, Miles opened his door with a Miller in his right hand, his head rang spotted and uneasy as he weighted the ground, swayed to height, his equilibrium slanted before a shadow came from a distance, glowing and burning with a bright light.

Nathaniel stepped back to his Dodge and reached to his passenger's-side mirror for the spotlight. Thumbed the button to turn on the light. Shined it down on the sideways slant of white that lay wedged and what Nathaniel thought sounded like Waylon Jennings blaring from the vehicle's interior.

Glancing at Shadrack he told him, "Stay put."

Stepping from the concrete slab, making his way over the crushed rock that surrounded it, with the rush of air expanding in and out of his lungs, Nathaniel walked through the knee-high field grass, taking in the vehicle, hearing the engine popping from cooling, recognizing the El Camino.

The passenger's side was dammed by tree. The driver's

side screeched open. A dome light burned with the shape of a passenger and out stepped the hulking heft of Miles with the tune of "Willy the Wandering Gypsy and Me" seeping from the car's stereo.

Miles stumbled. Raised a can of Miller to his lips with his right, his left shaded his vision, one eye wide, the other pinched. The glare from Nathaniel's spotlight offered a look of bewildered madness upon Miles's complexion.

The only thing coursing through Nathaniel's mind was that he needed answers, and he wondered if anyone else was in the vehicle, maybe Shelby, but he didn't see any outline or shape; looking to Miles, he wanted to make sure he was okay, but half joking, asked, "Who the hell taught you how to drive?"

Everything around Miles seemed strange, expanding and spongy, as if he were in Alice in Wonderland's forest. Nathaniel's skin appeared rubbery, alien-like, the bright burning light from behind him caused his outline to glow, and he told him, "Kill that goddamned flare, you're blinding me."

Looking around, Miles seemed dazed or lost; as Nathaniel eyed the vehicle, he pressed his hands to the passenger's-side window and saw nothing but an open case of Miller and a tapped bottle of Maker's. He kicked the tires and told him, "You were reaming the hell out of your car down the driveway, ran your fucking wheels off the gravel. Other than a few scrapes, I believe the Camino is still drivable."

Holding his beer, stepping away from the vehicle, Miles's footing wasn't secure. Planting his feet down as if walking in deep snow, stopping and taking a swig, he looked over his car at Nathaniel and asked, "The shit are you doing at Shelby's?"

Before Miles could take another step, Nathaniel made his way around the vehicle and approached him; the man wasn't acting right, staring off into the darkness, up at the sky, trying to focus his vision. He was two sheets to the wind and smelled like a pub, or maybe the wreck spit a concussion upon him, rung his bell, but getting a closer view, his eyes' pupils were expanded and Nathaniel told him, "I got some questions that need answered, Knox."

Knowing each other, fishing, sharing drinks and conversations over the years, there was no distrust between the two of them. Only mutual respect. Miles's face took on a crunched-up wrinkle of confusion, knowing something was off, regardless of how out of his head he was.

"Kind of questions could you have for Shelby?"

Miles took a healthy swig from his can of Miller, then his grip went slack and the beer fell. Legs swayed in a two-step motion but stayed rooted. Nathaniel came forward to catch his stumbling. All at once liquid oozed from his nostrils, unswallowed hops foamed from his lips while his eyes rolled like dice without dots into his head. Nathaniel caught the hulking heft of Miles's balance, steadied him.

"Damn, you weigh more than a feeder steer."

Positioning an arm around Miles's neck, balancing out his weight, he guided him up the hill of grass toward his Dodge. "Where's Childers?"

The man had more in him than booze, he was on something, Nathaniel thought, seeing his dilated tadpole pupils. Unable to stand, he wasn't slurring his speech, but he'd barreled down the drive like he was in a demo derby. Nathaniel grunted, "Who's Childers?"

Laughing, he told Nathaniel, "My drinking buddy, he's in the passenger's seat."

The man was talking crazy, confused. "Only thing in the passenger's seat is a case of Miller."

Nathaniel needed to get him sobered up, get some questions answered. Getting him up the hill, Miles removed his heft from Nathaniel. "I'm good. I'm steady Eddie now."

Getting to the rear of his truck, Nathaniel told Miles, "Rest on the truck, get your wits about you." Miles pressed his deadweight against the truck. Trying to shake something off, he asked him, "You didn't answer, hell kinda questions you got for Shelby?"

"I need to find her brother, Wylie."

"What's your beef with Wylie? He stealing wire from building sites again?"

Nathaniel got quiet, swallowed the lump in his throat, then said, "I wish. Got reason to believe he might've murdered my brother Bedford and his wife Judy."

Shapes began to form around Nathaniel, men coming

from the night like dead zombies with split features. Eyes missing. Mouths broken and busted. Childers spoke over Miles's shoulder, "Think you can just up and leave me?"

Turning quickly, Childers's shape dissolved. Shaking his head, Miles tried to ignore the images and the words being offered to him, fighting the wave of numbness that coursed through his insides. Holding it together, Miles told Nathaniel, "I ain't heard from Shelby in a week or better." His vision adjusted. "Was hoping to catch her here at the house, but her car ain't here."

Taking in Miles's eyes, his jerk and tilt, hoping he was telling the truth, Nathaniel told him, "Only car here is Wylie's."

"It's always here. Don't run. Shelby's always taxi-driving him around."

"Think you can get us inside without busting the door down?"

Fumbling around at the door, Miles found the spare key hidden within a turtle that sat among the ceramic dwarves and giant mushrooms that created a Snow White–themed landscape. Miles swore the dwarves were pointing at him and mumbling to one another. Only thing he could do was squeeze his orbs tight. Stand up and unlock the front door.

Entering Shelby's home, Childers told him, "This ain't

cool, dude, going into your woman's home when she ain't around."

Under his breath he replied, "Make myself at home, she always said to me."

Nathaniel turned to Miles. "What'd you say?"

"Talking to myself."

The interior of the house sat unlit. Flipping a light switch, everything appeared clean. Wasn't messy. Nathaniel thought about those heroin heads at Leon's, two retched flavors of men lying about the broke-down sofa. Their eyes scorched into the rear of their skulls. Mouths open to the thickness of a two-by-four. Necks bent back as if broken. Didn't look as if he'd find the same forms of occupancy inside of Shelby's even though her brother was an addict.

It was hard to swallow, Wylie murdering Bedford and Judy. As Miles walked behind Nathaniel, everything in her home glowed within his vision, the smell was electric, a flowery scent reminiscent of her skin, that warm he felt when they were in one another's company, a positive flow of energy, recharging his human side every time they met, it was a scent that lit up his inhale. Traveled throughout his body. In front of him, Nathaniel studied the interior as other shapes of men followed, lurking around in their cut and ripped fatigues, and Miles told Nathaniel, "I can see it, Wylie doing what you said."

Looking off to the left, where the living room was located, Nathaniel said to him, "What I recall, Wylie had always been the one without words. Kept out of trouble. Unlike their father."

Shadows fell on a large-screen television that sat at the far wall of the living room, bay windows gave moonlight to a L-shaped couch, wooden end tables, and lamps. Memories of sinking back into the couch, sipping bourbon, watching Clint Eastwood Westerns, kindled in Miles's mind and he told Nathaniel, "Yeah, their daddy had a jealous rage toward his ex-wife, took it out on Shelby and Wylie. Whitey's a scarred vet, always proclaimed to be a dangerous wad of meat."

Stepping toward the kitchen, Nathaniel said, "Did Shelby or Wylie have much to do with their ole man?"

Following behind, fighting the oncoming hallucinations, Miles told him, "Shelby does. Always catering to him. Picking his drunk ass up. Keeping his house clean. Getting him to the grocery. No idea why. Wylie always crashed here."

Heading toward a hallway, flipping a light switch on the wall, Nathaniel said, "You add the number of local vets, young and old, that've fought in wars, add that to the changing climate of the rural class, the blue-collar types, they don't have a chance between the oxycodone, methamphetamine, and heroin, and that's on top of the boozers or drunks. Sounds like Shelby's got a hectic family situation seeing as her father and brother fit into those categories."

Down the hallway, flipping the switch to the bathroom

light, still no sounds; the scents were female, fresh berries and cocoa butter, detergents and lotions. Clean.

"Yeah, they've each taken their toll on Shelby, but it's about enough to wring out anyone's life," Miles said, noticing the Kimber tucked in Nathaniel's waist.

Stepping back down the hallway, into the kitchen, Miles saw it was devoid of dishes. No bread or potato chip crumbs. A long wood table and four settings. Wilting daisies held in its center from weeks before, bought by Miles. *Something isn't right*, he thought as soldiers stood around him, carrying their M16s, poking about.

Searching the bedrooms, Miles fought visions of the men who surrounded them, these dead men's ghosts. "This is Wylie's room," he told Nathaniel.

Clothes were tossed about, a mattress on the floor, no sheets, a pillow, and a blanket. Scented candles and a plug-in air freshener. A cup of water and a few pills that'd been crushed in a bowl. Nathaniel rummaged through the possessions, unsure what he was looking for, hoping for some clue. He found nothing.

The second bedroom was arranged on the far end of the home, two large mirrors served as walls to one side. A waterbed rested in the center with zebra-striped sheets. Many long nights spent in that bed; some were sexual, some were talking, reminiscing of childhoods roaming the fields and woods, egging and corning cars, running from cops when parties got busted for underage drinking, their upbringings, the good and the bad of one another's lives. *Where is Shelby?* Miles wondered.

Thong panties and matching bras lay on a dresser. All colors and designs of lace. Picking one up, it was perfume scented. CDs lined hickory bookshelves, Janis Joplin, CCR, Mötley Crüe, Pantera, Slayer, Nine Inch Nails, and Lynyrd Skynyrd. Being a stripper, the mirrors were for practicing her dancing routines. Miles fingered several heavy-gauged pieces of steel, some were hoops, earrings and curved piercings that lay scattered on a nightstand next to a framed photo. A man with silver hair, box cut, raw boned, bulky arms and shoulders and talking with a group of younger men at what looked like a party. Turning to Miles, Nathaniel said, "Guessing this is you?"

"Back in the day."

"Looks like a beach party."

"Little R and R on China Beach."

"I've heard you tell the stories, never seen the pics."

The dead soldiers who surrounded Miles and Nathaniel laughed and Miles said, "I'm one of the few who's been through hell and lived to tell about it."

Eyeing Miles, Nathaniel saw there was a torture that bled from the man's vision. Something unblinking and fearsome that Nathaniel wasn't too sure he wanted to awaken and encounter. He walked past Miles, back down the hall, through the kitchen, into the living room, questions hemming Nathaniel's mind. He was missing something. The house was neat. Intact. The dead flowers. Clothing laid out.

Untouched. It was as if she'd left, planning to return but never made it back. Miles held the same feeling as Nathaniel. He followed Nathaniel, who paused and turned to him, asking, "If Shelby was working, what time would she be home?"

Staring off into nothing, it was as if he had read Miles's mind and he fought hard to keep his composure, searched for a focal point; actions kept rummaging throughout his body, tense sensations of energy, visions of war combined with these dead men following him through the house and his wonderings about Shelby, everything came to him all at the same time and he told Nathaniel, "Late, works nights, she keeps graveyard hours."

"But if we found her, she'd know where Wylie hung out if he wasn't here?"

"I know another place to look for Wylie."

The phone rang, bumped each man's nerves. Rang four more times, then an answering machine beside the couch chimed in. Nathaniel and Miles stood near it, waited, and a voice spoke, "Shelby? Monica. Girl, what is up? You done missed another shift this week with no call, you's MIA and Crout is pissed. I covered for your sweet ass again. Bet you's all laid up with that Knox fella. Call me. ASAP!"

Looking at Miles, Nathaniel told him, "She's not laid up with you, nor has she been at work."

Scenarios scrolled through each man's mind.

If Shelby hasn't been at work in a while, where the hell has she been? Miles wondered.

Nathaniel began running scenarios. Told Miles, "Let's acknowledge the pink elephant in the room."

Watching Nathaniel's features grow waxy, his eyes foiled over like onyx beetles and Miles held his composure, what pink elephant, was this son of a bitch fucking with him?

"Pink elephant?"

"What we're both thinking—the possibility that Shelby could be involved with Wylie." Miles tensed up and Nathaniel continued. "Hear me out, I'm not saying she is, but if Wylie holds a gun on her, forced Shelby to drive, she could be the transit, an—"

Miles cut him off. "—An innocent accomplice."

"And she drives an old '68—"

"—An old souped-up '68 Camaro."

"The other side of the coin, just hear me out, I'm not accusing her, but she's employed at a gentleman's club. Could sell to other girls, keep their bump-and-grind routines fueled. But here's the kicker for me: her home is way too neat for an addict or a dealer, let alone a murderer."

Miles's mind was running a million miles a minute. He was angered by Nathaniel's insinuation but kept focused with his body vibrating, growing numb. The quiet in the home was so clear it sounded like static and he said, "The girl just said she's not been at work."

"Right, so the other scenario, if you find out your brother killed someone, robbed them, what would you do? Hide him. And if you did, where at?"

There was the thought of beating Nathaniel senseless,

but then that wouldn't find Shelby or Wylie and Miles kept as calm as he could and told him, "I can't see Shelby taking another person's life, but she'd do most anything for Wylie; still, I don't see her hiding him from the law. Not willingly."

Being inside the house was driving Miles insane with the scents of Shelby, the silence, the suffocation of dead men floating around him. He watched Nathaniel walk over to the phone and glance down at the machine, the numeral two blinked. Curious, Nathaniel pressed play. "Shelby, baby, Miles. It's late. Call me."

"When'd you phone her?"

Miles gritted with rage. Was wasting time standing here. And he said, "Earlier. Like I told you I haven't spoken to her in a week."

"Where's the other places we can look for Wylie at?"

"It's rough trade. Lot of pot smoking, pill popping, whiskey, beer, gambling over card games, bitching about politics and basketball and the occasional fistfight. Chucky's."

"I know the way, I'll navigate, you can ride shotgun."

Exiting Shelby's home, stepping out into the night, Miles was in an orbit. Each step he sunk deeper into a strange world, pieces of jungle began to grow all around him. Getting to Nathaniel's truck, the passenger's-side door unlocked, swinging the door open, and inside sat a small boy. Nathaniel opened the driver's-side door and the boy said, "He didn't shoot my mom and dad, did he?"

Nathaniel slid into the seat and said, "No, he didn't, but he's gonna help us find the person who did."

Nathaniel fired the diesel up, looking out the front windshield, watching the darkness of night become tunnel vision. Everything had transformed into jungle for Miles, watching it slowly come to life as something like burning headlights blinded him and he closed his eyes and drifted back into the battle.

His mind pinched. Closed off the light at the tunnel's end. Floated him on a lukewarm skiff down those lost channels of memory where he and others hunted the savage and nomadic.

The enemy they'd been battling for the past six months had spandex flesh stained yellow around walleyed vision, and talk that needed to be translated. They were men whose vices clung to beating and thieving from those who would not bend toward the communist direction.

Miles had scavenged the rut roads in and around Da Nang, participated in search-and-destroy missions throughout villages. Survived gun battles that omitted platoons and now he was riding saddle in the jungles of Chu Lai.

Walking the center. Three other marines lined in front and three more behind. The point man and the man who carried the rear, the caboose, held the timeline zero. Would be the first to see action. Take fire from snipers hidden within trees or succumb to booby traps.

Miles had volunteered for recon when Lieutenant Sigmund needed a grunt who'd been in the dirt. Could blow shit up or defuse it. A jarhead nicknamed Canteen, a real cowpuncher from Iowa with Popsicle-stick dentitions, elbowed him. "Fuck you doing, Knox, them crazed fucks hop from planes, rappel from 'copters. Hide in the brush for weeks. Live on rations, bugs, and stems like hermits awaiting the Second Coming."

Knox told Canteen to mind his own. If Vega had volunteered, so would he, as Miles'd bunkered down with demise, masticated the shell shock of battle and not lost his shit. Lieutenant Sigmund took this seventh body to replace the one who'd been retired by an NVA sniper. He wanted a combat engineer with field experience, who held an eye for mines and booby traps; he wanted Miles Knox to be a part of the marine reconnaissance unit he'd assembled. Someone who'd make shit no longer exist. A man who'd earned the nickname Devil Dog after an intense firefight during Operation Allen Brook, where a heavily armed enemy had ambushed and pinned Miles and other marines down. Round after round of mortars came whistling from the heavens and cleaved the earth, while suppression fire dotted and pierced man after man. When one jarhead went to drag another wounded jarhead to shelter, a sniper'd mangle the marine's insides with an AK-47. Leave them to be baked by the monsoon humidity.

He'd lost over half the unit he was attached to after eight hours of hell. When support arrived, Knox didn't waver, he dodged the spray of metal elements and the knock of soil, aided the wounded and the dead across five hundred meters of terrain to the chopper LZ, helped unload ammunition, and later accompanied another unit to destroy enemy ordnances.

At the base camp in Da Nang, Miles knew recon soldiers kept to themselves. Never spoke to anyone other than their own. Anywhere they went at base camp they ran. To and from the shower, they ran. To the bathroom, they ran. To eat, they ran. Always running. They bunked away from the infantry grunts. They disappeared for weeks, were predators for intel.

There would be no screening. Training was hands-on, learned in the field of battle.

Miles was placed with a group of elite leathernecks: Nafus, Bull, Rut, Crust, Skipper, and one man he'd fought alongside of, Vega. They'd be flown out into the bush and dropped within earshot of the opposition.

Now, a fist was raised by Rut, a Durham man from North Carolina. Dropped out of college to fight the evil that lay in Vietnam, where he could use his mind and athletic skill. The men took shelter in the dense plant life of braided vines and leaves that window-blinded the sunlight. They sat motionless, their faces coaled black. Sheened by bitterness, toughened by the drive to never quit, their rifles in tow, safeties off, fingers printing the trigger guards, weighted with pistols, knives, ammo, and rations, their boots pasted with jungle grime. Carving out their own trails, they never followed trails formed by others; those were the enemy and they knew where they went. Recon were the shadows, the perimeters of the unseen, unheard. They were the silence.

Miles craved a smoke in the early-morning steam that lifted from vegetation like a pot of boil. To taste a cigarette would give scent to their trespass. Bodies were already saturated by jungle heat. The men sat irritated by the dart of insects peppering their lobes, orbs, and flesh as they watched for a sign of movement from a hamlet, careful not to break foliage to offer hint of their trespass.

Their mission was to hunt and exterminate an NVC guerrilla unit believed to be delivering genocide to innocent villages throughout the Quang Tin province. Miles and the unit had been lowered deep into the hills south of Da Nang. Embedded within the rashly green jungle of Chu Lai.

With nothing but jungle quiet, Rut whispered, "Move." They filed into the sanctum of huts framed by bamboo, banked and roofed by vegetation. A few iron kettles hung over ashed heat. A hum grew in pitch like a swarm of jackets upon a honeycomb. Marines inhaled the rancorous odor that grew from the lair with each step.

The norm, Miles recalled, when entering a village, was barefoot children coming with the beg and plead for nourishment, especially for meat; some spoke broken English while the half-assed stares and sunken facades of *papasans* and *mamasans* were plagued with the worry of a soldier's encroachment and what it sometimes yielded. Questions about an enemy they feared would kill them for speaking. But on this day, there was nothing.

Miles's eyes snapshotted the scenes. Between the walkways and within the huts, human hides lay strung. Some with scalps macheted from crowns, others' brainpans speared into the earth, gazing into the heavens above with hairlines split by carbine, creating unconnectable ends of mess pooling around them like busted pans of fluid from vehicles. Miles lowered his vision and shook his head.

Skipper, the team leader from Tennessee, didn't wanna work carpentry for his father, signed on Uncle Sam's dotted line and never looked back. He gave the proclamation, "Don't touch so much as a pissant's leg."

"How about its antennae?" spat Bull.

"This ain't the time for shits and giggles."

Miles stood watching flies pad about the heated stink. No amount of training could have prepared him for this encampment of slaughter.

Every step Miles took was slow and calculated. In a garden about the size of four king-sized beds, he found two men seated upright, back to back, their charcoal pj's weighted by moisture. Lips and lids removed. Their outlines no longer scaled by soul. Miles kneeled down, studied the soil around them, took in the imperfections of earth, the tire-track-sized footprints and the tarnished brass that lay around them.

Behind Miles, Nafus, an ole boy from eastern Ohio, asked, "Shit you eyeing, Knox?"

Miles said, "Indentions."

"What for, some NVA wandering around with your same-size kicks?"

"Seems the heel is longer than a sandal, the heel overhangs the tread."

Then came the shouts of "Goddammit!"

Miles and Nafus took to the rutted ground, entered a hut not twenty feet from the garden, where a man, woman, and two children, who looked sketched by pencil and colored by spilled paint, were counterpaned across the hut's center, their dank clothing curtained from their frames, identical to the men Miles found in the garden. As though they'd been tortured for hours, toyed with for amusement, then dissolved of their simple lives.

The radio man, Bull, and the medic, Crust, and infantryman, Vega, just a Pennsyltucky boy who liked stringing in the fish, stood over them with horror in the black balls of their vision, taking it all in, shaking their heads. Bull said, "Anyone that'd kill the young is to be branded a dead motherfucker in my way of thinking."

Miles studied the earth floor where they were strewn, noticed the dirt where Bull stooped.

Miles kneeled, pointed. "See there?"

"What?" Bull questioned.

"Found the same outlines in the paddy around two other dead VC."

"Tire-tread sandals," Vega said as he looked down.

Miles touched at the edge of the print. "Bare heels longer than the tread."

"So a *mamasan* or *papasan*'s got a swell of a foot," Bull smarted.

"Know what they say about big feet," Vega joked.

Miles cleared his throat. "What if it ain't NVA doing the slaughtering?"

"Fuck you spitting, Knox?" Bull questioned.

From the entrance came another voice. Skipper. "He's saying if it ain't NVA, every one of us could be going home like an assortment of seek-and-find. That's what you're saying right, Knox?"

"What I's saying is some of these villagers, they's missing ears. Digits. Been scalped."

Bull chuckled. "You check they tongues?"

"No. But why'd NVA slice off their body parts?"

Bull said, "Know what I say, we torch this goddamn weed lot. Let Buddha figure it out."

Miles's words hung in the air with the steady flow of silence. Wondering eyes getting a feel for his words. Railing through everyone's mind, no one would come out and say it but they knew what he was saying. And Miles finally said, "Only men I ever seen do things like this was American soldiers."

Skipper said, "American or NVA, that's why we're here. To find the killers, decimate accusations. Report back before some whistle-dick journalist breaks the story on the evening news."

His head ached from the gunshot within the cabin and Katz pleaded, "Why you doing this to me? Keeping me here?" Shelby had fired the pistol into the ceiling, gotten Katz's attention, motioned him to lay face-first on the floor, again. Now, he twisted his view to a sideways glance, Shelby didn't stare at him, her eyes were heavy iron sinkers as she looked through him. Her features swimming in a stupor. No smiles. No emotions. No words. Katz held no assurance that she would not pull the trigger and end his life at any second. And the pisser of it was, no one knew he'd paid Miles's camp a visit. That he'd come out here to check on the place. He was alone. Was without a partner as driving a semitruck and breaking the seal of a bottle night after night, gambling on card games over at Chucky's, was a heavy tolerance for most women to tolerate.

He watched her feet within untied boots, laces clicking over the tile, walk to the kitchen.

Katz was, as some assholes referred to him, an Ingine or an Indian, Tonto, Cochise, or Crazy Horse, as he was called at work by gum-rotted black-tooth rednecks. Joking? Sure, but after the second and third time, it wore him thin. Ate at his demeanor. He never accused them of being inbred, of their mothers and fathers being brother and sister, of having intercourse and creating a bastard child. But in all honesty, he liked being alone. No one to answer to. He was his own boss.

Blinking his eyes, light sprayed over the floor at the eruption of mess; spots of blood, a few empty beer cans and a Walmart sack, from the back-and-forth Katz had witnessed but did not comprehend. He couldn't label any of what he'd witnessed to anything other than derangement or madness.

Now as he lay, the loosely booted feet came back, knelt down over him with a towel from the kitchen, strung and wrapped the cotton around his jaws, used the towel to gag his mouth. Tied it in the rear of his skull.

Back in the dining and living room area of the cabin, Shelby stared at something, Katz was unsure of what. And she started having another back-and-forth episode. A conversation, like two hand puppets on *Sesame Street*.

Remember those nights in that four-by-four space. Lamplight burning.

"Yeah, while they screamed and rattled the walls and floors with words."

They sure grooved scars and fear into our minds.

"And we wondered, when will it end? 'Cause we knew when they quit the screaming, the back-and-forth—"

—he was gonna tread back in there once she was gone and tell us to do things to each other while he watched.

"We sat there, like we was hidden, holding one another. Garments hung from hangers above us."

On the walls of the closet we'd chiseled letters with one of the many blades Daddy had bought us.

"Or we inked pictures of stick figures with a pen, or trees, rocks, waving streams, and skies."

All them circle heads with single-line chests, arms, and legs. Scribbles that turned into a giant mural of make-believe people and places we'd escaped to over those years of belittling.

"Our safe place to visit created from our imaginations, hiding from Daddy's salty skin and vodka words."

Him and his smoky locked chaos of slurs and shouts ping-ponging throughout the interiors of the house with his male dominance and Mama's female rebuttal.

"A father and mother who could not make their ends mend."

Katz closed his eyes, listening to the monologue; it was in some ways incredible, but also sad and terrifying, catching glimpses of Shelby switching back and forth between personalities. But also an abusive upbringing. And then she went stone-cold silent. Shelby stared into a void and asked, "How much longer can this go on? These memories I've survived. This part of me that's somehow frayed. I want you out of my head!"

Then Wylie's expression traced across from Shelby's lips with his sinister grin, and she gritted her teeth and shook her head. Dampness creased down her cheeks.

"No, you're dead. You and your gray skin, molded and shriveled similar to a wadded-up paper cutout. Those pills took you. Swallowed you 'cause you couldn't listen to me, couldn't quit crushing and snorting them, then that was no longer enough to block out the memories of Daddy. So then you had to break them pills down with the liquid. Suck them into a needle and stab it into the streams that lined your arms and legs. And by the time I found you, it was too late, I couldn't bring you back, you was gone."

Fuck you!

Pressing the metallic element of chrome to her temple, Shelby thumbed back the hammer and said, "No, fuck you. We'll end this here and now!"

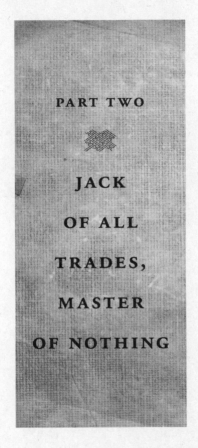

PART TWO

JACK
OF ALL
TRADES,
MASTER
OF NOTHING

As soon as the world regards something as beautiful,
ugliness simultaneously becomes apparent.
As soon as the world regards something as good,
evil simultaneously becomes apparent.

—*The Complete Works of Lao Tzu*

Dear Miles (Turtle),

Goddamn our war was no movie. It was a real beating, breathing thing. Been damn near 25 years since we trounced down on the Communist rule of Victor Charlie. I bet you thought it'd be another 25 before you heard from me. I was never so surprised when you phoned on that Sunday morning, Dee comes to me and says they's a Miles Knox asking for you. Hearing your voice. Be damned if you didn't sound just as you did when you used to sing "Come On Baby Light My Fire." I've since tried to return the call. You didn't answer. I'd have left a message but you don't got no machine brother. I know we seen some shit. And we're the only ones who are telling the tales seeing as everything we did was classified. The best thing that happened to me over there was you joining the Recon unit. You're the only one who took things seriously. And I was the only one that knew that. Only one that listened. And you kept me alive. Remember the time

just you and me held off 300 gooks with nothing but
a .45 and two grenades. Actually we beat up two PFs
and screwed they girlfriends. But seriously it was one of
the best days of my life the day you called. Dee said if
you'd have told her "it's *Turtle*," she would have known
who you was. Hope you don't mind being called
Turtle, I know they sometimes called you Devil Dog,
but I'll always remember you as Turtle. Cause you was
slow, took your time, and always finished what you
started. Just like the Bugs Bunny cartoon, the turtle
always won the race. I had some pictures duplicated
a few weeks back for you. I especially like the one of
you with the grenade launcher and the Chuck Taylors.
Reminds me of John Wayne. I bet your woman is
saying "What a Man!" Miles you was a tough son of
a bitch. Could carry a thousand pounds of equipment
and could do it all damn day long. Anyway I'm looking
for the papers you asked about. You deserve a Heart.
I always tell people your story. Tell them you deserved
flight pay for all the time you spent flying through the
air before we met, after losing half your unit. That's
how you became one of us, got recruited to Recon.
Whether you wanna acknowledge it or not, you're a
goddamned hero to us and the Vietnamese. If you'd
not caught those heel prints, we might never have
known what we were dealing with. Semper Fi Brother!

Bull

Heated, Miles felt weighted down with a warm, waxy salve fertilizing his complexion, climbing down and coating his frame like how he figured a clay detox mask might feel, as if his entire body were dipped into the sludge. Outside the truck, foliage passed by like tracer rounds, rainbowing through the dark sketches of timber that bent, curved, and swayed. Beside him Shadrack's young eyes glared up, two hands resting on the comic book in his lap. "Why you sweating?"

The words were foreign to Miles at first, coming from a long tunnel surrounded by static, melding with the clamoring in his brain, until the English broke through his bubble of understanding and he told him, "Steroids. They cause a man's body to repair quicker, build muscle and burn his food at an accelerated rate because of the extra fiber."

"What're steroids?"

Miles gritted his teeth. Wanted to growl. But didn't. The kid asked one question and that was one too many.

Navigating the steering, Nathaniel butted in before Miles could answer, telling him, "Drugs."

Surprised, Shadrack said, "You're on drugs?"

Taking shape in front of the glove box, Childers stared Miles down. "Gonna answer him? Or just sit there like a fucking POW?"

His jaws were stiff, there was too much happening at

once, but still he told Shadrack, "Yeah, I do roids. Age is an unwelcomed friend. Delivers hair in places you never had it, and subtracts it from places you don't wanna lose it. Wake up every damn morning with bones creaking, joints cracking. Muscles dissipating. You're just waiting around to become a crustacean, to retire and buy a walker while chewing on cholesterol meds and filling up an adult diaper."

Shadrack wrinkled his complexion with confusion, looked to Nathaniel. "What is he talking about?"

"Getting old, buddy. Getting old."

"I don't ever wanna get old. I wanna be like Batman. Help people. Find who killed my parents like Batman found the people who killed his."

"Smart kid," Miles said, trying to focus on where he was at, what he was doing; he felt lost, out of touch, his head was processing sounds in and outside of the truck, seeing colors swirl and arc, while his body felt as if he were free-falling, never hitting the ground, and it was all happening at the same time, over and over, again and again, and he questioned Nathaniel, "Sure you're headed in the right direction?"

Nathaniel didn't answer at first, being acquainted with and trusting Miles, he sensed something was off with his demeanor, something deeper than booze; the man's pupils were the size of onyx-coated dimes. He'd keep an eye on his actions, his cop radar on alert, but it wasn't like Miles had a criminal record or was a cold-blooded psycho. Steering the Dodge truck off the road, fighting the roar of wind velocity, navigating through a mess of cedar that lined both sides of the potholed road before him until a small crimp of light shone through the trees, opening up to pieces of a house that formed into view. Some distance from the home were various makes and models of vehicle, the structure itself was nothing more than an oversized modular home that sat upon a concrete basement with a green tin roof and lights at the corners bolted upon poles shining down as if a prison, highlighting the features of the patrons.

"We're here," Nathaniel said. "When I's a county cop this fuck tried putting me on payroll, wanted to make sure any of the tweak-head dealers that trespassed around the property when he had these parties didn't get out of line and start too much of a problem, he wanted his gambling patrons to have a safe passage, be able to drink, do some drugs and get indebted to him, and he wanted to have me on speed dial in case he were to get raided for partying, maybe give him the heads-up or to give the word and possibly cut him loose, sweep his actions beneath the rug."

"That's what Chucky has always done, holding these card games, letting working folk from around the surrounding counties gamble lots of hard-earned wages," Miles mumbled.

"I hear he even lets folks wager their homes and vehicles, lets them get in deep hock to him. This guy's got more money than graves got bones."

Miles grunted in agreement.

Metal poles lined one side of the yard with airplane birdhouses faded and peeling. Stacks of unused lumber cut to odd lengths sat piled and molded. Masonry troughs for mixing concrete lay with shovels, spades, and sledgehammers, corroded and scuffed.

Childers asked Miles, "What's your plan, Devil Dog? You gonna go all Josey Wales?"

Miles just wanted the voices and images to leave him alone. His body flushed with adrenaline; closing his eyes, searching for focus, he asked Nathaniel, "What about the boy?"

"He stays in the truck. The doors locked."

Even though Miles was on a psychedelic roller-coaster ride, he said, "The people who frequent here, they're not *Green Acres* types."

"I know the shade of characters we're being dealt, but something I don't got a lot of at the moment are choices or time. I'm Shadrack's guardian. And I won't rest until Wylie's been found; you can either help me or stay with him."

"I'm helping. Just questioning the boy's safety is all."

Parking the truck some distance from the home, they saw bodies outside on the lawn, drinking, conversing, sounds of Chris Knight's "The Lord's Highway" blared loud and distorted from inside.

Ignoring Childers's outline, glancing at Nathaniel, Miles searched for his center. He wanted to help find Wylie, believing and hoping it would lead to Shelby, help discover answers to what the hell was going on. He felt she was in danger; he felt a strong fear for her safety. And the LSD intensified those feelings. Feelings that something was wrong. He questioned Nathaniel: "You being the ex-lawman, how you wanna approach this? I was Recon, I just watched and then I took out whoever needed taking out. We can't walk up to these folks and be all Buford Pusser."

"We're not gonna walk up and split some skulls. We'll toss up a jar of questions, see what answers fall down for us. You just follow my lead and find your opening. Someone's gotta latch on to our small talk. I've done enough interrogations to know how folks' minds work."

Shapes and colors danced around Nathaniel's head that weren't real and Miles snorted, "Now you're fucking Matlock?"

"Look, wiseass, we need to say you're looking for Shelby, that's our in, and if she's maybe been here, or possibly brought her brother out and dropped him off, last thing we want is to be suspect in searching for him. If we spook him or his acquaintances, he'll run. So no, I'm no fucking Matlock."

"Well then, Quincy, what if they haven't been here?" Miles smarted.

"Cut the seventies crime bit. It's like this: if they've not trespassed through here, maybe we can get a lead, find out where else they might be, and if not—"

"—if not I know another place he'd venture."

"Well then we're wasting dark, Starsky," Nathaniel sniped.

"You know these folks won't be none too kind with an ex-cop."

"Why I got you, ex-Recon. You can help me persuade them."

Persuade them, Miles thought. He was seeing images of dead people, hearing wicked noises, colors trancing around and struggling to figure out what was real. But there was also this body buzz, he was numb but felt strong, like he could conquer or crush someone or something. Call it confidence, more so than normal. Whatever shit Kingsley gave him was casting a real mind fuck of a spell in his head. He'd no hard feelings toward him, but he was 50/50 on the chances of whether he'd accept or decline his offer to drop acid again. There was still plenty of night left before the verdict was in.

Outside the truck, Nathaniel eyed Shadrack, hair clipping over his calm eyes. He mouthed, *Lock the doors*, and waited for the locks to click.

Moving forward, Miles felt like he was on combat patrol, canvasing and searching out the enemy, studying the surrounding hillside, watching limbs waver and creak in the wind; his mind was unsteady, sounds echoed in his head like everything was in stereo sound, crisp and clear, gunfire and grenades with visions of war. The shapes they approached off in the distance were shifting complexions like a funhouse of mirrors, looking like VC villagers and wounded marines; there was something dark brewing all around him. Childers's frame arched and hunched beside him like the walking dead. His shirt stained similar to splotches of consumed oil, suctioned to his rib cage with his organdy pigment oozing as though a plastic film.

Approaching a group of men in a circle, smells of tobacco twisted from the orange that coaled between digits, laughter spewed from foul mouths, all of it combining and echoing. Childers asked Miles, "The hell are you gonna do, play soldier with the miscreants?"

Feeling eyes sweep over Nathaniel and himself, Miles met the nodding of men, some women, and even teenagers; he nodded back and struggled to hear the whispering words under their breath, hissing like a million termites feeding on lumber, gnawing and hollowing out their routes. There was a paranoia embedded in his brain that they weren't welcomed and it hung over him as if a looming shadow. Breaking Miles's thoughts, Nathaniel told him, "Let's canvas as we work our way toward the house."

A factory worker Nathaniel had arrested years ago on a DUI made eye contact. "Well looky who decided to rub elbows with the working folk, even hanging out with a factory grunt."

"Kirk. How goes?" Nathaniel asked.

Dressed in a red Cleveland Indians T-shirt and thread-busted ball cap with a face of patchy reddish-white beard,

Kirk told him, "Ah, working lots of twelve-hour shifts over at the factory before it shuts down." Eyeing Miles he said, "You know what I'm talking about, don't you, Miles?"

Miles nodded. "Twelve hours is half your damn existence, but we ain't shutting down anytime soon, some nights we're so busy we can't find our asses with both hands."

And Nathaniel cut in with, "And you're still at Keller?"

"Yeah, still slaving so Uncle Sam can earn his right to regulate what I can or can't do. How's it being self-employed?"

"Better than dealing with the same dipshits doing the same stupid shit, over and over again. You staying out of trouble?"

"Well I ain't had no more DUIs, if that's what you're asking."

"Good to hear and if you do get arrested for drinking and driving again, don't tell them you're having suicidal thoughts."

"No shit, right. About froze my fucking dick off in a cell all by myself."

"That's what you wanted," Nathaniel said.

"A cell by myself, yeah. But you all came in and made my ass strip down to my boxers after that lady gave me all them damn questions, you all even took my blanket, all I had was flip-flops and boxers. Was fucking freezing."

"Protocol, can't risk you hanging yourself. That's why you don't lie, just sleep it off till morning."

"I know that now." Pausing, he took a draw from his smoke and said, "Heard about your brother and sister-in-law, really sorry."

The words stung and irritated Nathaniel. But he let them slide. That was the reason he was here.

"Appreciate that."

"Any idea who offed them?" Kirk asked.

"Not a clue," Nathaniel lied.

"Guess you don't got no ties to helping out the county fuzz no more?"

"Naw, that's above my pay grade, no longer a concern for me." Clearing his throat, Nathaniel asked, "What brings you down here?"

Taking a swig of his Pabst, Kirk swallowed and said, "Same thing that brings all of us here: smoke a little weed, drink some brews, get in on a card game, maybe earn some cheddar that Uncle Sam can't claim, listen to everyone bitch about their job, the government. You?"

"Miles here was looking for his girl, thought she might be down around this way with her brother."

Giving a one-eye-wide, one-eye-small stare, Kirk said, "You talking about Shelby and Wylie?"

Trying to hold his composure, the son of a bitch's head had flashes and stars circling around it like sparklers, it was the LSD stressing his mind, and Miles chimed in, "Yeah. Wylie always has a taste for weed, pills, booze, and the cards. And Shelby's always his taxi."

"She's always been kind when I seen her."

"Too kind, always offering help to her brother and he won't help himself."

"What happens when you offer handouts, folks take advantage of you, become dependent on the handout," Kirk said.

"What's wrong with this younger generation, don't wanna work for shit," Miles said.

Raising his beer, Kirk took a swig, eyes gooing out of their sockets, and he told Miles, "I hear that, but not my boy. No, sir, he works over at Deavers farm, shoveling chicken shit, feeding the cows, bales hay. He knows he's gotta earn his way in this life."

"That's good," Miles told him, and asked, "So you ain't laid eyes upon Shelby or Wylie tonight?"

Trying to keep a straight face, Miles watched Kirk as his whiskers kept oozing off of his jawbones and falling to the ground, only to grow right back as if a video being re-wound. He said to Miles and Nathaniel, "Naw, ain't viewed either of them, but a word to the wise, you might not wanna say Wylie's name too loud around here."

"Why's that?" Nathaniel questioned.

"You ain't heard?"

Considering he hadn't spoken with Shelby in nearly a week, Miles asked, "Heard what?"

Before Kirk cold answer, the bodies of patrons who stood talking began to spread apart, as a deep slurring-but-familiar voice barreled at Miles: "You rotten son of a bitch!"

All eyes burned into Miles and Nathaniel, the bodies of men, women, and teenagers huddled around them, and Miles turned, looked forward, taking in the dark, off-balance shape that limped toward him in his denim overalls; it was Bill Shivers.

Childers chuckled. "Look what the heifers let loose."

"Think you can rough me up, embarrass me, then come trespassing on my brother-in-law's property?" Bill yelled.

Fighting the tilt of Bill's clam-chowder skin, the crazy noises the wind kept whistling through the surrounding woods, through Miles's head, anger pulsed down his arms to his digits; he wanted to ball his hands into fists, club this loud mouth all the way into a dental reconstruction, and he told him, "You was the one pissing all over the VFW's tile, I'm just here looking for Shelby."

Nathaniel whispered to him, "The hell is this about?"

"Shelby?" Bill slurred. "You hear that, boys, this fucking VC murderer is looking for thieving Wylie's sister."

Before Miles could answer, Nathaniel butted in. "Miles just wants to know if Shelby's been here."

Between the LSD and the booze bubbling through Miles's body, there was another feeling that combined with it, an unknown dread that doubled as a body buzz compacted with adrenaline.

"Got an idea: why don't we all go in the house for a visit, let you ask Chucky," Bill said.

Wanting to manacle his grip around Bill's skull, compress

it as if a vise being tightened down, Miles spat, "Lead the way, you flaccid-organed fuck."

Nathaniel shook his head, whispered to Miles, "The hell did you do to piss this shitbag off?"

Twisting his head to Nathaniel, he told him, "He was being a public nuisance, offered him a lesson in civility."

All around them, mouths chuckled at Miles's recollection, as Bill turned away with a complexion that appeared heatstroked and started toward the house. Miles and Nathaniel followed, felt the tension that grew all around them; for Miles it felt as if he was entering a VC village, as if they were walking into an ambush. His body becoming more and more anxiously pumped. Muscles hardened with an underlying tension. He tightened his fists, making his way through the swarm of bodies, wanting to clothesline or punch the people who surrounded him, there was a rage and violence from within similar to the air he was inhaling and exhaling from his mouth as he stepped onto the creek rock that led to the creaking wooden steps that gave with the girth of his weight. Behind Miles the wind nearly scalped Nathaniel as it rattled the warped wood of the patched screen door that Bill opened for them; each man passed through the chipped-paint entrance and stood in a kitchen where cigarette smoke hung in the air thick as homemade jam.

Several circular fluorescents burned overhead, a stereo boomed and muffled from another room of the home with Black Sabbath's "Paranoid." Men sat gathered around a table, cards fanned out. Idle chatter of speech. "That baby Bush was the biggest drunk in college," G-Town John said, glaring through the bulky lens of his glasses at his cards.

"Yeah, well, he ain't near as cool as a president who can smoke pot without inhaling," Hunger Strike Led fired back. Guy was one breath away from anorexic, like he binged on meth and chased it with whiskey for nourishment.

"That son of a bitch is like Arkansas mafia, you cross him and you end up dead or just plain disappear without a trace," John said, digging a finger up his nose like nobody's business.

"Hey, you digging-for-gold motherfucker, cut that shit out, we all gotta touch them cards after you pick your fucking boogers," Led told G-Town.

"Makes no difference to me," said a shapeless man in a stretched-out black T-shirt, more hair on his arms and neck than on his head; he went by the name Porno Harry. He studied the creased and worn cards fanned out between thumb and index finger. "I made a helluva lot more money under Clinton. That guy is straight-up a pimp in my book."

"Bush's a fucking frat boy turned born again. The Baptists down around here would beat him with a Bible and drown him in the creek, show him some true religion," Led said, slurping his beer.

Decorating the table were sweating cans of Meister Bräu beer and glasses of Early Times whiskey with crimped wads of earnings piled in the table's center.

"Always boils down to politics, boys. The truth is it's

our damn money they blow on other countries, after they stick their noses into foreign troubles, demolish all their shit and then rebuild it instead of helping take care of our own country. Funny how we vote these fuckers into office and they're making around 150K a year, then they serve a few terms and they're millionaires, sign me the fuck up," said a man with flaming red hair in bibbed overalls, a cigar hanging between his lips.

"No shit," G-Town John said.

Sounds lit up Miles's brain. The kitchen door caught by the wind, jerking and slamming the side of the house, a fan buzzing overhead. Surveying the interior for a threat assessment, Miles viewed two shirtless men with overstuffed sack-like bellies off to the side of an entryway to what he guessed was the living room, their eyes, wide and red veined, swiveled to him and Nathaniel with heated surprise. They'd be out of breath after the first attempt to attack them, Miles thought, as he tried not to stare, and they morphed into NVA soldiers.

Miles's insides kept tense and uneasy as he blinked his eyes shut, opened them, felt that the room was filled with bad teeth, bad gums, bad breath, and bad vibes, floating and infecting his every inhale of air.

Led dug a hand over his black carpet-fiber locks, and said, "The guy creates NAFTA, begins a mass exodus of American jobs. Says free trade is good. But it also affects Mexican workers, destroys their wages for agriculture down in Mexico. It ain't just us that got affected."

Looking over his cards, G-Town John sipped his beer and said, "Can't blame immigrants for wanting to come here, I mean fuck, I'm going where the work's at."

"No you can't," Chucky said. "No you can't," ashing his cigar onto the floor.

Porno Harry said, "Yeah, but look at how many folks have come here."

"How many?" Chucky asked.

"I don't know, but it's a bunch, can bet your ass on that," Harry said as he twisted an oil-stained index finger into his ear.

"Yeah, well, this country was built by immigrants. So who gives a shit how many comes here." Shaking his head, changing the subject, Led asked, "How about Kentucky basketball?"

"What about it?" Chucky smirked. "You're in fucking Indiana."

"Don't remind me. Mike Davis? He's a clown," Led said.

"I don't know about a clown, but he sure as shit ain't no Bobby Knight." Chucky laughed.

"That's one coach who took no shit," John said.

Butting in, Miles added, "Three NCAA championships, one National Invitation Tournament, and eleven Big Ten Conference championships. The man gave zero fucks."

With his back to Miles and Nathaniel, Chucky turned around in his worn-out bibs. His fire-red hair was greased and sticking crooked in all directions, hence his moniker.

He chewed on his harsh-smelling cigar, which ashed from his lips, as he said, "Miles Knox, the great war hero, accompanied by Harrison County's finest lawman, Nathaniel Timberlake. For what do I owe the honor?"

Honor? Miles thought. *How about disrespect? Fight for others' freedom, see and live through more hell than any of these types give two shits about, all they did was bitch, drink, and smoke weed to blow off steam.*

Feeling the intensity of glaring orbs shadowing him, Miles said, "I didn't come here to sit around a card table bumping dicks, I'm looking for Shelby McCutchen."

Pulling the cigar from his mouth, Chucky spit, "As your eyes can attest, that tainted piece of ass ain't here."

Anger rifled through Miles like the Rifleman cocking his 1892 Winchester .44–40.

And Nathaniel pushed the barometer temperature in the room with, "What about her brother?"

"What about her brother?" Chucky responded with an acidic tone.

"Seen him?"

"I haven't. But if he were here, he'd be laying with eyes to the heavens and a bullet between his swelled sockets."

Dead silence found the mouths of the men around the table, who kept their glares upon the cards. "Paranoid" by Sabbath ended. The stereo found the form of silence. Only thing that could be heard was the wind and voices outside the home and Miles's heartbeat drumming within his ears.

The stereo switched to another tune, "Gun Street Girl,"

with Tom Waits picking strings, and Chucky asked, "Tell me, war hero, is it true you hunted American GIs?"

Wind vibrated the screen door upon the frame. Miles's entire body was full of fury, livid over how others spoke about Shelby, disrespected her. The features of every man in the room morphed into wounded soldiers, GIs. Chucky's complexion looked like a glazed donut expanding and contracting, and Miles told him, "None of your concern what I hunted, it's classified."

Nathaniel's lungs wrestled with the fog of cigarette exhale clouding the room; it was suffocating. The temperament in the space went from jovial to toxic. His tension gauge redlined.

"None of my concern? Really, come trespassing on my property, into my home—"

Interrupting, Miles told him, "No more trespassing than any of these folks you're bleeding of their wages. Besides that, I was invited, led into your home, by Krispy Kreme."

"—Oh there you go, interrupt me, how many times you gonna disrespect my brother-in-law, Bill. Tossing his ass out of the VFW, then to come in here asking for your damaged-goods female girlfriend, I don't care who you are, what you done, I'll fucking—"

A switch flipped in Miles's brain. Coming forward, his left hand grabbed an ear, his right hand was a sledgehammer that came down across the center of Chucky's face like an ice pick, splitting nose cartilage with not a single blow but three quick ones, up and down in succession, then right and left hands gripped Chucky's jaws, fingers dug behind their hinging, and thumbs buried into his eyes. The air in the room bubbled with tension, tasting the violence, everyone's sphincter muscles drew tight.

Two men at the table, G-Town John and Led, became sick. Turned and retched thick, chunky liquid all over the scuffed vinyl flooring. The two men who guarded passage into the living room started to come forward. Nathaniel lined them to another direction of thought. Reaching behind his back, pulling his .45, he said, "Steady Eddie, boys. We'll be on our way soon as Miles here gets his reckoning. Right, Miles? Miles?"

Overhead lights blinked and dimmed as Miles's head became a helium-filled balloon, words being volleyed from Nathaniel's lips distanced like a crowd cheering from a ballfield, sounds of words lengthened and bounced down a tunnel as the distance grew further and further and those sounds were lost along with the volume in the room, until everything around him—the people, their syllables, the music—became stretched out to a big minus. The volume nob had been turned to a negative.

Miles drifted and slipped into a world of frogs speaking English through a bullhorn. His digits and limbs felt detached. Flexing his body for feeling, his flesh tight as cellophane pulled over a dish's opening to seal in freshness, muscles hardened like a lead pipe full of concrete, the images of war came as scratchy black-and-white film. Breathing deep was the scent of sweat that clogged and soured one's self with the mash of a week's worth of body odor. Seated in the jungle, moisture padded upon leaves, as Miles had been in the bush for days, tracking an unknown enemy.

Feeling the cold steel tattooing her temple, closing her eyes, seeing Wylie trail through the entrance of her mind, fighting his face, blackened and bruised, indexing the trigger of the revolver, she imagined knocking him backward across space.

There was a sudden disturbance of sound in her ears, a grunting and gagging, pulling her attention from Wylie. Opening her eyes, Shelby looked down to the floor beside her. "Nuh more! Nuh more!"

It was Katz.

She was holding the pistol to her head . . . what the hell was she doing? Was she really gonna blow her damn brains out to rid herself of Wylie's control? Lowering the pistol she felt something like a thud to the side of her face. Only it wasn't a thud, it was pain creasing her cheek. Her teeth felt like they'd been pried by channel locks and a chill divided her spine as she began to chatter her teeth. Running her tongue around in her mouth, she tasted the warm fluid within and spit blood to the floor. What damage had she pressed upon herself?

Katz rolled around on the flooring, struggled to his knees, pressed himself to the wall. Watched Shelby standing incoherent, staring off into nothing, her one hand weighted by the .38, the fingers of her opposite hand ran over her face, touching the bruising and claw marks.

Shelby paused her actions, glared at Katz, watched him trying to tuck his chin into his chest, to create some space, remove the towel from his mouth, and he gagged, "Halp muh!"

With the .38 resting at her thigh, Shelby started to step toward Katz, to help remove the towel from his mouth, but her feet stutter-stepped, her leg joints locked up, and she began to shake, she tripped across the foundation, and the wind reared outside, blew the front door open, mashed into her complexion. Stunned Shelby, and she dropped the pistol.

Pressed into the wall, Katz wasn't taking any chances, saw his exit, his hands tied behind him, he maneuvered his stiff frame around Shelby, trying to get feeling back into his knees and legs again as he half limped and ran out the open door.

Lights flickered in the cabin and Shelby thought it was her head at first from the door slamming her in the face; gaining her balance, she watched Katz run down the gravel road, passing his old beater of a Ford, shrinking with distance, and she smirked. *Run, motherfucker, run!*

In that moment, watching Katz run away, she realized it was a multitude of actions, stressors that had led her to this trauma within herself. Her childhood with Whitey. Verbally abusing her mother, who then abandoned them. Her caring for Whitey and Wylie, never expecting anything in return. Placing their care, their wants and needs, before her own. Her father's directing her and Wylie to caress and fondle one another as they grew up. And Wylie not listening to her pleas to help himself, only to find him dead, seeing the Oxy, it crushed her, fried everything inside her. Created this split, like an alternate dimension of self.

Then all at once she felt Wylie pushing her to stand up, to step out the door, and into the wild winds that ripped from all directions. She began to run. Fighting against the air, fighting the control Wylie had on her. There was no rain. No lightning. Just harsh, strong air coming on like left jabs and right crosses. Similar to when she and Wylie were in their teens, riding their Honda XR600R dirt bike up and down the country roads, hair raked back over her head from the acceleration of speed, only to make a sudden turn, off into a hayfield, the air shifting as they cut over the foliage and onto a deer trail, navigating over the packed-down soil. Sting of insects and tree branches pelting their skin. But those days were long gone and she asked herself, *What happened to you, Wylie, what happened to you?*

In the distance she passed a push mower on top of a large snapping turtle walking down the driveway.

"What the hell?!"

Shit! I done forgot about the turtle I caught, placed a mower on him so he wouldn't get away!

Lungs burned as Shelby passed the turtle, eyed Katz hobbling off the gravel drive, cutting into the woods to her right. Following behind him she knew the old man was headed toward his home. Knew he lived just back a path that led to his barn. She hoped she could reconcile, gain control of her actions, help Katz free his hands, let him escape, if she could just get Wylie out of her head.

Following him over the land, into the woods, her lungs were on fire, heaving with a burn in her chest; her heart was ready to burst through her breasts. She hadn't run hard like this since childhood, she and Wylie taking to the wooded areas around their home, bear-hugging up trees, climbing to their higher limbs to look out beyond the tree lines, viewing the bordering properties and roads, or building forts and playing soldier in their army field jackets. Taking turns running away from one another while one held a BB gun, tried to shoot the other in the back. Hearing the pop of the BB gun, feeling the tiny thud that couldn't penetrate even the material of the coat. Sometimes pretending to fall to the hard soil, play dead. Roll over the wilted, dried, and crumbling blanket of leaves and twigs. Whitey watching, shouting, "Good shot!" in between taking pulls from a bottle of Jack or Jim. Where had those days gone? Those days of youth, uncaring and just being free and clean of want and need. It was remembering those times that fueled her affection for Miles, his carefree ways, taking her and Wylie fishing here at his camp, grilling, drinking beers, listening to Chris Knight or Ray Wylie Hubbard or John Prine. Talking about their upbringing. Their nine-to-fives that sometimes felt like they were in an alternate realm or a prison, punching the clock to rent their time.

From nowhere the heft of a limb came into Shelby's gut. Delivered her to her knees. Swiveling her view up, another branch indented across her back. Pulping her face-first into the leaves and then the dirt. She felt pain across her chest and spine. Followed by burning as she took small gasps of air, gulping and then coughing. From the corner of her vision came a boot. Katz held the log that'd done the damage, grounded Shelby.

Looking down into a face of heaving red madness, Katz yelled at Shelby, "You crazy bitch! Why, why you doing this to me?"

With the gusts swerving Katz's locks in all directions, flecks of bark, soil, and foliage flinging in his face, he hoisted the log back across his body, just above his shoulder, winding up like he was preparing to split a monstrous fastball down the center, Shelby held one hand over her gut, the other up at Katz, her body aching, moisture dotted and plagued around her eyes and cheeks as she pleaded.

"It's not me! It's Wylie. I got something wrong in my head."

Looking at her kneeling, crazed frame, Katz told her, "You got that right, something's all misconfigured up in that brain of yours."

"Just go. Go. I need help. And you can't offer it. I'm broken."

Angered and amped, Katz still held a restraint to batter a woman, to hit Shelby again; even though she'd brutalized him, Katz felt something similar to sympathy to her unwinding, to her frayed state of being. Holding on to the log, stepping backward, acknowledging her plea, raising his head up and down, he was lucky he got the restraint of fishing stringer loosened, then untied. When he'd felt a comfortable distance from Shelby, he turned and he ran, he ran as hard as he could holding on to the log.

They'd fallen back into the green cover of jungle leaves. Keeping distance from sounds and eyes, scouting, staying out of view from those they hunted. Taking notes and coordinates on terrain, what they'd come across and what Knox, and the rest of his unit, now believed. Their enemy wasn't NVA. It was Americans. And the question remained: "What'll we do? Deliver the intel back to the hill or engage the enemy?"

But that decision wasn't Miles's to make.

"My guess, they's six to eight of them. Seven of us. If

they's a secret patrol, a unit sniffing out the spies, and the VC plays sides, then what'll we do?" Bull asked the men.

"Know damn good and well they ain't sniffing out spies, might've started out that way, but after the butchering we seen, this platoon or group of mercs, whatever you wanna call them, they're just killing innocent VC, no one's letting them play sides," Vega said.

"I say radio the hill, give 'em the goods. See if they want us to pursue or abort, give us coordinates on an LZ pickup," Nafus said.

"We abandon this, we lose all that we been tracking," Bull said.

Finally Miles broke in with, "What if we capture one of them? Drag his ass from the herd. Break him down. Get intel. The whys. What the fuck this is they're doing. No wasted time nor words. Find out what needs finding out."

"That's all good and well until the cat's got the soldier's tongue and he don't wanna talk," Skipper said.

"Drop a man's drawers, trying shaving his nuts with a Ka-Bar while another man throws a blade into the soil around an unbooted foot for mumbly-peg, he'll fucking talk," Bull snapped.

And from a distance came the echo of automatic rifle fire.

The phrase "he'll fucking talk" bounced over and over, ringing in everyone's ears. Miles blinked, glared at Chucky's face in his grip, coated with sweat, a battered nose dripping fluid down his upper lip. Miles's digits spread out and dug in behind Chucky's ears, thumbs buried in his eyes, which were tearing up like he'd been huffing ammonia, with Chucky screaming, "Stop! Stop! Let go of me!"

It felt like hours but had only been mere seconds; Miles had blacked out. Nathaniel stood with his .45 drawn, yelling, "Miles? Miles?!"

Looking at Nathaniel, Miles blinked, his heart pounded in his palms, he couldn't speak.

Looking around the room, the smell of vomit combined with cigarette smoke. Two men doubled over. The other two held a fear unlike anything Miles had seen. Bill stood trembling without expression, white as a ghost, shaking his head in defeat. Two men at the entryway to the living room were pent-up nerves, one portion pissed off, another recognizing defeat.

Looking back down upon the begging shape Miles clutched, slowly he released the pressure from his thumbs, his palms and fingers, lessening their grip and squeeze. Childers whispered in his ear, "You done went shithouse rat loco on this wannabe kingpin."

Where he was at finally sunk in: Chucky's house, looking for Shelby and Wylie. He'd had enough of Chucky's words, had become angered, and he demanded, "Apologize, you piece of shit."

"Apologize for what?"

"Words you spoke about Shelby," Miles told him.

Chucky tried to talk tough. "Fuck you! Come in my home, attack me, you—"

"—Drop it. She's not here, Miles. Let's make trail," Nathaniel hissed.

Chucky sat digging his palms into his eyes; they were bulbous and his skin reptilian, the man was shaken, but there was an anger that burned within him, an anger created by his fear of Miles, who towered over him like an aged beast.

Bill raised a can of beer to his lips and Miles swiveled his eyes at him. "Give me one."

"One what?"

"One of them beers," Miles demanded.

Hesitating, Bill turned to the water-stained brown fridge in the corner, popped the door open; it squeaked, echoed loud and quaking like a knife scratching paint from a truck's hood. Light spilled out, creating a phosphorescent glow that fucked with Miles's mind. Watching Bill pull an iced can of Meister Bräu from inside, he gritted his teeth, seeing Bill and the other men in the room, bodies expanding and contracting in portions, as though each segment was a separate living, breathing organism. Miles couldn't hear the music but he could see it, "Smoke on the Water," the notes were etching around in the air. Every sensation in his body was heightened. He was radioactive. Wanted to explode on each of these men with an opera of violence for their wasting of lives, bullying and taking from others during these gambling sessions, watching men gamble their homes, their cars, their properties and paychecks, while bitching about politics and for what? There was no gain.

Bill tossed the beer to Miles, who caught it with one hand, popped the tab, brought it to his lips, inhaled the crystalized foam. His head fell back, tasting the iced-can tilt, soothing his mouth's thirst, the golden pilsner within was electricity in his mouth. He took all twelve ounces in one maddening gulp. Crushed the can in its center, tossed it onto the floor where the aluminum clattered.

Bill glared at Miles. "Want another . . . war hero?" Childers shook his head and told Miles, "Got a smart mouth, even after you tossed his ass out of the VFW. Maybe you need to tune his ass up again."

Sounds of knocking whistled from outside the house. The noises were playing tricks on Miles's mind. "I'll take as many as you got," he said.

Turning toward the fridge, Bill opened the door once again, reached in, removed another beer from a shelf, tossed it to Miles.

The two men guarding the entranceway gathered their courage; though they feared Miles, they tried to stand their ground, stood tense. They were ready to move when Chucky offered direction. Even though they knew Miles could bushhog them down like wheatgrass, they had to save face in front of Chucky.

Behind Nathaniel, the screen door belted hard against the frame, opening and closing.

Chucky's irritation was redlining, being belittled in front of his minions, eyes globing from sockets, appearing large as two freshly leathered baseballs with beet-red stitching. "I've had enough of eyeing you on my premises, drinking my damn booze, war hero, don't you know when you've wore out your welcome."

Outside, patrons drank, cursed, and talked louder and louder. Trees waved back and forth as the vinyl siding of the house rattled. A squirrel got cupped from a limb, circling in the air until it hit the ground, landed on all fours in shock, darting its head from left to right. Then took off running as though drunk into the night as people doubled over with laughter.

Miles's mind was lightning in a bottle, ready to pounce, and Nathaniel whispered once more, "Let's get."

Looking up at Miles, Chucky turned his head sideways. Tilted it like a pup learning commands. "No idea what kinda shit you're on, but your pupils is the size of olives, can't see no color other than black, no wonder your ass come acting all lunatic-crazy, you got the Vietnam voodoo dancing in your head."

Fed up, Nathaniel grabbed Miles's arm with his free hand, feeling the bulge of his triceps and biceps, tugged on him as he pedaled backward to the screen door. Keeping his .45 raised, out the door they went, down the steps, and into the yard, wind howling.

"The fuck was that, Miles?" Nathaniel said. "You blacked out on me. Went fucking AWOL. Thought you was gonna spoon his eyes out of his skull."

Only word Miles could muster was "Kingsley."

Bumping through the outlines, Nathaniel asked, "What about Kingsley?"

To Miles, the shapes kept shifting to bullet-riddled bodies, faces busted and ears missing, the children begging for food, VC wanting "*number one chop chop*" and he mumbled to Nathaniel, "He slipped me some LSD at the liquor store. It's got my mind lit up like napalm."

"For fuck's sake. Let's get your ass to the truck."

Working through the bodies, behind them the air combusted with buckshot from a twelve-gauge shotgun. "Whoever gets those two motherfuckers gets a thousand in cash!" Chucky shouted from the open door of his home.

Next thing Miles and Nathaniel knew, hands were reaching, gripping, twisting, and pulling at them. They pawed and punched back, trying to keep the furious mosh pit of grasping hands away from them.

Dragging her weight of swelled fiber over the leaves, up the gravel road, Shelby felt as if her lungs had been soaked in butane and someone had struck a match from within. Her every inhale was an incensed wheeze of burn.

Each bend up the gravel drive, one step after the next, up to the front door that was hinged wide open, delivered a lesson in hurt; she entered the mouth of the cabin, her mind blurring and fading, the wind spurring behind her,

feeling the hurt encasing her chest and back. She made a
fist with her right hand, felt her tiny muscles knot. She released the tension. Repeated the action several times to work
out the stiffness. It wasn't just the wielding combustion
from Katz's log that bound her up—she was dehydrated
also.

Looking down, seeing the revolver on the floor, bending her knees, they pained; she reached for the .38, scooping her digits around the handle, hefting its weight, and
slid the pistol into the front pocket of her sweatshirt. Walked
slowly across the floor to the kitchen, where she opened the
fridge, found bottles of water. Grabbed one. Twisted the lid
from the water. Placed it to her lips, gulped it down. Tasting the clear, cold hydration work its way through her body.
Thinking to herself, her mother was right, she'd told her
she'd always been the responsible one. Even as a kid, playing with Legos, Lincoln Logs, puzzles, she'd be the one
who could build, figure things out, organize the puzzle
pieces, finding all the corners first to build the frame, and
then it was just a matter of filling it in. When she was done,
she'd clean everything up. Not Wylie. Sure, he could build
things, but when he got frustrated, he was done, he'd just
leave it laying for someone else to clean up, meaning Shelby.
And she was still doing all the cleaning up all these years
later.

With a moment of silence in her head, no Wylie over-
taking her thoughts, speech, or mind, she stood taking
in all that had transpired. The killing. The beating and

abducting. The back-and-forth in her head. And now, an escape.

Still, she knew Wylie was here, somewhere inside her, and she directed her words into the open kitchen of the cabin.

"You fucked up royal, Wylie."

No one responded. Tears stressed her cheeks.

"You OD'd, went and scrambled my brain, killed Nathaniel's brother and sister-in-law, began this spiral. It was all you!"

All she could hear was the wind and the erratic pound of her heartbeat.

Pressing her palms against her temples, she screamed.

Visions of purple lips and floured pigment danced within her mind, needle marks like stars in the night pricking bends between arms, between toes and fingers; a bubbling madness heated Shelby's brain, a Zippo lighter with a Grim Reaper, a blackened spoon, tearing of cotton and absorption of melting liquid, her sight became molten, her eyes fluttered and from her peripheral a shadowy image dispersed like exploding atoms until it was no more.

Shelby held her breath for two or three pulses, released it, knowing Wylie was as shriveled as a corpse. He was dead. Then he spoke to her.

Wanna blame someone for all this? Better look at our daddy. Me being a doper, you a stripper, come on, sis, we's practically forced to be lovers once he ran Mama off, until we

was old enough to keep him in check, by then it was too late,
we was damaged goods.

Regardless of who was saying the words, Wylie or her,
they were correct. There was only one person to blame, and
she knew that was Whitey.

Wind pounded over the bodies of men, drunk, crowding
and elbowing. Grasping at arms, clamping on to Nathaniel, who rolled one grip after the next from his body, punching and elbowing back. Working toward his truck, where
Shadrack waited inside, some distance away.

Huffing for air, adrenaline escalated, with digits digging at locks of hair, Nathaniel jerked backward as he
ducked and spun, bent a man at his elbow, twisted it up
into his spine. "I got no quarrel with you!" he shouted.
Only to feel more hands scratching at him, and he released
the man's arm and kicked him in his ass, pushing him away
while more men tugged and pulled, awkward and drunk,
until an arm wrapped around Nathaniel's neck from
behind.

Pushing the man off, Nathaniel saw that he was a
weighted obscuration of ink, with clowns, crowns, and
crosses expanding over left and right shoulders, the wind
beating down over a skull peeled to a sandpaper hide of
baldness, a patch of fur beneath his lower lip and a

snakeskin belt rimming oversized Dickies pants, his fists scarred and knuckles flattened from barefisted boxing. He stared at Nathaniel and Miles, ready to earn the purse Chucky offered for their hides.

The surrounding drunks created a circle around Miles, Nathaniel, and the bruising miscreant of a man, already forgetting about the thousand dollars. "Beat their asses! Beat their asses!"

Beside Nathaniel, Miles took a breather, glared at the surrounding faces that glowed with shapes expanding, compressing, and sloshing into one another with heads fumbling and bobbing. "I got this," he told Nathaniel.

In Miles's mind the surrounding drunks started chanting, "Blood! Blood! Blood!"

"Got this?" Nathaniel said. "You're half out of your fucking mind on psychedelics and these lunatics are wanting to collect our hides!"

"Look, you wanted to find Wylie."

"Well, he ain't here and if you hadn't went AWOL on Chucky, we'd be down the road by now!"

Everything was Fourth of July in Miles's mind and he turned his tone down low and told Nathaniel, "When I rush this rhino-headed fuck, you draw your piece, fire a warning shot, make some of these blue-collar turncoat bastards scatter, then you make for the truck."

"What about you?"

"I'll break for the woods. They're all drunk, and it's harder to attack two targets when you're this banked up on booze. Meet me down past Green's old schoolhouse, back before the condemned bridge."

"In White Cloud?"

Looking wild-eyed, Miles told him, "You know of any other schoolhouses owned by Green?"

"Seeing as you're haze-eyed on fucking hallucinogenics with a mean storm brewing, be careful," Nathaniel snapped at Miles.

"Wouldn't be the first time I's stuck in the wilds with bad weather and a buzz."

Booted feet came stomping over the dirt, gritting teeth; Chucky came down the house steps, working his way through the patrons, and yelled, "Hell you all waiting for, beat those bastards!"

When the beast of a man rushed toward Nathaniel and Miles, Miles pivoted, stepped toward him, a blur of bodies and voices all around him feigning and echoing slurs, sloshing and spewing alcohol, the big bastard of a man gritted and huffed like a mad bull ready to charge a matador. Nathaniel held his .45 up at a sideways angle over his head and tugged the trigger. The gunshot let the surrounding bodies find the earth. Beers dropped while other bodies were running for cover. "Crazy son of a bitch has got a gun!"

Nathaniel placed one foot in front of the next and ran, navigated through the beat and aged vehicles in the yard, making his way toward his Dodge Dually.

All around Miles, it was war; the gunshot rifled his

memory into a free fall, the monstrous man before him planted a foot and pumped a hard right hook to his ribs. Miles's chest cringed and his lungs coughed air as he slid back into his days in Puerto Rico, absorbed the body blow, stepped to his right in a southpaw stance, returned a garbage left hook into the beast's shoulder, followed by a straight right jab down the man's center, feeling teeth scrape his knuckles.

Off-balance, the man stepped back, his knees were wobbled as blood gushed red from his gums and teeth, combined with the ooze of tobacco juice.

"This guy's not near as tough as a chicken gizzard," spat Childers.

Somewhere in the distance, doors unlocked, Nathaniel huffed air, his lungs fast expanding, and his heart pounding as he slid into the driver's seat, door slammed and locked. He laid his pistol upon the dash and Shadrack came from the floor, as he had ducked down and hid, his eyes and face relieved to see Nathaniel, he asked, "Are them people shooting at you?"

"No, buddy, everything's okay, nothing to be afraid of, they tried to get unruly and I fired a warning shot."

Revving the diesel engine, shifting to drive, Nathaniel stomped the accelerator, threw soil, leaves, and rock.

"Where's the drug man?"

"He's meeting us down the road."

Red taillights flared back down the driveway while Miles stood facing the hulking man who again rushed him, expanding his mastiff arms wide around Miles in a bear hug, squeezing and lifting him off his feet. Miles came with a hard headbutt, driving his forehead down across the bridge of the beast's nose, once, twice, until he released Miles. The bovine-sized man brought his hands to the oozing swell of fluid from his nostrils. Miles's eyes expanded wide with the bellowing of voices all around him, and he came forward with a straight hard left, then a right to the brute's hand-covered face. Miles heard and felt the bones in the man's hands give and fracture. He dropped his hands, cursing, and Miles grabbed the man behind his ears and delivered headbutts to the man's nose until it was pasty and flat and the man dropped to the earth, pleading, "No more, man, no more."

Miles pivoted away from his shape and ran atop the boot-indented yard, headed toward the woods, when wind was replaced by misting rain, and with his back turned, another shotgun explosion delivered a pelting sting across the rear of Miles's back and upper shoulder, followed by a voice screaming, "You're a dead man, Knox, hear me, a dead man!"

But Miles didn't stop. He kept moving at a trot within the darkness, which took on the appearance of a black light, causing trees and weeds and foliage to glow as he disappeared into the woods.

Back at Chucky's, with Miles gone, another blast exploded, peppered the man he'd just fondled a beating to, and the man bent at the waist, patted his knee and thigh, hopped backward, screaming, his right shin dispersed blood from holes like paprika below his knee, dampening his denim. The man was no use to Chucky as he'd let Miles and Nathaniel both escape.

Chucky's face was red-charred fury as he stood balling a fist in the air, angered and shaking his one fist at the fighter, the other hand gripping the sawed-off twelve-gauge pump, yelling, "Shit! Shit! Shit! You're a useless inbred!"

Down the road, Nathaniel navigated, trying hard to calculate what had taken place. The crazed banter of drunk bodies. Miles blacking out into some alternate reality, returning into a psycho LSD rage. What he knew was that he'd make it past Green's property to the bridge, but feared Miles would not.

Scratch of briar and whip of branch came across arms and face as sounds bounced and crept around in Miles's brain. The sounds spreading like an Ebola outbreak sourced into a stick of dynamite with the fuse sparking with germs, waiting to combust into a monstrous infection.

It was something Miles couldn't contain.

Wind kept howling, dropping down from the sky overhead, thunder exploding like mortar fire off in the distance. The center of his vision was full-on black as if staring at an eclipse of the sun; Miles was wigging out, touching the heated flesh on the back of his neck, fingering his rear delt, it was pasty with blood. He pressed a single digit into what felt like an entire area gored by BB. Looking at his fingers, he realized he'd been hit by bird shot and hadn't felt it. His heart stiffened in his chest, his mouth was chalky, and in an instant his brain pinched and tilted. Blinking his eyes, rubbing his digits over the wound once more, feeling the tiny pelts of broken skin, he realized that he wasn't gored, it was a hallucination.

Miles chewed on a rush of energy unlike anything he'd ever felt. His mind held on to a clarity that was rich in sound and sight. A near-religious out-of-body feeling.

He kept moving. Knowing he couldn't stop. He had to somehow find Shelby, help Nathaniel and that kid find Wylie. Figure this shit out, see if Wylie really killed Nathaniel's brother and sister-in-law. He had to keep these objectives in his mind right. Whatever *right* was. He had to get centered, balanced somehow, but everything was going erratic, his senses heightened. The wind tilted trees, bent lumber to the earth, clattered limbs like drumsticks. Debris of leaves and bark and soil flung about like shrapnel, daylight sprayed bright, and Miles dug his boot prints into the maddening weather. Things kept shifting. From one world to the next.

He climbed up a hillside, panting like a winded hound on the trail of a rabbit or deer. Came down onto the broken pavement of road. There was no trespass of vehicles. No sign of Nathaniel.

Moving on, lungs flamed, hefting the weight that

tendoned about his frame, Miles followed the blanched pavement, too many sensations to understand, to regulate, to grasp, coming in on all channels at once, and Miles thought to himself, *This must be what it's like to be a beagle, a cur or a walker hound, bluetick, redtick, or bloodhound, able to experience so many scents and sounds.*

Miles's legs tightened with each step as he passed the old gas station that stood restored; it was a white wood-slatted shotgun-style house, two red pumps standing out in front with the glass housing on top. He was supposed to meet Nathaniel but couldn't remember where he'd told him. His brain kept blinking but his knees kept bending and his legs kept walking.

Rounding a bend, Miles took the curve to the bridge that was no longer in use. To his left the road ran up a steep hill of trees and rock, Miles stepped to his right, walked to the abandoned bridge, pressed a booted foot to the iron beam that connected one side to the other. It ran over Blue River. Boards were rotted and weak; to make his way across the condemned structure would deliver him to the opal-green muck of running water below. *It'd be a helluva drop*, he thought.

He stepped off the lumber, which gave and creaked, not wanting to fall through, not trusting his reflexes. Walking off to the side, going down to the water, Miles eyed the embankment on the opposite side, the incline of soil and timber; he couldn't remember which side of the river he'd told Nathaniel to meet him on, and decided to cross. Maybe Nathaniel was there. Waiting in his truck, he had to already be here, somewhere. Miles made his way down, until his footing gave and he slid until he was stopped by his feet splashing into the water. His legs wobbled as he waded out in the river, water up to his knees, then he stumbled. Felt the solid pound to the rear of his skull bring a vibrating shudder, and suddenly he was riding the current downstream, his eyes to the sky above, and all at once the war came with the combustion of automatic-weapon fire from a distance.

Farmers were dressed in village rags running beneath the sticky sun, while Miles and his recon unit held their cover, keeping position, watching from afar as the flare of a rifle opened up one farmer after the next, a domino effect, flesh-and-blood target practice fertilizing crops with human matter.

From the opposite view of the field came men wearing black pants, sandals, long-sleeved shirts, and conical straw hats armed with automatic rifles that donned bayonets. Their faces charcoaled black, each of the men stepped to the fallen, speared their hides and skulls until there was no lifting or lowering of chest, no begging from galvanized lips, confirming their departures from the world.

Through binoculars, Miles and Skipper studied the faces of the guerrilla unit they were sent to hunt. Miles lowered his, same as Skipper, who'd a look of sickness and mild madness painted upon his complexion and who whispered, "Ain't no fucking NVA, you were goddamned right, Knox."

Miles nodded. "They're American skin, Section Eight motherfuckers."

And then unexpectedly came the combustion of rifle fire that ignited the air, pelting foliage, soil particling into the air as Skipper hollered, "Fall back! Fall back! Our coordinates have been compromised!"

Limbs felt split and beat, ribs ached, her throat was parched and gravelly. Seated in her Camaro, the key hung from the ignition, and Shelby's foot rested upon the accelerator.

In her head, Wylie's voice was silent.

Lifting her right arm, her hand making contact with the key, her shoulders felt chewed and worn, high winds belted outside the windshield, vibrating the hood.

What have you done?

Flashes of gunfire. Combustion of skin rifled through her head as she twisted the key, her Camaro's 350 small block fired to life, and she thought about her mother, what she'd warned: *Your father, he's toxic. Why do you cater to he and your brother's bullshit?*

Shifting into drive. Pressing the accelerator, Shelby steered down the driveway from the cabin; her mother had come from a loose life until she met Whitey, who, her mother told her, treated her like a queen. Giving her flowers once a week. Taking her to dinner and movies. Her mother became settled. Wanted a family. Had kids. Once the kids were old enough, her mother got a good factory job. She was happy. She'd grown up, come full circle. But then something in Whitey changed, the booze and the memories of war created a monster; then came the arguments, the name-calling, and her mother couldn't tolerate the verbal abuse and left, but Shelby couldn't leave her daddy, and Wylie wouldn't separate from his sister. Shelby thought she could help her daddy. And even now, as a grown-up, she recalled her defense of Whitey and Wylie, telling her mother whenever she called her these days;

It's my daddy and my brother. My blood. Someone has to help them.

Her mother told her, "It don't gotta be you. You got a job, a house. Money put back. You got a man that treats you decent. With respect. He's older. Matured. Go be happy."

I am happy, but if something happened to Daddy or Wylie, I'd never forgive myself. I only have one daddy and one brother.

"They're not your responsibility. They're grown men, for God's sake. I love my son, but you gotta cut the cord or he'll never learn."

Following the granules of gravel, trees swayed and rocked on the sides of the driveway. Her car moved a bit on its shocks. Reaching the driveway's end, hanging a left onto the county back road, Shelby knew her mother was faultless in her telling. Mashing down the gas pedal, her brain fog was clearing, her mind was tired, but her sentiments were on point, she was going to confront her father over his abuse to her, her brother, and her mother, something she'd never done before. She knew it contributed to her brother's drug dependency, to her mental split. She needed to hold it together long enough to confront her father. And after that she'd have to take responsibility for her wrongs. Turn herself in. Admit to what she'd done, though she felt it wasn't completely her doing, there was something within her that wasn't quite right, something in her brain had frayed, no longer fired correctly. Like a word without a definition, or a definition without the word, she'd draw a blank, unable to place her finger on what was happening. Being the tomboy that she was, changing the plugs in her Camaro, checking the gap of the plugs, or changing the oil, unscrewing the bolt from the pan, draining the black sludge, removing the used filter, she'd draw blanks, sat stone postured as if she'd looked Medusa in the eyes, blanked out. Only to snap back to the present, seeing the actions she started, wrenches scattered about, not remembering when she'd started on the task. It was an admission she'd realized or maybe she'd known it all along; she wasn't sure as her brain kept changing channels, finding static reception while flipping through emotions. The ups and downs. It was a dopamine roller-coaster ride, navigating her through hell.

Wind rocked the truck taking the curvy back road and the sky overhead lit up with lightning. Shadrack closed the distance on the front seat, butted up next to Nathaniel as though he were a dog and needed reassurance.

With one hand upon the wheel, the other comforted Shadrack. "Nothing to be scared of, buddy."

"I don't like this."

"The storm?" Nathaniel asked. Thinking about Miles, hoping he got away from Chucky and the crazed drunks. Hoped he could make it through the woods in his drunken-psychedelic mental state.

"Yeah."

Glancing in the rearview, not seeing any headlights behind him, Nathaniel sat in the saturation of paranoia, as if someone was following him; every now and then he swore he caught a glimmer of approaching headlights, but then they disappeared, and he told Shadrack, "When we's kids on the farm, your dad didn't care much for storms either."

"Really?" he asked with curious surprise.

"Really. We always knowed when bad weather was in the works, though."

"How?"

"Animals. Chickens. Ducks. Horses. They got all worked up. The air pressure changes. We had this bluetick hound, Old Pete. He'd come sit with your dad when he lay on the couch or in his bed, lay his wrinkled neck over your dad's neck until the storm passed."

"I always wanted a dog, Mom and Dad wouldn't never get me one."

"That dog was something else. Real protector. Followed your dad everywhere. Lived on that farm with us until he was probably sixteen years old." Getting choked up, Nathaniel cleared his voice. "Maybe we can get you a pup when all this mess is straightened out."

"Really?" Shadrack said with excitement.

Thinking about Miles, Nathaniel hadn't even looked back to make sure he'd gotten away. Firing off the shot. Everyone scattered. Nathaniel ran straight for the truck. For all he knew, Miles could've gotten hit by the shotgun blast he heard as he drove off.

"Really. And if I recall correctly, it wasn't long after he passed your dad moved out. Met your mom. He'd saved enough from working at Keller's to buy that place you all lived in. But man did he love that dog."

No longer paying attention to the storm Shadrack asked, "How—how did Pete die?"

"Was lucky, never suffered, he got slow in his old age and he went to sleep one night and didn't wake up the next morning."

"He never woke up?"

"No. He didn't wake up. He'd slept in bed with your dad until his joints started to give out and he couldn't jump up into the bed no more. Your dad built this cedar crate, placed a thick pillow made from duck feathers inside it with an old comforter, kept it next to his bed for Pete to sleep in. Sometimes he even slept on the floor next to Pete."

Holding tight to the wheel, wind rammed the truck. Coming to a stop sign. Looking left, seeing no hint of headlights, Nathaniel hung a right, headed toward White Cloud as his pistol started to slide across the dash.

Removing his hand from Shadrack's shoulder, he grabbed the .45, leaned forward, slid the pistol down into his holster, and reassured Shadrack with, "Like I said, once we get things straight, we'll see about getting you a pup. Every kid should have a dog. Learn some responsibility. And a pup would keep my hound dogs Ruby and Ring company, too."

The surrounding wilderness and sky lit up with lightning and Shadrack asked, "We going to meet the man?"

"To meet Miles."

"Thought he's down the road?"

"He is, down this road in White Cloud."

"He walked?"

"Yeah, took a shortcut through the woods."

At least that was what Nathaniel hoped. If he didn't make it, they'd now be hunting for Wylie, Shelby, *and* Vietnam-crazed Miles.

The road curved and rose off to the right; down a hillside was the Blue River. It ran along with the road some thirty to forty feet below them. Coming to his turn, Nathaniel slowed and hung a right, the back road narrowed,

and they passed a yellow sign with black letters that read
DEAD END.

Passing Green's schoolhouse up on his left, they drove
by Carney's place, which sat some distance off the road, the
low glow of a bonfire sparking with the wind, then on
down past the service station that had been out of business
for years, the gas pump still sat in front of it. Navigating
beyond several houses located around it, he drove toward
the rotted bridge that was no longer in use. Slowing to a
stop, Nathaniel looked around. Shifted into park. Wind
and a light mist of rain whipped against the truck and he
told Shadrack, "Sit tight."

Getting out of the truck, walking to the driver's-side
door, he flipped the spotlight on, aimed it at the bridge and
the rusted iron, nothing. Then he aimed the beam of light
at the weeds, worked his eyes down the hillside at the green
water, and saw something move.

Gunshots still rang in Miles's memory after spotting the
US soldiers dressed as villagers. Stumbling from the murky
bed of water, Miles eyed the toss of foliage being scattered
and uprooted; squeezing his sight closed, hands palming
his face, the world around him was a flutter of violent
sound and energy. Leaves milled from the soil, lumber
cracked, the wind and light rain pelted a tune of kaleido-
scope color upon his soaked frame.

Opening his eyes, his feet sunk and mud suctioned each step as he muscled his way through the thick, weighted pudding-like earth, his calves and hamstrings burning from the steep incline of the hill, when from somewhere came a bright ray of light burning down behind him. Freak-out mode kicked in as hands grabbed at small trees and sharp mossy rock that seemed almost cartoonish in appearance, climbing the incline all he could think was *NVA, fucking mercs are closing in on me.* Sounds of foreign voices, screams that sounded like a chorus bellowing his name followed by the rattle of machine gunfire cutting a hole into his perception of era and time, like time traveling, a hole to another dimension ripped open, and his sight was filled with shapes running from tree to tree, taking cover as he climbed to the top of the summit, worked his way through a grove of briar and berries bending and swaying, being gouged and pierced by thorn, causing red to vine down his hands.

Coming to a hayfield's edge, he ran with the mist of black and gray overhead, leaving the chants of his name echoing behind. He fought and pressed his torso through the gusts of heated wind that burred his complexion, he leaped like an aging deer only to land in a mess of barbed wire, his body entangled, rooting around his flesh, his every pull or tug carved and cinched deeply into lean tissue, and he screamed, "Motherfucker!"

Punching, twisting, and kicking, feeling the jag and tear of metal burrs, his body felt as though it would combust, cleave apart like polymer being heated and pulled. Teeth gritted, mouth foamed, he broke the restraint of wire, lugged posts from the ground, and ran mad and quaking through the leafed ground, the wind dive-bombing his body with barking chatter.

Shaking free of the barbed wire, walking with the smack of air and moisture in all directions, Miles paused, blood inking down his arms and face like condensate on a bathroom mirror, took in a thin strand of fishing line, a trip wire, strung about six inches from the earth, one end attached to a poplar tree, the other to a section of briar. Miles stepped over it, his heart pumped heavy, punched his sternum, when the smell of Irish Spring soap rose up in his face, circled his inhale like flies to a fresh pile of shit.

Bars of soap had been cut into strips the size of Wrigley's gum and hung by bread ties from tree limbs with beer and pop cans rattling. "Booby trap, some SOB's hiding something," Miles muttered to himself. He dug his digits into his head, his wet clothing bringing on goose-bumped skin and Miles began to run once more, caught a glimpse of monstrous sections of thick ivy greens, and the heavy aroma of skunk bud, before he figured out he was standing within the center of a dope patch.

Working his way through the thick gummy foliage of red hairs, Miles came upon a dilapidated structure with a rusted roof, the windows covered by clear plastic, wood siding once red now chipped and flaking to a weathered and rotted pigment.

Shelter, Miles thought, as he punched and pounded on the door to no answer, ripped the wooden screen ajar, slammed it against the house. Miles tried the doorknob, it twisted clockwise and in he stepped.

Inside the smell was fungal and mildewed. He stood within a room where walls curled and expanded with cotton-candy webs spread over the heads of cobwebbed trophy bucks, attached and lined with animal skulls; below the wall were horns strewn about a dusty, malformed countertop, yellowed newspapers and coon-hunting magazines, children's hardback books of the Hardy Boys, Agatha Christie, and Barbie doll and baby doll heads, arms, and legs lined and scattered over the floor.

Miles's frame was soaked with vibration and nerves and river stink. As he tramped across the holed linoleum, his boots squishing, a chill traveled up his spine, the animal heads eyeing his each and every step, the walls breathing and swelling until one of the deer twisted its neck and began laughing madly at Miles. He shook his head, his brain beginning to rattle with the air flogging the house from outside. Miles walked through a jamb into a connecting room when a rifle's butt cut the air and split him between the eyes, hammered him backward. Eyes blinking, he staggered his footing, the deer head still in hysterics, laughing and drooling, all he could do was glare into the wavy screams of derangement before him, when memories whistled and tormented his mind with the flashback to barbarism.

After being spotted and fired upon, their position was compromised, Miles and the soldiers discussed the merc/executioner unit they were hunting as Skipper devised their removal. Telling how they'd surround the encampment's perimeter at dark. And when the signal was given, they'd remove them. Miles questioned with, "Shouldn't they be observed? Apprehended? Taken in for war crimes? They've murdered innocent VC villagers."

"Knox, our orders are to seek out the executioners. End them. Come back to camp."

"But they've committed—"

"—Murder? War crimes? Top brass knows this. Don't wanna be reminded of it or the weight it'll carry if the media gets a whiff of it to run a print in *The New York Times* or the *Chicago Tribune* or the *LA Times*, have ole Cronkite spilling the bad beans all across the evening news."

Day passed from sticky heat to shadowy night with timed naps and turns for lookout, until dark stained the retinas' view and each man was in position, watching the bounce and glint of flame from a spit. Several of the hunted sat around the flicker of light. Each with facades shaded black, decorated like Indian war paint. Then came the screams and a large man in Vietcong village attire dragging a female by her locks, creating a trail with her bare feet, skidding over the ground and warm piss releasing from her bladder, sheening her legs. The man dragged her before the orange heat of flames. Kept her on her knees. Behind her he tugged her locks with one hand, wet spat from her eyes, mucus from her nose, and a blade appeared across her throat, creating a bloodline from the flesh that was parted.

Several men encircled her as the man sheathed his blade. Ran digits beneath the river he'd created, raised them to his lips, and licked them. "Have at it, savor her spoils of soul."

Miles eyed Bull with saucers, who eyed Nafus, who eyed Rut, Crust, and Vega. Skipper gave the hand signal that traveled back to Miles as each man sighted their rifle on the hunted. And gunfire tore open the night like strobes of heat lightning.

Treading down the mossy concrete steps to a basement door, Nathaniel felt the tug of Shadrack's hand on his back pocket as this time he'd not wanted to stay in the truck alone. Nathaniel'd driven back the way he'd come, crossed over the Blue River, taken Harrison Springs Road, which divided abandoned homes along the river and fields of corn, dead-ending at the frayed pavement where the condemned iron bridge lay constructed on the opposite side, and Nathaniel had killed the truck, stepped from it, and found no sign of Miles along the opposite hillside, shining his Maglite down the mud-slick decline to the river, glimpsing movement, only to hear the crunch of booted feet. Turning to his left, he caught something, a shape some distance away was cutting through the stalks of corn. He yelled, "Miles!" But the shape kept creating distance.

What the hell is going on in that head of yours? Nathaniel wondered.

Irritated, Shadrack and he followed, passing into pasture, the fling of itch from the graze and brush of leaves over skin, discovering soap strung from tree limbs at the field's border, hiding the growth of marijuana, avoiding the obvious booby trap on the perimeter. Moving forward they came to the rear of a deserted home. Nathaniel worked his way to a decline of steps that led to a basement door. Now, with a Maglite in one hand, .45 tucked down his waist, Nathaniel lit up the spongy green steps that ended at a chipped rough-cut walnut door, wondering if Miles had maybe entered the home. Nathaniel tried the handle and the door creaked open. Waft of a million gummy skunks knuckled Nathaniel's inhale and Shadrack muttered, "What's that smell?"

"Weed. That scent can never be mistaken," Nathaniel whispered.

Eyes adjusted and searched the webbed ceiling rafters, finding worn Romex wormed from two-by-eights with bare bulbs, and Nathaniel told Shadrack, "Keep close."

The room was lined with large wire crates that looked to have been used to board dogs, and scattered about the cinder floor were mattresses pocked by ringworm lounging. Rusted log chains hung from four-by-four posts at one end, while at the other end, sawhorses sat spread out with four-by-eight sheets of plywood. On top sat scales and gallon-sized Ziplocs.

"What is all this?" Shadrack asked.

In his right hand Nathaniel gripped his .45, Maglite in his left, meeting the side of his pistol, sweeping the area as he took in the corroded cages and discolored mattresses. Along a far wall were long green stalks and dried lime-green leaves spread out and hanging from meat hooks; below them were large silver tarps. And speaking aloud to himself, he muttered, "Looks like we've trespassed upon a grower's harvest."

Shining his light, Nathaniel made his way toward a makeshift table. Shadrack tugged at Nathaniel's pocket and questioned, "What's a grower?"

Thinking of what his nephew had viewed over the years, the situation began to settle into Nathaniel's psyche as they stood looking at the table, and he told Shadrack, "Person that grows weed, makes a living from it, it's illegal trade. Now I need you to keep your tone down in case they's someone other than Miles present."

"Bad people?" Shadrack whispered.

"Let's hope it's just Miles in here, taking shelter from the wind and rain."

Shining the light back on the piss-stained mattresses, then the stalks, from what Nathaniel recalled the property had been sold after old man Mercer passed to someone out of state. A war veteran. Nathaniel didn't know the man, only that he'd served in 'Nam, similar to Miles; some said he was chewed up, kept to himself, was what some referred to as an antisocial, committed suicide in the house years ago. Regardless, once the crop dried out, whoever grew it would have to cut up, separate, and weigh it up. Get it ready to sell and transfer around the surrounding counties. Least that was Nathaniel's way of thinking.

What he needed was to find the stairs. Shining the light, he saw what he believed was a side view of a stringer hidden by a makeshift counter, where wooden crates were stacked upon it and below it. Walking toward it, Shadrack released Nathaniel's pocket, bent down, started to nose around, getting brave, a bit too comfortable, and Nathaniel whispered, "Don't touch nothing."

Shadrack turned to him and asked, "Where's your friend?"

Maneuvering around, keeping Shadrack with him, Nathaniel turned and looked to his right, realizing he was standing at the bottom of the stairs, getting impatient, Nathaniel pointed. "Hear that? Maybe my friend's up there."

Behind them, wind rolled and trees creaked through the open door he'd not latched closed. Above them, footfalls stomped, slammed, and thudded down. Then muffled words, a voice, loud and angry. Followed by more feet hammering onto the wood above, bringing the sag and creak of the flooring. Nathaniel eyed Shadrack, put an index finger to his lips. Pulled Shad into him and whispered, "Don't talk, we came here to find Miles, let's hope we ain't rustled upon some kinda bad."

Feet kept a repetitive mashing back and forth over the flooring upstairs. Nathaniel walked slowly up the stringer of stairs, bending his knees, and Shadrack came behind him. What he couldn't do was abandon the home, but he also couldn't place Shadrack in harm's way. He was in a fishing net with a blade to cut his way out—only there were hooks in the net as well, digging into him every time he chose the wrong movement. Miles could be upstairs, maybe in trouble; he was sauced to the gills on hallucinogenics and booze.

Footsteps kept tromping back and forth over the floor. Nathaniel and Shadrack kept taking one step after the next. The steps gave and squeaked until the two of them reached the door. Nathaniel hadn't planned this far ahead, and handed the light to Shadrack, whispering, "Keep the light on the door." His left hand gripped the aged metal knob, twisted, and listened to it click. Opened the door as if moving it through honey, in an exaggerated action. Once it was wide open, they heard the barking echo of a madman's voice and Nathaniel turned back to Shadrack's trembling hand and whispered, "Give me the light."

There was this static movie reel playing in her brain of how it started, but she couldn't remember how or even why. Only that her daddy persuaded Wylie and her with words. Telling them, *It's okay. You're just touching. It's called curiosity.*

But trying to normalize it, place the actions within one's psyche, there came an understanding of it being acceptable. The touching.

But it wasn't. And it never was.

The things that had passed between she and her brother represented a sickness from her daddy. From Whitey.

She often questioned, in the years after, where it came from, maybe from the war he served. What he'd seen or done over there with others.

Either way it started after his drinking increased, along with the verbal abuse toward their mother, and then once their mother left Whitey, the episodes became weekly and then nightly, but instead of a sitcom, they were like a sickcom. An addiction for her daddy.

Touch him, he'd say.

That was what he'd told her. And she did.

Touch her.

That was what he'd told him. And he did. Wylie's dry-as-a-cornhusker hand caressed pale cheeks, fingers tickled down her neck, his palm maneuvered over her early developed shapes.

There were sensations they'd each felt in the beginning. Warmth. Things their bodies did that they'd no control over.

Kiss her. Kiss him. His words would become unnerving, but acceptable at first; they each knew something wasn't right about what they were doing, what they were participating in, like they were acting or playing characters in an unknown game devoid of rules or boundaries, but being younger, impressionable, and her father being the figure of authority, she and her brother feared disappointing him, though they each felt their actions weren't correct, there was something wrong about all of it, but it was also exciting, yet as time passed and those commands, those actions, became recognized as feeling dirty, wrong, even shameful, they each felt as if they were just going through the motions, like actors in a movie, they would remove themselves from the situation, let their minds wander off to someplace else, like swimming in the river or playing in the woods, not wanting to anger their drunken father, fearing repercussions from him.

All the while, Whitey sat watching, sipping his brew.

In their teens they were addicts to these unknown endorphins. Hormones. These experiments, as Daddy referred to them as. But Shelby and Wylie never felt this was something normal that a brother and sister did with one another.

The movie reel in Shelby's brain became scratchy and went black. It was too much to remember. What she knew for certain was that as kids, Wylie and she had slowly became emotionally exhausted. As adults, they'd grown, never really dealing with what had transpired between them, trying to normalize it even though they never accepted it as normal, they just tried to ignore it. Forget it. They buried their actions in their work. In their daily routines and choices, replaced by music at bars, drinking with friends or somewhere alone, fishing from streams, dancing, or even hiking with Miles, she knew she'd buried most of what happened by focusing on a task when memories flared up, though there were some actions Shelby spoke to Miles about openly. And he listened, held her, and comforted her. Never judged, only listened.

Now, driving, these memories echoed and burned red-hot in her mind. Tears fell from her sight, warmed her cheeks like molten syrup. Shaking off the bend of pain-filled confusion, the lost gaps of time, there was a maddened fury from within as she steered the vehicle to her daddy's house.

Sound of gunfire bubbled from Miles's eardrums like a hydrogen bomb exploding beneath the ocean, turning, he realized the gunfire was upon he and the other marines. Then pain siphoned his spine, sunk and wormed into the rear of his skull. Hands became a liquid paste and he dropped his M16. Followed by the feeling of hands gripping and squeezing his arms, lugging him through the jungle foliage; around him others were being dragged too, the blades of growth nicking and splicing their arms and faces, a grip of bodies rushing him toward the clearing of flame, where a crazed-looking man stood over the female whose neck was a pasty tint of dark crimson from her throat being divided.

Nomadic in appearance, his dome-shaped head held locks that appeared like muddy stalactites all over his skull; he'd a sunken face half-painted by designs that danced with the shadows of the fire, the other side darkened by oily moisture and camo paint, looking as though he were the leader of the Mighty Mongrel Mob gang from New Zealand.

Miles's eyes rolled around within his head, everything was grainy and blurred, it was as though he were suspended in the air, hanging from a meat hook beneath each append-age, until the man smirked, and sound was reintroduced to Miles as the man spoke: "And what do we have before us? Purveyors of *war*? Spies of an *American* regiment? Or sabo-teurs of our *exodus*?"

Slowly his surroundings twisted the volume knob and there was the thump of grain sacks being released, of weight crashing to the earth, coming from Miles's left and then his right, he looked, one was Nafus, just an expanse of skin, fiber, and bones, with features flagging and sopping of blood, rolled over on his back, intestines splayed and half-removed, squeezing his lookers. Glancing to his right, Bull lay on his shoulder blades, stiff, paining for mercy, his chest rising fast, his right shoulder appeared to have been opened up by gunfire. The others? Miles had blacked out, had no idea how much time had passed, where or what happened to them, his mind was crisscrossed and disoriented from the blow to the rear of his skull.

One of the men who dragged Miles spoke. "Located

them several clicks back in the bush, lurking with rifles, taking aim, ready to engage us, left three others dead for feeding later, if needed, Captain."

The man chuckled, rubbed his chin, zeroed in, and pointed to Miles. "And what do I call you?" Miles looked up at him, unable to decide whether he'd speak. Trying to focus, to unblur his sight, which kept fogging, Miles was stealing glances to the perimeter, gathering a tempo, a means of escape, to figure a way to save his recon team; he was fighting for his bearings, because he viewed what they'd done to the female, recalled what these sick psycho fucks had done to the other villagers, the fog was lifting from his sight, and what he could make out were outlines embedded in the darkness, descending from trees upside down as though Christmas decorations, and he told the freak, "Knox, Miles. Knox."

"My men reference me as Yama. Lord Yama. We, my men, we're carnivores. Do you know what I mean when I speak this word?"

Miles nodded. "Meat eaters."

"Do you like to dine on meat?"

"As long as it moos."

"A comedian." He laughed. "And what branch of service are you affiliated with, Knox?"

"Marine. First Engineers."

The man chuckled. "Ha! For God's sake, a marine, I'd think you'd eat the ass out of a live Bengal tiger."

"Like I said, I prefer meat that moos," Miles mumbled.

"Do you know why men eat meat? Why they partake in the letting of fluid and tissue? The flesh of other mortals? 'Cause the blood of the enemy, it strengthens men. You're savoring their soul. Their strengths. It makes you stronger."

From the surrounding dark, sound of gunfire bounced. The cannibal stood earthy and silent, his attention to the darkness behind Miles. Then came the tussle of feet brushing through the surrounding foliage. And two more men appeared dressed down in jungle-patterned camo; in their grips they tugged and dragged Vega and Rut. Each broken open by carbine fire. Their uniforms dark with moisture, their appearances damaged and busted.

"More?" The nomad gestured.

"That one"—he pointed at Vega—"kneel him before me."

Vega was shedding a trail of damp, his boots' toes raking over the ground as two men held him before the leader, who reared down, held Vega's complexion beneath the chin.

"Such bone structure."

And before another breath was expelled, the nomad clung to a blade, raised it to the left side of Vega's head, met the fold between ear and skull, sliced Vega's ear from his head as though parting a radish. Vega screamed. And the carnivore screamed with a deviant laugh along with Vega. "Ah . . . Ah! Ha. Ha. Ha!"

Miles tried to break free from restraint, but hands gripped tighter, constrained his fight as his stomach rotated and hooked into a sickness, watching the carnivorous man slip it into his mouth, chewing and crunching the ear like he were ingesting a pork rind. Crunching it slow and deliberate.

From the ground Rut screamed, "You crazy son of a bitch, we're not the fucking enemy in this war!"

The flesh eater laughed. "This war? What you've been brainwashed to call this fucking cesspool of propaganda, where men bestow violence and ill will upon one another? It's a war of numbers, bodies opened up, dismembered, and scattered like fertilizer by whatever means necessary. Over here, everyone's the fucking enemy, have been since the treaty of 1954 and the country was divided at the seventeenth parallel!"

Miles lowered his head, counted his breaths, searched for his center, his composure, blocked out the history lesson, let his eyes gaze quick from side to side, pretended to be weak, feeble of mind, broken of spirit. He glanced to the shadows that bounced from the flames. Miles metered for disarmament, a way out. He needed an opening before he himself was opened up and became a reenactment of Jamestown's colonist cannibalism. So he listened to the psychotic propagations of this soldier who referenced himself to be King Yama, the Hindu god of death.

"Many have fallen to slaughter. And for what?" Yama said. "'Cause Ho Chi Minh declared war on the south, declared he was a communist? Then our government says sign up or be drafted? Defend your country? Destroy communism? Ha! What value does the US government place upon our lives? Is our government's life more meaningful than ours? Is that what they're saying, sending us to war to die 'cause these yellas are too weak to reap their own freedom? Fight their own battles? Is that how it's always going to be, we're too fucking weak to fight our own battles, let's get some good ole boys from the USA, the sons and daughters of the working because they fight harder and bleed better?"

Trample of foot punches the earth behind Miles; he can feel the heat of shadow lingering over him, then a hand digs into his scalp, the cold steel of an edge scrapes his neck. Miles quakes with a chill. He isn't ready to die. He *won't* die, as he fingers the cold pommel attached to the leather handle hidden in a scabbard on his thigh. Rolling his view to the side, he looked to Bull. Bull met his eyes, saw that Miles was a real marine. He wasn't laying down.

Pinhole of flame came through the black tunnel that Miles's mind had sunk into. Fighting the darkness, treading the black, until the gloam brightened. Expanded with the full-on explosion of color, followed by the feeling of his skin being pierced and pricked by pointed steel. Miles awoke to the spread of a split thumb and index at his lids. A man parting his vision. Barking questions like a rabid beast.

"Thought you's dead, your eye did a double deuce, you went weak-kneed on my ass. Now answer me this, why the fuck you trespassing in my home after all these years, huh? Can't you knock?"

"The hell are you spitting?"

"What are you after?"

"After?"

"Spill it to me, Knox! I wasn't born yesterday!"

Miles eyed the old man in front of him, who then rolled his head in a maddening direction to the opening behind him, keeping his right ear to the doorframe. He seemed to be listening and suddenly screamed, "Shut the fuck up, bitch!" He paused again and asked, "What? No, goddammit, I told you, I ain't taking no more of your shit, woman. They's uninvited company in here. Have some goddamned manner about your rotgut ass."

Miles was stuck in some madness again. Who was this man talking to? Better yet, who *was* this man? This was some alternate world of crazed lunacy he'd stepped into.

The old man twisted back to Miles, leering hard, fucking him with sight. From nowhere a length swung up from the old man's right side, smacked Miles's cheek with the barrel opening of a sawed-off 30/30, and said, "You fucking left me. Left me for them sons of bitches to feast on. I know you know what you done. Don't think I don't recognize you, sure, you're older, bit bigger, meatier, but you're still Miles Knox. A fucking *Devil Dog*. Leatherneck!"

Miles sat speechless, his muscles cramped, tendons ached and twitched with something like electric shock, deciphering the man's complexion of spiderwebbed skin and cigarette burns. Wrinkles. And a gray clawed cotton beard, hair a mess of uneven wires with singed ends. There was the taste of astonishment and even a bit of disillusionment—it was Vega. And he puckered his lips and spat at Miles, "Goddamned lucky I made it out."

"Made it outta where? I never left nobody over there, I saved who I could fucking save."

The man belted Miles across the face with the modified pistol butt of the 30/30, bellowed, "You spiny son of a bitch, calling me a falsifier, a deluder, a fucking liar? Gonna play webbed brained on me? I know where you been, what you done, you been in my patch, haven't you? Think 'cause we served together, that it somehow entitles you to my fucking hooch? That's why you come after all these goddamn years, ain't it?! Heard about the crazed farmer and his gummy purple-haired dope, didn't you? Heard ole man Vega got the premium red-eye smoke."

Miles spat blood. "No. I just crossed through it, on accident. Needed shelter from the fucking wind. The rain. Was . . . was . . . meeting Nathaniel." He remembered, he finally fucking remembered.

"Shelter? Nathaniel? Who the fuck's Nathaniel? Loose-lipped son of a bitch, you crossed through it. Got a mind to whoop your ass until cartilage in my elbows wears to bone on bone. I know you know they ate them others. Chewed they skin like tomcats lulling fresh bluegill guts. Just stringing it out in long greasy strands as if ramen noodles."

The bastard is crooked and rabid, Miles thought. Hadn't had his distemper shots. Needed to be dewormed. No way was this Vega. Wasn't he from Pennsyltucky? As he called it, which was actually Pennsylvania. He damn sure wasn't a Hoosier. Besides that, Vega didn't make it. This lunatic needed his head chopped off and sent to the US Naval Research Laboratory for observation. Talking about things he couldn't know, shouldn't know. How did he know Miles's name? About the war? The shit he'd witnessed and couldn't forget? Shit that was more than scarred into his psyche. The drugs. It was the LSD. This was all in his damn head.

Miles clasped his eyes shut. Gritted his teeth. Only to open them. Hoping the crazy was gone.

But he wasn't.

Miles stared into the man. Studied his features. The longer he stared, unblinking, the more familiar the man's features became. On the right side of his mangy facade, there was a numbed mess of folded skin where his ear should've been.

No. No. No, Miles told himself. *This isn't real.*

The old son of a bitch got up in Miles's face and began barking like a rabid hound. "Why are you eye-fucking me like uncured meat? Huh? The fuck is wrong with you? Your eyes, they's dilated like fucking onyx marbles, Knox!"

Miles jerked back. Clasped his eyes. Sweat smeared and

ossified his frame. He tensed and flexed his muscles. Felt as though he was ready to separate, to rip out of his own pigment. Veined and bulging, he rocked back and forth, listening to the rattle of air from outside slamming what sounded like the screen door, and the man yapped, "What? Woman, I told you, they's fucking company out here."

Miles exhaled a deep breath. Quit rocking. Peeled his lids open and listened. Only hearing the beat and spanking rhythm of his heart behind his sternum; he could hear no woman's voice. No lips gabbling. No tones for speech. Nothing female. No woman. Nothing beyond the storm that trounced against the home, with the smell of mildewed lumber and dead foliage hovering around the room. The old man got back up in Miles's face once more. "Remember that loud and vicious son of a bitch. Remember him filleting Nafus before your fucking lookers? Huh? Do you?"

Keeping Shadrack close to him, the light shining on the water-stained and rotted lumber of the home, Nathaniel saw nothing but relics of times past, ceramic dishes, pictures of men and their hunting dogs coated by dust. A table for eating with an arrangement of chairs. But somewhere a voice bickered and bounced off the walls, the floors, the ceiling. Only it was distant and muffled. With the Maglite in one hand, the .45 in the other, Nathaniel followed the sound that grew louder.

Flames danced across Miles's complexion with the blood-stained Ka-Bar across his throat. His digits brushed the ribbed handle of his blade. Yama held up a hand. "Let Miles be the voyeur to the expiration of his fellow brothers. Let him view their demise. Their reckoning. And let us start our actions upon that one." Yama pointed to Nafus.

Miles was on his knees. A man at each shoulder. A hand gripping each flank of arm. Nafus was dragged, screaming, "Let go of me, you fuckers!"

"Oh yes!" Yama barked. "Yes. Yes. Yes. This one's got fight in him. A true warrior. His blood will bring us great strength."

Nafus was forced down onto the ground before the square-shouldered barbarian of a man, held and pressed into the earth. Yama reached down, ran his fingers over Nafus's jawline, and gripped it. "Love the sharp-edged marrow of your face." His other hand coursed an edge across his complexion as if it were a whetstone for sharpening, then came the slice, the cut and crank of cartilage and dividing of flesh, followed by the screams as Nafus's nose was severed.

Blood rivered and coated the ground. Panic and pain ribbed Miles's ears, his eyes scoured the perimeter once again. He had to do something. For whatever reason boot-camp came roaring into his brain with the drill instructor training them, M1 raised over head. Marines shouting the words "Kill! Kill! Kill!" echoing in his brain until he had no other ambition, only reaction.

Yama delivered the nose to his lips. Miles's stomach twisted as the man's teeth crunched down on the cartilage; it sounded as if he were eating potato chips. Yama chewed. And chewed. Nafus welled and moaned. And Yama questioned, "Tell me, Knox, how do you like your meat—rare and bloody, somewhere in the middle, or over a swelling spit of orange flames and well done?"

Everything in that moment lost its sturdiness; everything was tossed into the air and floating down, scattered like snowflakes, delivered in snapshots of all that he'd endured and viewed, the roads he'd traveled on the rear of a tank, oil covering the dirt, C-4 fused and ready to blow ordnances, village women posing with GIs and the jungle and all its hellish traps. Fields of rice. The hooches they'd built. The reason Miles had enlisted into the Marine Corps, to be tough. To serve his country, to kill communism. Then silence coated him. A chill beset his flesh. And everything was one motion. Removing the blade from his side as he was being pulled to standing, as Yama turned his eyes away from him, his outline monstrous and thick, flames from the fire shifting and bouncing like strobe lights over everyone's shape, Miles jerked his left arm free, the blade cutting the air, swiping one of the men's vision, painting the air with blood and screams as the man dropped to his knees, his face buried into his hands. Turning to the man on his

right, Miles redirected the blade into the man's rib cage
with a thud, passed bone and stabbed his lung only to pull
it free, the release of fluid followed and Miles came forward,
meeting Yama as he turned to his men's screams. Yama's
stomach took Miles's thrust quick as a shank in a prison
takedown, but he still drove a palm into Miles's right eye,
dropped Miles to his knee. The knife was dug into Yama's
kidney, fingering it, he could not pull it free. Laughed until
he began to cough. Fell to the dirt, eyed Miles. Then M16
gunfire punctured the floodgates for sound. Bull held a rifle
and began shooting, tearing open Yama's men. Bodies
sprayed and enriched the surrounding air.

Then everything came in flashes. Snapshots. Yama and
Miles eyed one another. Their hearts pounding. Bull indented Yama's temple with the rifle's heated barrel. Yama's
arms were damp and soiled from hands to elbows as though
he were coated in latex. It was Nafus's blood. The knife
protruded from his kidney. He laughed. "Just remember
you're removing me, taking my breath from this world, but
it will change nothing. We soldier for the same government. There's more men like me doing the same all over
Vietnam. Killing the guilty and the innocent 'cause they're
one and the same."

The shot came hard. Marrow and skull and crimson
flaked over Miles's face. Followed by a world of dark. Sound
of air being sliced. A broken rhythm, radioing base camp.
Giving coordinates to their location. Salvaging what could
be salvaged. Miles only wanted to forget.

And some of the actions he did forget, because now he couldn't remember what happened to Vega.

Cabin pressure raised within inner ears of sound, popped with the wielding of butt stock stampeding Mile's forehead. The old man came at him. Belted him between his lookers once more. Knocked him against the table that scuffed the floor. There was the punch of air all around the home. Cracking and splitting. Miles, muscled and hefty, came from the table as though bouncing from the ropes of a boxing ring. Slingshotting at the bony cocktail of an elder man, he howled a whooping cry of war.

Wrapping his arms about Vega's circumference, he drove him through the entrance to the next room, running him into an old fudge-colored Buck Stove. Shower of dust, crunch of dead insect shells underfoot. The old man belted Miles in the face with his forehead. Miles shook it off, rode a right cross into Vega's sternum. Raised a left leg and kicked him into the wall. The rifle pointed upward, gunfire rang out. Ceiling fell onto the men, the clench of pinching and stinging, Miles swatted his arms, pissants, hundreds of them raining down from overhead. The rifle came at him baseball bat style; Miles held his biceps at his side, protecting his ribs just as he did in his days of boxing, took the blow from the rifle, grabbed at the stock, swung the old man across the room. The wall gave and Sheetrock crumbled to the floor. Vega huffed, "We's just young men, you and I, we were sons, trained to kill."

Miles stood with the wind thrusting outside the home, wobbling and creaking the house's siding, the sounds of laughter echoing throughout the walls. Miles shook his head, clasped his eyes, and palmed his ears, trying to make it all stop. Not knowing what was real any longer.

Opening his eyes and lowering his arms, Vega came at him once again. Fists coming on like granite, Miles loaded a hard left jab into the man's face. The give of nose went liquid over his knuckles. Vega fell into the next room, where a wooden rocker sat in the room's center, a shape residing within it, ragged clothing and skeleton hands; the person was expired, and Miles came at the old man, drove a right cross into his sternum, knocked him into the shape within the rocker, knocked the shape to the floor, where it crumbled.

"No!" the old man screamed. "No! You've whittled her to bones. Broken her to pieces."

"You crazed old bastard."

From above the roof rumbled, sounded as if it were going to be torn from the trusses and tossed across the wilderness. Miles dropped to the floor, wanted to find shelter, fighting the sounds and images, keeping his eyes closed, in his mind the air rained purple all around him, the shear of bones, the rattle of meat, there came the faint chatter, whispers within the wind like steel carving through tin. A maddening rush of blood banged around in Miles's eardrums.

Opening his eyes, lowering his hands, turning, Vega stood shaking, looking at him. "Don't recognize me, do you? Vega. Remember Yama cut my fucking lobe off and ate it like cracklins?"

"No, everyone but Bull and me was dead. You . . . you're haunting me, you're not real! It's the drugs!"

"I'm real, real as you and your flesh and this goddamned rotted hardwood our boot soles is mashed into. Ain't dead. You only wished I's dead."

Rage balled in Miles's gut. "Fuck you, old man, fuck you!"

Left foot then right, Miles approached Vega with a straight right cross only to feel the crack in his ribs, the 30/30's pistol grip hatcheting into him. Followed by a burning light and a booming voice that erupted from behind.

There was the flesh of a smaller bone structure rattling against the ranch house's scuffed door. Wind had scooted the chairs across the split slab of concrete front porch, tossed them out into the unmowed yard. From behind the door came the creak of flooring, the door opened, and a whiff of salty sweat layered with booze and a complexion greasier than a Lay's potato chip met the stench of an unbathed woman.

With thinning hair glossed back over his skull, Whitey belched pure grain alcohol from sandpaper lips, his eyes hazed by a glaring of not recognizing the outline that stood before him.

Mashing his cheek up into his eye, Whitey stood in thought, reaching below a lard-colored gut of red and purple stretch marks, and dug at his crotch with one hand, the other hand postured a fifth of Dark Eyes Vodka and he parted his mouth with, "The fuck happened to you?"

Something like electricity pulsed within Shelby's frame and through gritted teeth she said, "Where do you want me to start?"

Taking a long draw from his bottle of booze, he swallowed and told her, "Great, you come by to toss me the blame game, that why you're here?"

Smirking, Shelby told him, "Oh, we're gonna do more than toss words."

"Then talk, quit wasting my time, I got drinking to do."

Tired of standing with the wind howling behind her, Shelby elbowed past Whitey and stepped into the living room, where beer cans and empty liquor bottles decorated the coffee table and Brillo pad carpet. A mirror hung behind a worn leather sofa that sat with reclining ends; the overhead glow of dusty ceiling fan lights and lamps in the corners flickered. Taking in the home's appearance, the gnat-stained ceiling that appeared like dots of chocolate bubbles in spots, Shelby observed how her daddy had let the home fall into a deeper state of disgust from one visit to the next.

Closing the door behind him, following Shelby, Whitey told her, "Been a while since you come to visit your ole man, usually I'm calling you."

Shelby turned around to face Whitey in the room's center. "How ironic."

Standing red-eyed, he said to her, "You've brought a helluva wind storm as your passenger. So what is it you got on your chest, you look like hell warmed over."

Taking another swig of the vodka, Whitey fell down into the couch and looked up at Shelby with pink-smeared eyes.

All Shelby could think was how pathetic of a human being her daddy was. Worked up with the fragments of memory in her head, of everything she'd been through, Shelby was itching to leap from her own hide. Twitching, she ran a hand over her complexion and through her wrung-out locks of hair; pushing strings behind her ear, she felt her own filth as she stared at Whitey and said, "You, you're a bastard. A monster and—"

Looking angered and confused by her words, Whitey cut her off with, "—You going through daddy issues? What is it I done that's so horrific, caused you to shed your clothing for wads of cash, date a man as old as me? You telling me that's my fault?"

"Asshole, you know what you done to me and Wylie. Shit you pushed us to do while you watched."

"This why you come over here, to bark about your

upbringing? Know what, I never forced the two of you to do nothing that wasn't already born into you. It was curiosity was all. Don't go blaming me for silly kid shit you two done."

Anger coursed through her entire body and she pointed at Whitey, her voice rising. "You're sick, you tried to weigh Mom down 'cause she wanted to work, to earn her own way, her own money, you enforced hell upon her 'cause she wasn't dependent on you for anything, called her a slut and a whore knowing she was none of them words."

Shelby remembered her mother working late nights at an aluminum plant, coming home and dealing with verbal bruisings from a drunk husband. Leaving work to bail Whitey out of jail for bar fights or drinking and driving. Whitey gambled money away on lottery tickets, card games, or ball games at the bar instead of paying bills. Her mother could only take so much.

"Wait a damn minute," Whitey sputtered. "Your mother, she was a real piece of work, leaving you, Wylie, and me at my lowest. I can't take all the damn credit." Whitey took another tilt from the Dark Eyes.

"At your lowest?" Shelby scoffed. "You didn't *want* any help, all you did was lay in a bottle after work and gamble, you quit being a daddy to me and Wylie and a husband to Mom. Treated us like we's some incestual lab project. And all these years later, Wylie can't even hold a job, got hooked on dope, fucking overdosed, and here I am playing the role of mother to you!"

"OD'd? I just saw him last week, you . . . you're talking crazy, hell, you *are* crazy, sound like your madcow-brained mother. You want some cheese with that whine?"

Whitey's words removed the training wheels from Shelby's mind and she started pedaling for herself and Wylie both as a shit-eating grin painted her face and her voice changed to a squeaky Bob Dylan whine.

Last week? Hear that shit? Way he talks about you, about us, Mom, like we ain't no count.

Whitey paused with the bottle in his hand, held a look of complication about his face. "Who the fuck you talking to with that fake-ass mouse voice?"

Reaching into her hooded sweatshirt's front pocket, Shelby tugged the revolver free, pointed it at Whitey's head, and thumbed the hammer, speaking in that mousy voice:

You need to be ended!

Whitey posted a glare at Shelby and shook his head. "Think you're scaring me into some kind of admission of guilt with your little *acting* routine? If you're gonna end me, best pay a second visit to your mother, do the same to her, she's anything but innocent."

Shelby and Wylie, speaking as one, holding the gun, replied, *Anything Mom's done was brought on by you, your taking advantage of her, your drinking and verbal abuse.*

Whitey chuckled and belched, reached into his stretched-out shirt pocket for a hard pack of Camels, thumbed the lid open, shook one loose, fished a lighter embedded down in the side of the couch, fired up the cigarette, and blew smoke.

"Yeah, Miss fucking Innocent," he said. "I come home from 'Nam, had a head full of war, didn't even lose my way, I wanted out, wanted to forget. Then I go to the Four Way Pub in Elizabeth, shoot a game of pool one night, and in your mother walks, bare feet and dirty footed with cutoffs and a goddamn tube top, skin the stain of hickory, she sent shivers down every vertebra of my spine, still does to this day just thinking about her, she wanted me to buy her a drink. Next thing I know she got her tongue down my throat, legs around me on the pool table in front of the customers. Years later I find out she raped a fellow in the bathroom in front of a crowd of onlookers, poor son of a bitch was too drunk to fight her off of him. Your mother was deflowered behind the skating rink before she's outta middle school. We had you and Wylie, made the most of it. She changed. Grew up. But then wanted a job, got a good one, but I never wanted her to work."

Switching back to Wylie's voice, Shelby told Whitey, "Yeah, but Mom never forced us to touch one another while she sat back and watched."

Drawing hard on his cigarette, Whitey offered a confused glance at the switching of Shelby's voices. He shook his head and said, "You never been where I been, seen the shit I seen. Men killing children. GIs forcing village mothers to have sex while their husbands watched, tossing grenades between the legs of males and females that backstabbed soldiers with bad intel, created casualties. That shit, it weighs a man's soul, erases one's moral compass. Soots whatever heart you got into a tar pit. You can try to bury it, but it's always there waiting to be unburied. Not making excuses, I had some kinda unfiltered crazy in my head."

Still training the .38 on Whitey's head, Shelby bent and contorted her body forcefully. Her eyes cut through Whitey, and, in her own voice this time, she told her father, "I got no more room for the baggage you're carrying, the pain you caused."

Taking a hard pull from his cigarette, Whitey exhaled smoke and told her, "I don't gotta listen to this horseshit in my own damn house. I did what I did." As he tried to stand up from the couch, his face red, his one hand holding the bottle of vodka, cigarette coaling from his lip, Shelby pulled the trigger.

Couch leather exploded to Whitey's left, the smell of gunpowder and burned hide filled the air, and Whitey's ears rang while his eyes globed round like two fresh scoops of vanilla ice cream; he fell back into the couch and lost his grip around the bottle of Dark Eyes, spilling it on the floor, as the Camel cigarette dotted the air with ash. Raising his hands, which twitched, he coughed and pleaded, "Hold on a goddamned minute, Shelby. I'm your damn daddy, put that gun down, I done seen too many men die and lived to tell it and I won't be put down by my own daughter!"

"You shoulda thought about that when you's making Wylie and me fondle and rub one another while you watched, telling us to do things that wasn't supposed to be done between brothers and sisters!"

"Done told you I never done nothing wasn't—"

Shelby tugged the trigger once more.

Mascara smeared down her cheeks like a Rorschach test. Slap of lead pierced and expanded tissue, fluid coursed from meat and vein, Whitey sat in shock, breathing heavy, his crimson face mashed up like a Shar-Pei, right hand holding his left shoulder, and he shouted, "You fucking shot me!"

Shelby twisted her face into an odd arrangement, looked to the blurred shape in the mirror behind the leather couch, shook her head, jaws chattered with a slight grinding of teeth as she watched her face eclipse and morph into Wylie staring back at her. Lips purple, face a cold blue. Hair long, wiry, and dead as field corn during a drought. Then came the static once more and the shape split into two faces, hers and Wylie's. Their lips parted and spoke, regular and whiny combined.

Things you done, *can never be undone*. You don't *deserve to inhale air* no damn more.

Palm to shoulder, red spit through the division of digits, and Whitey stuttered, "Fine . . . I . . . I—"

Don't matter *what you say, fact remains*, she and *I are forever fucked* 'cause of what you done.

"—I'm . . . sorry . . . I . . . things I seen in war, what soldiers made VC villagers do, I couldn't undo it in my head, what else do you want me to say?"

Tears began to drip and froth in the cracked red globes of Whitey's donut-glazed-over eyes.

We're *gonna* kill you. *End you.* Right. Fucking. *Now!*

Whitey looked up to Shelby. Frustrated. Teeth gritted. "The hell is wrong with you, your damn voice?"

Shelby stepped fast, gun pointed until it rammed into the fryer-grease complexion of Whitey. Flinch of his heart. Blood falling from his shoulder. Finger pulled on the trigger, hammer to firing pin. Combustion spit Whitey's brains out the rear of his skull like vomit. Rending fluid and matter all over the walls and carpet. Faint shuffle of moans and wails became screams. Eyes closed followed by silence.

Shelby released the pistol, which thudded to the floor. Stepped from in front of her daddy. Maneuvered from the living room and out of the house to the outdoor air, where nothing seemed real except the wind reeling over her face. Over her entire being. Fresh air.

It came like a barge light on the Ohio River, burning and blinding Miles. Shielded by a wall of dark, it was a voice. "Miles?"

Feelings of being strung upside down, all the blood rushing to his head, bones spongy, mouth watery like he could toss his gut from his orifice at any minute, Miles barked, "Kill that fucking light."

Thumbing the light off, two shapes stood in the mossy,

mildewed area, eyeing Miles, who tried to adjust his sight from the bright light; looking around, Vega was gone. If he was ever there.

"Who were you arguing with?" Nathaniel questioned.

"Not real sure."

"Didn't see another shape in here with you," Nathaniel told Miles.

"I think I saw someone or something in here with me, but the acid and the booze has got me in a destabilized state of mind."

"Thought we's meeting on the opposite of the river in White Cloud?" Nathaniel asked, annoyed.

"I got my wires crossed, lost what reasoning I had to do anything, came in here 'cause of the wind and rain, I think," Miles told Nathaniel.

"Lucky I caught a glimpse of you crossing the river, came around looking. Can you maneuver?"

"I can do whatever it takes to get the hell out of here. Why don't you navigate, let me get my bearings before whoever I's bickering with makes another appearance."

Out of the house, wind whipping all around them, wilderness bending and shifting, Miles followed Nathaniel and Shadrack, the flashlight cutting through the night, Shadrack clinging to Nathaniel's back pocket, glancing back at Miles every now and then. To Miles, one moment everything appeared rifled, chewed and spit through a wood chipper. Then he'd blink his eyes and everything would switch back to normal. He kept questioning whether he had seen the old man, the man who professed himself to be Vega.

Nathaniel said he'd heard one voice. Maybe Miles was out of his mind.

Miles's head rang and he wondered what time it was. The wind was coming and going as they worked through the cornfield. Then onto the road and to the truck. The world around him felt disheveled. Unreal. Approaching the large shape that was Nathaniel's Dodge, Miles opened the passenger's-side door. His mind welted. Helping Shadrack into the truck, then climbing in beside him, closing the door, everything was quiet.

Nathaniel turned the key to fire up the diesel. And all the quiet disappeared.

"Where we headed next?"

Miles glared at Nathaniel. The boy between them. "What time is it?"

Off in the distance, the sky was appearing less navy colored. Nathaniel laid a digit on the CD player of the dash. "Five thirty a.m." Then he pressed play. Roger Waters streamed from the speakers with "What God Wants." Jeff Beck on guitar.

"Whitey's. Wylie crashes there when Shelby's gone. It's time we pull the last of the cattle from the pasture. Bring them back to the barn," Miles said. "He ain't there, we're outta options."

Shifting to drive. Rotation of rubber against holed pavement powered them down the road.

Clearing his throat, his mouth was a rusted bucket in the summer heat, and he asked Nathaniel, "You really only hear me in that house?"

"I did only hear you," Shadrack said.

Glancing down at the boy, Miles smirked. "All right then, that settles it."

"Settles what?" Nathaniel asked, hanging a right at the end of the road, turning onto Highway 62.

"I'm batshit fucking crazy. And I ain't real damn sure about some other things either."

"Sure about what other things?"

Miles took a deep breath and swallowed hard. "Long story short, when I's overseas, I was drafted into a special unit to hunt some real bad men. We found them and got into the thick."

"What's thick?" Shadrack interrupted.

"A bad situation," Nathaniel said.

"The thick was, we got captured. In the end, only me and another guy that went by the nickname of Bull was pulled out, least that's what I can recall. There was Nafus that was dismembered. Skipper, Rut, Crust, who I can't recall what happened to. And a guy named Vega whose ear was severed. Only I don't recall him dying nor do I remember him being rescued. It's always been a black spot in my mind."

Miles went quiet. Only thing that could be heard was the tires on the road, the wind outside the truck, and the sound of the CD player playing Roger Waters. "There was an old man back in that house, one I was arguing with, accusing me of trying to get his dope, then of leaving him behind in 'Nam, said he was Vega."

"No shit?"

"No shit. I didn't know if it was the drugs, 'cause I keep flashing back to the war, keep seeing dead men I served with and hearing all kinds of crazy sounds."

"If it puts your mind at ease, when I's a county cop, the farmer that was said to have owned the place bought it after old man Mercer passed, committed suicide in the house, was a Vietnam war vet, some said it was haunted by his soul, he'd relocated here from another state, don't recall his name nor the state. Never met him. Squatters we busted growing dope there seeing as they didn't own the land, they couldn't be tied to it if it were discovered, but some of the folks we caught there was pretty shaken, saying they's a ghost or some such shit in the house," Nathaniel told Miles.

And Miles said, "Guess that only makes me part batshit crazy."

Memories came rushing in her mind, pin bruises imprinting on skin, hang of a plunger with the needle dug into a blackened hole of a forearm; his flesh was frostbite-cold-to-the-touch, her brother lay unmoving like petrified wood washed up on a riverbank, only it wasn't a riverbank, it was the floor in the spare bedroom of her home, the pill bottle empty. The pills smashed. Glass of water, still warm. Pills shot in the vein and setting up. Clogging. He was dead as roadkill.

Looking at Wylie then, Shelby drifted somewhere in her mind. Into a closet of names etched, carved, and painted on the interior's walls, same place she and Wylie took refuge as children, a bare bulb from a lamp on the floor, and their shirts and pants hanging from hangers. It was their hiding place as kids on a rainy day. She snapped out of it and inhaled deep, dug her hands beneath Wylie's pits, grunted through the tears, tugged, jerked, and dragged him. Dragged him through her home. Over the carpet and across hardwood. Out the front door to her car. To the trunk. She'd not have him dead. Not in there. And she'd not bury him. She'd not bury him 'cause . . . things went mad in her mind. Looking at him. He wouldn't die. He couldn't die. She wouldn't let him. He wouldn't let him. In her mind, she was him. He was her. Maybe it was a maternal thing or maybe she'd always been crazy.

The images smeared through Shelby's head, inhaling, tears glossed her cheeks and she remembered begging to God.

Why? Why did you take him?

She got no answer.

And her mental state frayed and split, and somewhere in there, she'd lost it. A volley of balls swinging back and forth. Never stopping. Momentum gaining and in her head things were wrong. They'd always been wrong.

And now, standing behind her Camaro, the wind blowing, the area was getting less dark, she told herself, it was over, Bedford and Judy were no more and her father was no more. There'd be no more hurt, no more bad, and from behind her, sound lit up her peripheral along with headlights, it was the sound of a diesel engine. The lights of a truck.

With the clink of gravel beneath truck tires, headlights shined on an image standing behind a vehicle, their back turned to Nathaniel, Shadrack, and Miles. Energy began to build and circulate, Miles's insides flipped a switch, heart rate sped up, and nerve became adrenaline.

Braking hard. Shifting to park. Gravel dust was confetti-fog. Motion lights on the corners of Whitey's house and the porch offered a quartz light that opened the surrounding shadows. Miles came from the truck. "Shelby?" His heart was racing. As he got closer he noticed the air around her wasn't lined with the scent of fresh flowers and perfumed lotions and powders, qualities Miles acquainted with Shelby. What surrounded her now was a stench, filth. Full-on rot.

Shelby stood stiff as sun-dried coral glaring at the trunk of her car. Behind her, lifting his arm, Miles gripped her shoulder, turned her toward him. She looked near catatonic, her lips the shade of blood. Eyes without sleep appeared marbled by abrasion. Nearly black, attired in a hooded sweatshirt. Skin bloodless and opal.

Unsure if what he was viewing was real or part of a hallucination, vivid colors and the swelling of shapes and objects danced around Shelby's head; regardless, Miles sensed something wasn't right. Grasping Shelby's forearm, feeling the cotton sleeve, it was caked with grime, stiff, and her face unwashed. Sunken. Holding a dumbed-down stare as if she'd no idea he was standing in front of her, sensing his grip around her arm. Reminding Miles of a crazed, flesh-eating zombie from *Return of the Living Dead*; he was waiting for her to jump to life, screaming, "BRAINS, MORE BRAINS!"

Instead, all at once, Shelby snapped, "No!" Jerked her forearm from his grip.

Behind Miles, Nathaniel's tone echoed as he told Shadrack, "Stay put."

Truck door slammed, followed by the clank and give of aggregation beneath boots, Nathaniel approached from behind Miles, as Miles tried to wrap his mind around why she'd pull from his touch. "It's me, Miles. I ain't seen sight nor hair of you in over a week, something's outta focus here and I'm too fucked up and stringy minded to place a finger on it, you gotta tell me what's going on, you ain't been at work nor called."

Twisting her head sideways in a maniacal state, Shelby said, "You ain't the boss of me."

"No, I'm not, nor am I your keeper, only concerned. There's some real trouble surrounding you, lotta questions that need cleared up about—"

Beside Miles, Nathaniel interrupted him, delivered a bit of pent-up frustration and barked, "Shelby, we're looking for Wylie, where is he?"

Shelby shook her head. Turning sideways from Miles and Nathaniel. Shoulders slumped, she inhaled deep, exhaled slow, and pointed. "In the Camaro."

Stepping quick to the passenger's side, Nathaniel opened the squeaking door, the interior light flicked on, he looked to the front and back seat. His truck lights burning away the remaining darkness around them. Looking back at Shelby, he snapped, "Kind of game you playing? Only thing that's in here is the smell of something that's lapsed."

Miles reached for her once more, gently touched her shoulder, and she rolled her body away. "Whatever's going on, you can unload it on me, Shelby. Your brother's tied to some bad shit."

Gritting her teeth, a single tear dragged down her claw-marked face, and Miles knew something horrible had happened, and in a low tone she said, "Don't you think I know that."

"Baby, then tell us where your brother's at."

Shelby's head turned awkwardly, slanted, and her tone swapped to a squeaky manifestation and said, "I'm right fucking here, idiot."

Miles stepped back, unsure if it was the LSD or if this was real and he raised his voice: "What the hell is going on with you?"

Nathaniel came from the Camaro, holding a disturbed expression, looking at Shelby, who stepped backward, with each man watching her face, her brows arrowed down over her vision, offering an evil stare. Miles looked at Nathaniel, said, "They's something not right in her head and it's not the LSD fucking with me."

Shelby told Miles, "Ain't nothing wrong with me. Clean the damned turtle wax from your ears, maybe you could understand my English."

Nathaniel shook his head, reached, and gripped Shelby's arm to shake some sense into her. "Tired of this charade you're leading us on. We've been through hell all night to find you and your damn brother."

Pulling her arm free, she demanded, "Why?"

"I got reason to believe he killed my brother and sister-in-law for Oxy."

Shelby laughed. "I killed them. Took they fucking drugs. They money. Your brother sold me a bad batch, then was holding out, lying to me. I wanted payback."

Rage filled Nathaniel's complexion. "The hell you spitting, you're Shel—"

Shelby's complexion blistered with anger.

Nathaniel and Miles stood without words. Suddenly the sound of ungreased door hinges squeaked, the Dodge's truck door unbarred, the sound carried with feet mashing down on the gravel, tiny pats and Shadrack stopped beside Nathaniel and pointed, with excitement and fear in his tone, sucking in mucus, he yelled, "It's the *regular*, *she* shot Mom and Dad!"

Nathaniel's eyes darted from Shadrack up to Miles, then to Shelby. A hollowness filled each man. Nathaniel shook his head in disbelief. "Why?"

And Shelby laughed. "He just told you why, your brother sold him bad shit, he wanted payback."

Losing all sense of discipline, of right from wrong, Nathaniel saw red. Started to reach behind him. Removed his .45. Miles moved toward Nathaniel quickly, placed himself in front of Shelby. "Don't! This isn't the way to handle it. She's out of her head! This don't add up."

"She's gonna be outta her head, brains and all," Nathaniel said, fuming.

Miles reached for Nathaniel's right wrist; clamping down, he had age and strength. "This is for the law to figure out. You got a dead brother and sister-in-law, a nephew to consider! To raise," Miles pleaded. Keeping the .45 pointed to the ground, Nathaniel's mantra streamed through his mind: force should get returned by stringing, burning, or beating, fair was fair, and he told Miles, "Don't strum me like an outta-tune guitar, she murdered my family, took Shad's parents from him, there's consequences."

"There are consequences, but you're not the decider of those consequences," Miles said.

"Best slide your grip from me you know what's best."

"Not till you release the .45, calm the fuck down."

"You ever lost something blood related, Miles?"

"I've lost plenty of blood. Seen and done things that'd wilt your fucking hide to a hot puddle of candle wax."

"Sure you have, but to lose your own flesh, once it's taken, it can never be gotten back."

"Anytime flesh is removed it can never be replaced, but you got a kid to worry about now, this ain't about me, I'm not gonna let you drive a nail in your own coffin."

Nathaniel paused. Darted his vision down beside him, his vision took in the shape of a small version of himself, wet eyes looked up at him, a tiny hand touched Miles's grip on top of Nathaniel's hand holding the pistol, followed by words, "Uncle Nate! Stop! Please stop!"

Staring back into the face of this monstrous wall of a man, Nathaniel thumbed the hammer of the .45. Miles eased his grip and Nathaniel raised his left hand up slowly, as if surrendering. "We're good," Nathaniel said to Miles.

Miles nodded. "All right."

Nathaniel slid the .45 down into his waist. Regaining his bearings, Miles said, "We'll find Wylie, phone the sheriff, figure out who done what."

Shadrack wrapped his arms around Nathaniel's right thigh, pressed the side of his moist face against denim. Nathaniel laid a comforting palm on the boy's back.

Behind Miles, Shelby said, "He's in the trunk."

Miles turned to Shelby. "What?"

"The trunk. Wylie's in the trunk."

Nathaniel asked, hurried, "The keys, where are the keys?"

With a face of rage and tears falling down her worn cheeks, Shelby told him, "They's in the ignition."

Going back into the car, reaching to the right side of the steering, Nathaniel pulled the keys from the ignition. Walked to the rear of the car. Pressed the key into the silver lock. Turned the key. Lifted the trunk.

Shielding his nose and mouth with his forearm from the stench, Nathaniel yelled, "Holy fuck!"

He stepped back away from the trunk. The soggy smell of rot reeked stronger and more defined. Miles pulled Shadrack away. Pressed a hand over the boy's face. "Don't need to be a witness to this."

"Shit!" Nathaniel shouted. "Shit! Shit!"

"Guess Wylie was in the car," Miles mumbled.

Shelby raised both hands, palmed her face. Low-level sobbing began to build.

"They's no guess. He's in the car. Plunger and needle is still intact. Looks to have OD'd."

"Take your nephew to the truck. I'll keep an eye on her."

"I got some zip ties. She needs to be restrained."

Swallowing his pride, Miles agreed. "Get 'em. Then watch her, I'll go in, use Whitey's phone to contact the sheriff."

Unbalanced in his brain, Miles left Nathaniel to watch Shelby. Stepping inside the house, smell of damp iron haunted the air, and it hit Miles all at once: Whitey hadn't come outside to address the situation, to confront the trespass upon his property. And seated on the couch, an outlined mess of brain and blood, Miles's boots crunched over the floor, viewing the graffiti of what appeared to be a single bullet hole opening Whitey's complexion, his face an exploded Crayola red crayon. Head bent back over the couch. .38 on the floor. Bottle of Dark Eyes spilled between his feet. Dead cigarette butt stuck to his lip. Shoulder expanded by gunshot. Blood turning black. The smell was equal to the energy in the home: death.

"You're too late. Too fucking late," Miles said, standing beside the couch. "She finally did it. Killed your ass."

Miles knew. Knew some of what her father had done to her. To Wylie. The mental abuse. Things a father shouldn't do to his daughter, his son. Destroyed them from the inside out. Miles thought he was changing that. Thought they were changing each other. Mending and soldering wounds. Looking over the house, the mess of magazines. Books. Empty beer cans, whiskey and vodka bottles. Clothes piled and strung, the stupor of existence. Crackhead wouldn't live here, they'd be ashamed. Wasn't like Whitey was without a good wage. He flew a chopper for law. Drew a government pension from the army because of an injury in 'Nam.

The LSD had pushed through Miles's mind, the colors had come and gone, and the world was breathing an ugly sound, leaving a texture Miles didn't care to feel. In the kitchen he found a shit-green rotary dial phone. Lifted it up. Dialed 911. Told the operator, "Harrison County.

"One man has been shot in the head. Another man appears to have OD'd.

"No, ma'am, neither man appears to be breathing.

"Yes, ma'am, that's the address. Name's Knox, Miles Knox. I ain't going nowhere."

EPILOGUE

DEMONS DANCED IN HIS MIND. Screaming and salivating. Flesh manacled and oozing over skeletons of men, crumbling from shape, only to re-form. Gunfire rang a soundtrack of guitars and evil shrieks. Miles, running among the skinless and veiny frames of muscle and tendon. Slags of artillery, heated soil, and combusting wilderness. Then came the kick of legs and the pant of breath from lungs being charred by steaming liquid. Roller coasters of sweat attained to a second layer of skin and he awoke. Sheets damp. Being pulled and changed. He'd slept nearly sixteen hours the past two days. No sounds within his home. Only his body popping and twisting from age.

Walking down the hall, beat and worn, he thought of her. Shelby. What would become of her? His mind was numb with her face, frame, voice, scent, touch, her memory.

Entering the kitchen, he pulled his needles from a drawer, removed them from their packaging. Grabbed his vials from a cupboard, pierced the top of his first glass cylinder, punctured the lid, loaded the plunger, and stuck his thigh.

Pulling a gallon jug of water from the metallic fridge, removing the cap, he chugged it down. He was dry, needed to hydrate his insides, drown out his thirst. Laying the jug down on the counter, he grabbed a dozen eggs and a pound of bacon, a green pepper, a whole onion, and a sweet potato. A can of almonds mixed with cashews. Mustered a frying pan from the oven to the stove top. A paring knife from a drawer. Diced the vegetables up. Cracked six eggs into a bowl. Olive oiled the skillet. Combined the eggs with the diced veggies. Dumped the matrix into the frying pan. Lined the bacon on a microwave tray. Slid them into the microwave and thought of the food he and Shelby had shared. The mornings she'd stayed over. The omelets she'd made with onions, peppers, eggs, and bacon. Memories would be his only connection to her now.

In his garage, he sat on his Olympic weight bench, with the door raised, thinking about her. Time they'd spent with one another. Listening to Steve Earle. Ray Wylie Hubbard. Son House. Grilling rib eyes. Smoking ribs. Baking potatoes. Searing broccoli in butter. How did he not see this coming?

He lay back, looked up, Childers no longer stood off to one side, and Vega, was he really a ghost in a farmhouse in Indiana?

Miles pressed his palms into the rough steel of the bar,

three forty-five-pound plates on each side. He inhaled deep, arched his spine, pressed his heels into the floor, flexed his back and shoulder blades across the bench, and pressed the 315-pound warm-up from the bench. Lowering it to the bottom of his chest slow. Exploding on the pressing of the weight going up. The pump of fluid through his triceps, back, and chest. The inhale and exhale of air from his lungs. He racked the bar. Stood up flexing and enraged. Slid a thirty-five-pound plate to each side of the bar. Rested three minutes and went back to work on the iron. Sat back up, envisioned the men from his platoon watching him, thought about the letter Bull had written. Maybe he'd give him a call, see about meeting up. And then he focused on Shelby. He'd tried to see her, but she forbade him any visitation. It was butchering his whole being. His entire self. He had money for an attorney, to defend her. What she done was murder. But she wasn't in her right frame of mind. She was scarred by the abuse of her daddy and then the death of her brother. Still, she'd murdered three people. Taken three lives.

On the garage floor he stood before a barbell loaded with five hundred pounds. His feet shoulder-width apart, he glanced across the room into a mirror, his grip chalked, he bent down, kept his back straight, not rounded, gripped the barbell outside of shoulder width, the bar against his shins he deadlifted straight up, veins punching beneath his flesh, keeping his lower back tight, air pressing his abdominals out against his weight belt, grunting and breathing, locking out at the top, not dropping the weight but lowering it, controlling all the way to the floor, he went for reps, up and down, explosion of pulling upward with each rep. Hip flexors burning. He lifted out of anger. Out of need. Of sustenance. Of needing to hurt someone or something to get answers because he'd never get her back and that demolished his soul.

Looking from the garage he watched Nathaniel's Dodge pull up.

"I think—" Nathaniel hesitated, and then said, "What the sheriff thinks after talking with some criminal therapist types and investigating all that transpired, that Shelby was acting out. That she had a division of self. She was channeling her brother and his actions. Several factors took their toll all at once, stressed her, triggered her fragmentation. Her unwinding."

Miles nodded. "Her daddy, Whitey, he was a no-good son of a bitch. He never treated her or Wylie worth a piss. Hell, he was no good to their mother neither, why she left."

"Why'd they not go with their mother?"

"Shelby wouldn't leave her daddy, and Wylie wouldn't leave Shelby. Least that's how she explained it to me. She always felt responsible for them two."

"Makes sense. At any rate, sheriff's guessing, Shelby found Wylie after he OD'd, and that sparked the wildfire

in her head or woke up whatever else she had going on under the surface."

Miles wiped sweat from his brow. "Then why kill your
brother, his wife? Regardless of what she was spilling to us,
it don't make no damn sense."

"What she confessed was the dealer of the drugs was
what took Wylie away, sold him bad stuff, maybe it was re-
venge. Being a cop, I seen similar shit. Most every shooting
rampage always goes back to that common factor, mental
health."

Holding on for a sliver of hope, Miles asked, "Then
they's for certain it wasn't Wylie that killed them?"

Nathaniel told him, "No, it wasn't Wylie."

Changing the subject, Miles asked, "How's the boy?"

"About as good as he can be. Misses his parents but
knows he has a good home."

"Give him some time and he'll be a better cat fisherman
than his uncle."

Nathaniel smiled. "We can only hope."

After showering, Miles thought about work, about that
night he handed Kimball his ass, about the truck passing
by in the street, turning right, then sitting there and watching. He thought it all made sense now, payback for an old
deed, someone he worked with who had a beef that couldn't
be undone, a burned bridge, so they snitched. Who, he'd a

good idea. And he thought about whether he'd have a job after the meeting with management and the union. He knew what he'd need to do before returning to work—he'd a man to track down who went by the name of Pie.

There'd been funeral arrangements to sort, people to contact, aunts, uncles, cousins, and friends. His nephew to care for and the memories from that night, the chaos at Chucky's and Leonard's, the sounds, tilts, and jerks Shelby made. Her eyes darting and the evil she spat as they waited on Miles to return from the house, and he delivered the news about Whitey. Shelby had shot and killed him, too.

Now, sitting at his desk, glancing out the window, at his yard, his land, Nathaniel wanted to reach for a bottle of bourbon, twist the cap. Change the color of a glass. Take a sip, taste the cold and icy burn. Wash all this crazy gun-fired world away. But he couldn't. He had Shadrack to think about now. Regardless of what the system decided, he'd have to live with the decision. Of course it'd take a year or better before Shelby went to court. At least he'd listened to Miles and not taken the law into his own hands.

Men lined the far side of the bar, beyond the rack of pool tables where balls clanged over green felt, cigarettes coaled and hazed the area where booze was sipped and guzzled and the smell of something fried reeked from the kitchen in back. Miles viewed Pie from the door, made his way through the bodies of sweat, smoke, cologne, and perfume, came up beside the old man, and said, "Let me buy you a drink."

"Ain't this some shit, cracker-headed son of a bitch gonna buy me a drink, you the same honky ass I see every time I drag pallets from that dirt factory," Pie smarted to Miles.

Sliding onto a barstool Miles told Pie, "Look, you know me only as a guy who watches you dig for pallets that sit out beside the dumpster at my work, but I know of you, that you played college ball and worked for Catalyst at one point and—"

Pie interrupted with, "—They's as many *and*s in between and all through what you're talking about. Cut the shit, what do you want, peckerwood?"

"A favor. I'll buy you whatever booze or food or whatever it is you want, you name it, I just wanna see right be made and it'd offer you some payback to a man that's always disrespected you."

"Payback to a man, for a drink? Big as you is why don't you go place a bruising on his hide?"

Miles smirked. "If I could, I would. It ain't that easy."

Pie picked up an iced glass of bourbon, rattled and finished it off. Told Miles, "Three things I lay no trust in: titties, tires, and white men making offers."

"Look, I've never done nothing to you, sure, we've traded curses back and forth, hell, if anything I always defended you, even when you got shitty."

Puckering his lips, Pie smiled. "Fair is fair, what's you wanting?"

"Ride with me, confront this son of a bitch about what he called you the other day, what he calls you every time he sees you."

"The one calls me coon? Your boss? Why?"

"'Cause it ain't right for one, and two, it might save my fucking job."

Pie tapped a Newport from his wrinkled pack, lit the cig, inhaled hard, blew the smoke from his lips, off beside them, pool balls crashed, men yelled, and women clapped and hooted. "You buy me any drink I want?"

"Anything. Pay for a tab. Food," Miles told Pie without batting an eye. "Hell, I'll buy you the damn bottle."

Pie yelled at the bartender, slapped his huge hand down on the bar. "Hey, Delma, give me three shots . . . Wait, hell with that, give me the bottle of Pappy, and the cracker here is paying."

They sat in Miles's El Camino waiting next to the Ford F-150. From the CD player Son House sang "Death Letter Blues," Pie twisted the cap from a ten-dollar pint of whiskey and said, "Shit, how long this motherfucker gonna take, he must be jacking it or something."

Looking at Pie, Miles said, "You ain't drinking the Pappy?"

"That's for special occasions."

"What, you got a lady friend you gonna share it with?"

"What? No, I ain't sharing Pappy with no damn body. That'll be for my private stash." Pausing, Pie chuckled and said, "All you white folks is crazy, share Pappy with a female. So, where's this fat body at?"

"Well, for one, I doubt he could find his pecker even if he wanted to jack it. And two, white folks are crazy."

"True," Pie said. "Least you's honest." And then pointed at the CD player. "What make a pale skin like yourself listen to ole Son House?"

"Emits feeling. Good music with strong emotion, you know when Son sings, his words, his voice, his guitar, they come from a real place. You can feel his music. The man was a God in the delta."

"Listen to your philosophical white ass. You might be the first white man I can hang with. Course *might*'s a pretty weighted word."

"Color isn't recognized in my world, Pie, a man is a man, a woman is a woman, got nothing to do with their pigment, gender, a person is a person."

"Oh you gonna give me that content-of-character jive?"

"No, it's how I was raised, my mother worked with

Black folks in a Black bar up in Pennsylvania when I's a kid. My father worked in the steel mills, many of his friends were Black or brown, some whites, Italians, they sweated their hides in the factory together and drank and played cards and partied together. Skin color or sexual orientation was never mentioned around me."

"What, your daddy or mama Black?"

"No, they was white," Miles said. Pie got quiet with thought and Miles told him, "Look, I served my country with all creeds and colors, I had their backs and they had mine, race was never a factor for me or the men I served with then and it never will be."

"Maybe you need to explain that to your lard-ass boss."

"Looks like we're about to," Miles told Pie, when the shape came wobbling back and forth from the Brown and Williams building toward the parking lot. Miles pulled the latch on his door and Pie said, "Seeing this pathetic fuck, I think I'd done this for a bottle of Beam and a two-liter of pop."

Coming from the El Camino, Miles and Pie leaned their asses on the passenger's side. Conrad was out of breath, his marshmallow face damp with perspiration, reeling for wind, and he shouted at them, "The hell you doing here with this coon?"

Pie piped up and said, "Watch who you be calling a coon, you sloppy joe motherfucker."

Miles cut in with, "Know it was you that went to management, it wasn't Kimball. And I know why you did it. Payback."

All the red and huffing began to clear from Conrad's hound-dog jaws; pointing a bratwurst-sized index at Miles, he said, "What if it was me? Huh, you was fighting, you beat the boy black and blue."

"Wasn't fighting on company property, it was the middle of the damn street, far as I know, street's owned by the city. Hell, it wasn't even on company time. It was lunch, and you came rolling through late, out drinking down at Steve's Tavern, if I was to guess."

"Knox, you're pissing up a rope. I'll see you in the morning with or without your rep."

"I don't think so. You're still pissed 'cause I fucked your ole lady when I's drunk, back when you's thin and carefree and fucking some snatch in the lab, you couldn't stay honest to your wife, got her a boob job, a gym membership, couldn't just love her for who she was. You're holding a grudge. Way this is gonna play out, you're gonna contact management, tell the fucking truth, there won't be no meeting tomorrow, tomorrow I return to work or else—"

"—or else what?"

"I go over your head with Pie, explain how you're a racist cocksucker, how you degrade Pie every time you come into contact with him. What you refer to him as just like you do every other Black man or woman behind their backs at work."

Conrad went pale. His tongue tied. "I-I-I . . . you—you son of a bitch. You . . ."

Miles pushed himself from leaning on the El Camino's door, got in Conrad's face. "You know I was drunk that night and so was your wife. You need to let it go."

Tears of anger begin to form within Conrad's sight and Pie stood beside Miles, told Conrad, "You's about a sorry-ass racist son of a bitch."

Steering around the lake, Katz's truck was parked up by the cabin. Braking, Miles shifted into park, got out of the El Camino. Eyed the truck, Katz leaning against the hood, arms crossed. His face bruised and scabbed.

The front door to Miles's cabin was open; finding it odd, walking toward Katz, he asked, "You sounded pretty serious on the phone, see the front door's open, you get into a scuffle, have to run some folks off?"

"Let's go inside the cabin."

They passed through the jamb. Miles eyed the interior, it was a wreck, leaves on the floor, furniture overturned, empty beer cans, pill bottles, a bag of what looked like wads of money, and Katz told him, "I read about Shelby in the paper, about a lot of unknowns to her story, well . . . I got some of the unknowns to her story."

Turning around with a sickness in his gut, Miles said, "I'm listening."

"I laid on that floor, right there, hands bound behind my back with fishing stringer. I'd come to check on your place, seen a Camaro parked out front."

Miles shook his head and lowered it, realizing where Shelby had been when Nathaniel and he were searching for them. Here.

"Figured it was you and that girl you been seeing, Shelby, let me tell you, she's got heavy issues. But I'm not coming forward. I don't want no part of whatever she might have or might not have done. I have a brother, he's got the issues, know how it is." Pausing, Katz told Miles, "Just wanted you to know what happened out here."

Miles pointed to Katz's face and asked about the bruises and scratches. "She did that to you?"

"She acted like she was someone or something else, arguing with herself, beating the shit out of herself. Throwing herself again the walls. Just plain lunatic shit. Back and forth for hours and hours until that damn door was open, she's in one of her fits, and I seen my chance, and I ran. She chased me, but I got loose, knocked her silly with a log, then ran again, didn't stop till I got home."

"Jesus, this is fucked up."

"Thought she was gonna kill me."

At a loss for words, Miles told him, "I-I-I don't know what to say, Katz, I'm really sorry she did this to you."

"Not your doing, just thought you should know, 'cause you'd wonder what the hell happened out here when you showed up."

Miles stood silent. Tried to put the pieces together of this woman, this other side of her that he never really knew. He asked Katz, "Did you go to the hospital?"

"Hell no, had me a few beers, some grub and a shower and a lot of sleep. She busted my head, but it's scabbed up. She rattled me, Miles, I ain't gonna lie."

She rattled Miles too, but he didn't say that. Couldn't believe what Katz told him. Too many questions that may never be answered.

He followed Katz out, shut the cabin door behind them.

"You need help cleaning up?"

"Naw, I'll get to it in a day or two, you probably done had your fill of this place for a while."

"If it's helping you out, I'll be fine."

"Maybe I'll give you a ring in a few days, we can drink a few and clean up the mess, then."

"Sounds good."

Watching Katz get in his truck, Miles waved; he got in his banged-up El Camino, feeling bad for what transpired here. Firing up the vehicle, shifting to drive, he navigated down the gravel, tree limbs and leaves lay strewn and scattered from side to side. Miles thought about the bad he'd been dealt during his life, serving his country in a war to help fight communism but was instead measured by a body count, given a medal, a pat on the back, lives lost that could never be replaced, holding a job that offered little more than a decent wage, insurance, and retirement. Then dating a younger woman that he loved, but had lost her mind, murdered three people, and would disappear into a system as if she'd never existed. And he wondered what any of it even meant. Turning out onto the back road, he thought maybe it was like the war he'd fought, which tattooed one's soul with scars that to this day still offered more questions than answers.

Growing up, there was a box full of three-by-three cardboard-framed Kodak slides that lay in my parents' closet upon a plywood shelf. The slides were a world I viewed by pinching the squares between index and thumb, holding them up to the light, and viewing the pics of young men attired in military-green clothing. They were soldiers. Marines.

One pic always stood out. It was a black-and-white photo of my father standing with a grenade launcher in his right hand, wearing a pair of Chuck Taylors, dressed down in his fatigues with a backdrop of hooches he and other marines had constructed upon their arrival. The pics were from my father's service overseas in Da Nang from December 1967 to January 1969, his tour of duty, twelve and a half months, two Christmases and two New Years.

During his wartime deployment, he'd snap pics of the men he served with, who were unknown souls to me. Men I'd never met. Men my father never spoke about by name when I was growing up, similar to his time in Vietnam.

In this box were pictures of villagers and villages, the

roads he swept for land mines, the different hills that were redline zones or free-fire zones, other hooches upon hills, like Hill 55, Liberty Road, which, as I'd learn years later, was nicknamed Dodge City because, as my father would explain, there was always a firefight, four to six combat engineers leading two squads of infantry grunts and a single tank, sweeping three to four miles of road for land mines and booby traps daily. That was his job.

There were other roads that led to other hills, like Hill 65, which was an artillery hill for grunt units. Hill 52 was an area for special forces. And my father swept these roads with the Thunderin' Third Herd, First Engineers, C Company, Third Platoon, tank division.

After my father's deployment, coming back stateside, Camp Lejeune was overcrowded, so he finished his time guarding an ammo dump with an M1 rifle in Vieques, Puerto Rico, where he was given one magazine with six shots. That was it. Telling me this, he laughed and said, "Who the hell was I gonna stop with that?"

When I was older, he told me that after the war he'd lost all his paperwork on the transition from Da Nang back to the States. That he'd been recommended for a Purple Heart, but never got it.

When the economy nosedived under Carter in the eighties, my father lost his job at a tobacco plant in Louisville, Kentucky. My parents had to regroup, reevaluate their employment. We'd move to my grandparents' hundred-acre farm, on my mother's side, the Bussabargers, when I was between six and seven. That box would find a new shelf in another home, a small two-bedroom structure, part stainless-steel trailer and part sheet-metal house with a slanted roof, which my step-grandfather had constructed for his mother when he'd inherited or bought the farm as a young man, depending on who you asked, but that's another story.

We'd live here until my parents bought another home in town next to my father's mother, my grandmother Myrtle Bill, who began her mornings early, sipping strong coffee from a frog-green coffee mug till around noon, when she'd start filling the mug with Meister Bräu beer. My grandmother was very proud of her son and his service to his country, keeping pictures from his marine corps graduation upon a shelf for everyone to see, along with the newspaper cutout citing my father's heroism in the Vietnam War.

Still, in this other house, as in the previous, that box and those pictures were never spoken about.

To start over career-wise, my father would enlist in night school to become an insurance salesman, selling insurance with his brother's company in town. His other job would be bartending, and also reenlisting in the military, but not the Marines: the Army Reserve. My mother would go from working as a cashier at a local grocery to landing a factory job just outside of town.

I'd grow up inspired by the military, by action-adventure and martial arts films, watching all of Stallone's movies, especially *Rambo*; Schwarzenegger's *Commando, Raw Deal, Terminator,* and *Predator*; Chuck Norris's *Missing in Action, Delta Force, Lone Wolf McQuade,* and *The Octagon*; and war films like *Platoon, The D.I., Full Metal Jacket, Apocalypse Now,* and *The Deer Hunter*. I'd play soldier with my cousin in the woods, hunting birds with our BB guns, strapped with survival knives, pocketknives, and ninja throwing stars until I'd get my first shotgun, a twenty-gauge Mossberg pump. Then I'd hunt with my father—deer, squirrel, and rabbit on my grandparents' farm—until I was deemed responsible enough to hunt alone.

In the woods, my father was cautious. There was no fucking around, I was to follow behind him, watching his hand signals, keeping my shotgun sure-handed and pointed at the ground, safety on, stopping when he stopped and trying not to step on sticks that'd crack and break and scare off whatever we hunted. He always held these traits that, even as a kid, stood out to me, his awareness of his surroundings and his sneakiness toward what he hunted.

There were hints of my father's service. Of his serving in the military. The reveille calls to get my ass from bed on school mornings. I never knew what they meant until I was older, only that they had something to do with his time in the military. He'd come into my room, sipping a cup of coffee, flip the light switch on, and holler like a DI, "Revelry, revelry, time to get up, time to get up!"

Then he'd laugh and walk out of the room.

There were stories he'd tell when he was drunk. Waking

me from sleep in the a.m. after he'd been bartending and
had gone out with friends for breakfast. Talking about
the NVA or the Vietnamese. Like I knew who the NVA
were. He'd talk about a senior leader they'd captured. And
the type of pistol he carried. The bluing metal of the gun.
Or the men he tried to save but couldn't. The parents he
wanted to phone. To explain that he'd served with their son.
Apologize for their loss. Things I didn't know, let alone
understand.

Weekends with my father were spent cutting wood on
my grandparents' farm, hunting whatever animal was in
season, visiting his mother for Sunday dinner, or going to
the local VFW or American Legion, where card games were
played over drinks among the local war vets, like-minded
men, men who'd served and fought for their country. To
me, it was just adults drinking beer. Smoking cigarettes.
Telling stories. But to my dad, it was being around those
who were similar to himself. These men had served in World
War II, the Korean War, and the Vietnam War. For him, it
was a feeling of belonging. In these closed-door rooms, cigarette and cigar smoke was a thick haze above conversations
shared over war stories or just stories about work or being
down on their luck. Sometimes these could fall into the
vulgar or rude area. Jokes were told, but feelings were never
hurt. I usually listened and watched or played *Space Invad-
ers* or plugged some tunes on the jukebox full of old-time
country and honky-tonk until my quarters ran out. At certain times of the year, my dad would take me to Turkey

Shoots, where men would bring their shotguns, pay for a ticket, stand some distance away, aim their shotguns at a paper target, and take a single shot. Whoever shot the best won a twenty-plus-pound turkey.

I wouldn't think much about it when I was ten or twelve or fourteen, but those times and those people would hold a place near and dear to me, make a real impact on my writing to this day. Those were real folks, the backbone and heart of rural, working-class America.

When I was older and my parents had divorced, my mother would mention stories to me about the nightmares my father had in the early years of their marriage. Things I never knew about, growing up. About dealing with the men he'd seen die. The battles he'd incurred. My father wasn't a violent man, but he was strict in the sense that if he told you to do something, he expected you to do it without back talk. And when he told you, he told you once. Then you got the belt. But he was also a cutup. A jokester. And he'd pick on a person until they cried. But he was also an avid storyteller.

For most, the military was a way to pay for college or begin a career. For my father, it was several things. He had something to prove, wanted to be a tough guy, wanted to be a New York City rookie cop, but at the time they had a height requirement. He was five-seven or five-eight; I believe he needed to be six feet tall. He was turned down. He did the next best thing. He enlisted in the Marines. He also wanted a new car, so he signed up and was bussed to Parris

Island in July of 1967, along with two friends, Jimmy Simcoe and Ervin Conrad. Ervin sat next to my father on the bus, waiting for the DI to wake up. When he got on the bus, the DI read out the riot act, giving everyone three seconds to exit the bus, and Ervin whispered to my father, "Think we fucked up."

The military would always be in the back of my mind. My senior year, I lived with my mother out in the country in a two-bedroom aluminum-sided rental home with a single-car garage, where I kept my weightlifting equipment. A recruiter had started calling me about enlisting in the army. He found out I studied karate and had earned a black belt. Thought I had discipline. Growing up on Stallone, Chuck Norris, and all the other action stars and their movies, I wanted to be in the special forces. My suspicion, my mother got worried. At the time, my father and I didn't talk a lot. I was a dog lover, raised around dogs, and I wanted a Rottweiler. The recruiter found this out. Told me he had a female that had had a litter of pups, and he was selling them but he'd give me one for free. That he'd bring one to my home.

I told my mother about this, and she phoned my father about the recruiter. I never realized this until years later. My father calls out of the blue the next day. Says, "I hear a recruiter has been calling you?"

I tell him, "Yes."

And he asks, "What did he say he'd give you?"

Taken aback, I tell him, "A Rottweiler."

He chuckled. "Did he give you one?"

And I say, "No."

He really laughed then. And said, "Don't sign anything. Don't trust him. If you wanna join, I'll go with you, but you should think about school or finding a good job or a trade. Not the military."

The recruiter called a few more times but eventually quit calling not long after that. And I never did get that Rottweiler. What my dad knew and what I didn't was war. And in war some people do not return. They die. But those who do return are no longer the same person they were before they served. War changes you. Forever.

From age twelve until my late thirties, I would train in, study, and teach martial arts, but I'd also become obsessed with strength training. I'd get my first weight set at age twelve. Between martial arts and weightlifting, that was where my discipline for everything else I'd do in my life came from. At age twenty, I'd land a good-paying factory job. Then I'd get married at age twenty-six, and around age twenty-eight or twenty-nine I'd have a midlife crisis and decide that I wanted to join the navy. Look into the SEAL program and the UDT program. Spoke with my buddy's aunt who was a higher-up in the navy, reporting to Colin Powell. She went over a few things with me. Explained the process and the vetting. Told me the UDT was a good backup plan. And for about four to six weeks I convinced myself I was gonna give up the security I had worked for—a good-paying factory job, a marriage, a home—and join the navy. I was running three miles every other day. Had quit lifting weights and started a pushup-pullup-dips-and-burpee program as outlined in *The Official United States Navy SEAL Workout* book I'd ordered. I'd become obsessed, reading one nonfiction book after the next about the SEALs. I'm pretty sure my wife was freaked out and a little worried, because I was very disciplined, keeping a journal, writing down my workouts, goals, and to-do lists for the next day. When I set my mind to something, I set forth to achieve my goals, and somewhere along the line she mentioned my wanting to quit my job and join the navy to my dad, and again my father would speak with me about it and plant a reason for not joining: psoriasis, a skin infection I have that can sometimes flare up severely. He told me that this would eliminate my chances, that being out in the field and during basic training, known as Hell Week, I'd not be allowed to use any medication to treat my symptoms, the hot spots that would begin to crust and crack and, if left untended, bust and bleed, the same symptoms he possessed that would eventually push him into early retirement from the army. And once again, my father had talked me out of enlisting in the military.

Fast-forward to years later, my obsession with becoming a writer would eventually pay off. After about six years of wasting a lot of paper, I started to succeed, started getting some short stories published in small journals, wrote a few novels that were close but not worthy of publication, until I found my voice and eventually landed an agent and signed with a publisher.

And that box and those pics would finally come to fruition, as my father would remarry, begin going to the VA for counseling, talking about the war in which he'd served. And he wanted to get those pictures blown up, somehow developed from slides to real pics. And he did that. And that world I never really knew when I was younger finally became visible.

In 2011, I'd start writing a rough manuscript titled *Back to the Dirt*. Sitting down with my dad to talk about his time in Da Nang as a marine, but also his basic training. The idea was to combine and merge my time in a factory and his time in the war. But also things that influenced me, strength training, and the things that haunted him, the war. Combining these ideas into a character who fought age while dealing with PTSD and being a steroid-abusing strength junkie. All against the backdrop of being a blue-collar rural worker.

A lot would happen between the idea, writing the rough draft, and rewriting the entire second half of the novel. When I'd begun writing the book, my father had been trying to get his Purple Heart. Over the years, time would take its toll, and he'd hit one roadblock after the next, trying to dig into his past; but there would always be some roadblock with the paperwork. Reconnecting with the men he'd served with, he'd build back the bonds they'd forged while serving and fighting in Da Nang. During the same time, I'd read a book for research titled *Tiger Force*, a true story about a special forces unit that had committed the ultimate crime during wartime: murdering innocent villagers in Vietnam. The war had become about numbers, a body count. I'd combine this with the story I was already writing.

My father struggled for fifty-three years with what he'd endured—being wounded during a routine road-clearing operation. Land mines were scattered over a road, and as he swept the area, a forty-pound anti-tank mine was detonated by the enemy, leaving my father wounded about his face and body. He'd tried to forget it, but in reality he couldn't. My stepmother, his wife, Julie, wouldn't let him. She pushed and helped him to unearth his past, writing letters, making phone calls, and eventually she helped him get his Purple Heart. Which he deserved. Reconnecting with the men he served with. Reliving what happened wasn't easy, but my belief is that in the end, it was nurturing, therapeutic in a sense, facing those old demons.

I had the honor of attending the ceremony where he was awarded his Purple Heart. Tony DiBlasio, who entered Da Nang in January of 1968 and left in February of 1969 as a Corporal E4, and Vaughn Seruby were in attendance and spoke highly of my father. As Tony told me, *Your father was a hero*. And to my father—and these brave men he served with, and all those who have served, those who made it home and those who did not—I dedicate this book.

Semper Fi.

Marine Lance Corporal Frank Merritt Bill Sr.

ACKNOWLEDGMENTS

After many false starts, I am forever grateful to my editors, Sean McDonald and Jackson Howard, for their spot-on input, which helped me shape these characters and discover this novel's center and power while working through a rough patch in my life.

Thanks to all of the men who served with my father through basic training and boot camp, and in Da Nang—those who made it home and those who did not. Thanks to my stepmother, Julie Bill, for not letting my father throw in the towel and helping him get his Purple Heart fifty-plus years later. Thank you to all the men and women who have served and sacrificed for our country.

Thanks to my book agent, Stacia Decker, and my film agent, Shari Smiley, for supporting and believing in my work. Thanks to the B Shift crew, George Savage and Kirk Vormbrock, for their support over the years. And thanks to Don Ross, Lou Perry, Thad Holton, Greg Ledford, Wes and Valetta Brown, Rod and Judy Wiethop, and all my friends and family.

Thanks to my beautiful wife, Jenn, and our rotten redtick hound, Emma, for always being there.

Third Platoon on Hill 37.
Top row, from left to right: Michael DaVeiga, Unknown,
Unknown, Frenchy, George Reed, Brewer, Tony DeBlasio, Joe.
Bottom row: Frank Merritt Bill Sr., Vaughn Seruby,
Francis J. Juranic Jr., Bennett.